INLAND

by

KATE RISSE

Book Design and Map by Mariella Travis | www.alleiram.com
Large Print and eBook Conversion by Sam Sheng | linkedin.com/in/samsheng

ISBN
978-1-961905-07-8 (Print)
978-1-961905-49-8 (Large Print Edition)
978-1-961905-06-1 (eBook)
978-1-961905-29-0 (Audiobook)

12 Willows Press
Winterport, Maine
www.12willowspress.com

For my family.

We've built a new earth. It's not as nice as the old one.

—Bill McKibben

MAINE
VT
NH
NEW YORK
MA
CT
RI
PENNSYLVANIA
NYC
DELAWARE
MD
WEST VIRGINIA
WASHINGTON
VIRGINIA
NORTH CAROLINA
SOUTH CAROLINA
GEORGIA
FLORIDA
1. Dog Island, FL
2. Carrabelle, FL
3. Wakulla, FL
4. Macon, GA
5. Charlotte, NC
6. Morgantown, WV
7. Mason-Dixon Line
8. Stockbridge, MA
9. Southern VT

PART ONE

The floods have lifted up, O Lord, the
floods have lifted up their voice.
The floods lift up their crashing waves.
Psalms 93.3

CHAPTER ONE

Juliet

At a brief pause in the rain, Martin, my mother, and I wedge ourselves into Duncan's banged-up, dark green F-150 pickup. Its oversized tires suspend the cab above the floodwaters, making it possible to ferry us to the boat.

"It's now or never," says Duncan, wading through knee-deep water in his black rubber boots, scooping my mother's dog, Pepper, into his arms and placing her on my mother's lap.

We pull away from the indigo beach house on stilts, unmooring ourselves from its vanishing stability. The marsh on either side swelled overnight and merged with the Gulf, swilling tobacco-brown water into our path, disfiguring the road, and washing away the last bit of serenity that has shined so hard on this island.

"What's going on, Duncan?" My mother asks as the truck lurches over submerged potholes.

"A whole lot of water."

"I see that. From where, though?"

Duncan has nothing to say as the truck bounces us through bloated lagoons that spill across sugar-white sands, leaching into the clear emerald waters of this central stretch of the Florida Panhandle.

Somehow, we make it to the dock. We get out of the truck with skepticism. Even Pepper makes a few false starts. My mother walks over saturated gravel, steps cautiously onto sodden, slippery wooden boards at the water's edge, and looks down at the roiling harbor that spits at her gray rain boots. With her hands on her hips, she pauses and turns toward the truck.

"No need to grab my bags, Dunc," she calls to him.

"Don't do something stupid," I warn her as the rain picks up again.

"I'm alone here most of the year anyway, with Duncan, Karl, Gypsy, and the doctor. Don't tell me what to do."

"The water is rising," I shout through drizzle as Martin and Duncan head down the ramp to the boat, their arms full of luggage, leaving me and my mother on the upper wharf.

She smiles, grasps both my hands, and looks into my eyes with a selfless resolution that marks the beginning of our separation.

"As with the phones, Juliet, and so much else, no one really knows anymore."

"I'm not crossing without you."

"You need to go home to your children." She smiles again, her heavy eyelids straining to convey some cheer. "And your students at the university. I'll be fine. The waters have risen before, and then they recede."

"This is different," I protest, my voice rising like an irritable adolescent, while Martin watches us from the flooded dock sinking in the swollen bay that's somehow supposed to collaborate with Karl's boat and get us over to the mainland. "This is madness. I'm not leaving you."

My mother's bemused laugh, her sudden joy under the circumstances, paralyzes me. I stare at her as she puts one hand on the sopping wooden railing and, with the other, waves to Karl, the boat captain, as though she's simply picking up a delivery of fresh Gulf shrimp, which she does on Saturday nights, or her mail, on Wednesday mornings.

Martin walks back up the ramp toward us in his determined way, oblivious to the flooded, slippery wood under his rain boots, arms swinging industriously, his steadfast gaze on my every movement. His drenched brown curls, usually cropped, have grown unruly from days of uncertainty on this island he fled to on a whim. As he approaches, I can see the Daltons sitting on the two seats under the awning of the cabin cruiser, glaring impatiently at us. Karl, at the helm, waves for me to hurry. Martin reaches for my elbow to pull me toward the boat. But my mother gets to me first, with a quick embrace.

"Godspeed," she whispers. "Don't look so worried. Duncan will take care of me."

From the bobbing boat, through the spray that splashes my rain boots and soaks my jeans, I watch her practical denim, yellow Gore-Tex, and red bandana fade into the fog. Her dog, Pepper, disappears against the shoreline, and the rain begins to beat against the fiberglass boat and canvas awning like bored fingertips on a desktop.

The Daltons have taken the two seats in the cabin behind Karl, so Martin and I stand to their left. We hold tight to a metal bar screwed into the bulkhead as the boat surges forward, soars through the air, and slams back against the white caps. The sonar isn't working. Karl squints as he strains to see through the mottled glass and overgrown strands of his damp blond bangs that have fallen over his brow.

"I got this," he says to no one in particular, rage in his rural-southern drawl, his teeth grinding.

Looking over my shoulder at the shore again, I fight back nausea. I can't spot my mother's red bandanna, can't catch my breath. Dog Island is just a cottony thread behind us now, the distance between me and my mother an expanding chasm. And because of what happened a few days ago with the pounding rain and swells off the Gulf that swallowed the base of the indigo beach house, inundating the shore, reaching Tallahassee, and pushing Martin south to Carrabelle and across the bay, I imagine that Karl won't make this journey again for a long time.

CHAPTER TWO

Juliet

Before the Ban, I'd considered hurling our smart-phones into the local reservoir for their insidious powers, pushing us into our own separate, silent worlds even when the four of us were together in the same room. But I'd made a bargain with the phone because it was the one thing that kept me connected to my youngest son, Billy, sixteen, who was slipping away from me. Through it, we messaged each other the most simplistic, inane discourse that otherwise would have eluded us both in a world that was getting complicated: *Why did you skip chem? ... When are you coming home? ... I need an apology.*

He'd break the silence and text back: *Teacher's a dumbass ... Soon ... Sorry mom.* I watched him sitting cross-legged on our jade-green velvet couch, shoulders hunched, head bowed in submission to the phone screen cradled in his hands like a small prayer book. It was too close to his face. His wide-set, stone-washed blue eyes, so alert and full of wonder as a child, gaped at the glow, spellbound by mysterious worlds that propelled him inward with their potent incantations.

He began to swipe up and peck at the screen, sifting through dozens of obsolete Instagram images from before the Ban, which he'd somehow saved. His smartphone had been archived in the basement, behind a steel door, in what he and I privately called the Vault. I'd planned to wean him from the phone, maybe in a week or two, to avoid the explosive reaction I'd seen from other kids forced to go cold turkey, which possibly had its benefits: a few days or weeks of disillusion, some bouts of rage, and then it was over.

I stood up from my armchair, deliberately grinding together the newspaper pages I'd been reading, hoping to break the soul-sucking spell on my youngest. But my gestures never worked very well. His eyes were like round balls of ferrous metal pulled downward by a magnetic screen. I stared at him for a while as he crouched on the couch in the grips of oblivion, his sweet smile weakening me. He looked up for an instant and winked, buying more time.

"Are you absent?" I finally asked. "Or am I?"

He laughed mischievously and looked around the room, blinking at the pale morning light that flooded our living room through big glass doors facing the garden.

"Who else still has one?" I asked.

"Sam Carmichael. He gave his parents a decoy."

"Jesus, Billy."

"You won't tell?"

"No. But when I return from the island with Grandmother in five days, you and I have to get rid of that thing."

He mumbled something and chucked the phone at the couch cushion as though the device had scalded his palm.

"It's too late now for the rebate," I said, looking through the bay window at a fat robin trolling for worms behind pale purple crocuses.

I wanted to show it to Billy and point out the pink popcorn buds on my cherry tree, but I was afraid of a disappointing reply or none at all. It was time to separate him from the phone while maintaining the camaraderie we shared over a homemade waffle breakfast.

He effortlessly flipped onto his stomach and buried his face into a cushion. His scream, muted by the plush green velvet, scrambled the compass of my motherhood, wiping out what little peace I'd just felt from the early signs of spring outside my window.

"Lock the phone in the basement," I told him. "Before Dad and George get home."

"Do you think the government will ban the phones?"

"The government did ban them," I replied, slightly alarmed that he didn't get it. Was he looking at messages online that made him feel invincible? Which my gutless decision enabled? "You should envision your near future without one. I'm getting tired of this."

He returned from the basement a few minutes later, empty-handed, whistling a tune I didn't recognize.

"Sam keeps his phone under his mattress," he said with a slight grin.

He paused, hesitant to give me more information. Unlike my older son, George, who was discreet with his mischief, Billy's plots often tumbled out with enthusiasm before abruptly halting, his smile fading, eyes shifting left and right as he gauged my mood.

"Go on," I said.

"I told him he was going to get cancer." His misshapen smile began to collapse. "You won't tell, will you?"

"Not my problem. But you can't use the phone when I'm on the island helping Grandmother pack up to come home. It stays in the box in the basement, behind the door, because Dad doesn't know you've kept it. And I hope to God you didn't tell your brother."

"Do you think I'm going to get cancer, Mom?" he asked, standing in the doorway.

"Not if you don't sleep with it under your pillow like Sam Carmichael, or the others who got sick."

"Can I have it for ten minutes after dinner?"

I shook my head, avoiding words. He often needed a concrete explanation, a repetition of the rules. But we'd gone over the dangers of the smartphone many times, the need to keep it vaulted except for a couple of ten-minute splurges a week when he was allowed to use it if his father and brother weren't home.

"I'm going to call Sam on your flip phone then and tell him negative," he said with sloppy resilience, running away from me as fast as he could.

CHAPTER THREE

Juliet

I turn from the dark plumes of storm clouds that devour the island behind us and from my stubborn mother who heads back, alone, to the sinking beach house. The coastal town of Carrabelle, partially visible for the first time in twenty-four hours, expands at the bow. The pines and the yellow buildings of the marina flash in and out of view behind dense filaments of fog, a cautionary welcome to an altered coast. Typically, on a dry, breezy day, George and Billy love this part of the journey home, sailing through the canal, past docks and pleasure boats, on the wide waterway. For them, it's just part of the trajectory of adventure from here to there, unconstrained by thoughts of grandmother, alone in the indigo house on the island.

Her refusal to join us on the boat confounds me. It was so last minute, with Karl and the Daltons waiting, water rising, and the rain pouring down on everything, no time to convince her otherwise. Martin's sudden appearance on the island and what that effort signaled, not to mention his unusual agitation, weakened me on all fronts.

But this has to change now if we're going to get anywhere.

The swollen channel begins to rock the boat. Martin, right next to me, white-knuckling the same metal bar just behind the helm, stares calmly at the expanding strip of flooded landscape until the boat plunges left, knocking us both off balance. He grabs my waist as seawater swills across the fiberglass deck. There's no hesitation as he sets me straight so I can grasp the metal bar again. I'm sick to my stomach that we didn't push harder to make my mother get in the boat, and furious at the Daltons, who pressed me to make a quick decision I'm deeply regretting. I lean into Martin, my legs splayed, our feet overlapping for balance and support, I tell myself.

"Don't worry too much about your mom," he says. "She'll be okay with Karl, the doctor, and that guy—Gypsy—who knows how to fix everything. You tried your best."

"Did I, though?" I ask as I survey the churning bay that pitches the boat every which way.

The invading sea has covered the empty docks, roads, and parking lots. It swells around the base of the marina, heaving itself with a force I've never seen, charging up the wooden stairs and battering railings and floor planks.

I look for the breakwater and the road to The Point, but it's all submerged now.

"Where is everything?" gasps Mrs. Dalton, bundled in her yellow rain jacket, sitting up front just behind Karl at the helm.

"Hell if I know," he mutters as he slows the motor and grips the wheel. He leans forward and looks purposefully past the wipers, searching for a landing that isn't there anymore. Grabbing the radio intercom, he shouts into it with alarming urgency that causes my grip to tighten around Martin's elbow.

"Carrabelle ... this is Dog Island." A rush of static, and he releases his thumb to long silence. "Marina, come in."

Despite his continued attempts as we reel through the channel, tipping and bobbing past the sinking town of Carrabelle, no one answers.

"What the hell! I'm going to hit the dock if I'm not careful," he says, straining to see in front of the boat. "I got no sonar, no radio. And now no goddamned dock?"

A moment later, he points at a man in orange waders, up to his waist in water.

"Who is that?" he bellows, killing the engine.

The man in orange holds a thick rope secured around a sturdy wooden piling that protrudes through the waves. As we pitch and dip in front of him, he lassoes the rope and hurls it toward us, one arm gripping what's left of the piling so he doesn't disappear into the bay.

Martin steps forward toward the bow and catches the rope. With help from Karl, who shouts, "Hold on everyone," Martin secures the boat and weathers the backlash by lunging toward me, throwing his arms around my neck, and grabbing the railing above my head like a child on a monkey bar, holding on for dear life.

I grab him this time with all I've got—for self-preservation and for his feat; he's made a split-second, possibly life-saving decision before it's occurred to anyone else in the boat to do so. I hold him tightly. Feel his strength and warmth in the disarray of all this. I'm glad that somehow, in this shitstorm of weird weather that came up so fast, so far from home, we've ended up together again.

I know him from VERT, our town's Volunteer Emergency Response Team. We trained together last year on the third Sunday afternoon of each month, blowing on the same rubber mouth of a latex-free CPR manikin, on our knees, suppressing nervous laughter as we fumbled with defibrillators, Narcan, and tourniquets. We've role-played everything from accidents to overdoses to natural disasters. I know what he's capable of.

"Everyone okay?" he asks, looking at the Daltons clinging to each other, braced against the side of the boat to the right of Karl, who's wedged against the helm.

"You okay, Juliet?"

"I guess so," I reply, urgently wanting to get off this boat that feels like it's going to capsize any minute.

"Grab your bags. We're going to jump," shouts Karl, pointing toward the sinking dock where the man in orange holds the side of the boat to steady it, or maybe himself.

Martin leaps out into waist-deep water and turns to help the rest of us. With our bags tight against our chests and pushing against the pressure of the cool salt water, we wade along the submerged dock, gripping each other's arms and reaching for the railing where the ramp rises out of the swilling bay.

Karl turns the boat around and shoots away from us through cresting white tops toward a simmering storm before I can shout at him to take good care of my mother.

Three days earlier, through the blinding sun reflecting off the white fiberglass interior of that same boat, I watched my mother waving at me from the upper wharf, her long white braid coiled down her shoulder from beneath a red bandana. Her skin was russet from years on the Gulf, where she'd spent summers as a child. After thirty years of teaching anthropology at a community college in Boston, and two years after my father died, she came back here for the birds, the solitude, and the weather.

"Where's the hat I sent you?" I asked, stepping off the boat and onto the dock with my backpack and small red bag.

My mother replied without much thought, "I gave it to someone on the beach who needed it."

"Watercolorist or ornithologist?" I asked, reaching out to calm Pepper, who waggled toward me, knocking herself off balance.

"Marie, the expert in prehistoric Native American burial sites."

"That wasn't very smart," I replied as I hugged her.

Karl interrupted to hand her a bag of fresh Gulf shrimp and ask a question about day visitors to the island. When she reassured him that she hadn't seen anyone dodging dock and airstrip fees, I realized how much I'd missed her pragmatism, particularly regarding my kids' reaction to the Ban.

We'd had some yelling matches in our home, some "I hate you's." But in the end, my boys surrendered their phones, grumbling for a few days, which seemed to fall on the moderate end of the spectrum of family battles. That Billy conceded without putting up much of a fight made my rash gesture of indulgence—secretly handing him back the device at the eleventh hour after his nemesis replaced him on the soccer team—seem much more reckless.

I waited a few more minutes on the dock while my mother finished talking to Karl. She told him she'd keep her eyes peeled for freeloaders, then turned to me and winked.

"That doesn't mean giving them gifts intended for you," I whispered.

"Yes, ma'am!" she replied, grabbing my elbow and spritzing my arms, legs, and back with an unmarked orange spray bottle of DEET that smelled of chemical lilac.

We walked home along the unpaved sandy road. The air smelled like citrus and pine tar and slightly medicinal from the wild rosemary, beach bay, dwarf pines, and oak scrub that abutted the banks of scattered brackish ponds clogged with cattails. When we turned into her driveway, I scanned the narrowing sandy path for cottonmouths, the common brown-green pit vipers on the island, coiled tightly under the sun, spitting and pendulating their trilateral heads in the carpeting of pine needles and reindeer moss, just in case passersby hadn't seen them.

"Your brother's children left this place a mess," she said, reaching the wooden stairs of her indigo house on stilts.

"It always looks like this."

"They know nothing about personal space."

"You say the same thing to him about my kids after we leave."

"Of course!"

But as we passed the ground-floor deck, cluttered with faded blue and red sun-cooked Boogie boards and a rainbow assortment of flip-flops, I felt the solitude of the island. I spied my brother's fishing rod leaning against a tall wooden cutting board covered in white polyethylene, where he cleaned his catch of the day, and suddenly missed him. He was loud, generous, practical, and handy with tools and machines. Like my husband, Tom, he got things done. And although impulsive and reactionary at times, he was the person you'd want to be with in an emergency.

CHAPTER FOUR

Juliet

At the top of the ramp in Carrabelle, we hit more submerged dock and step cautiously across slippery wooden planks and buried gravel before reaching a flooded parking lot, water up to our knees. I can't stop thinking I failed to get my mother into the boat. I drag my sopping rubber boots through the murky water, imagining that I might have convinced her if the Daltons hadn't given me a frosty glare from the deck, if the storm had ceased and the seas calmed.

The tide is rising faster now, flooding the streets and lapping at the tires of parked cars. It's like an endless high tide rolling in, pooling in areas I've always known to be dry, like the toddler park to my left, where a half-buried green swing set arches haphazardly out of the fetid water. The usual pleasant scents of pine bark, Spanish moss, and wild yellow jasmine baking in the Gulf Coast sun have fermented into a rank smell one might encounter in a pet shop.

Gripping our damp luggage, we slog along silently behind the man in orange, across the inundated main street and over soggy sod until we reach the center of the flooded town. Water punts the front doors of the closed bar, post office, and ice cream café like it wants to break in. Searching for higher ground, we trudge on in our rain boots and drenched clothing, through more seawater bubbling up from storm drains, until we rise on an incline and reach the shuttered doors of the IGA.

I unzip my backpack and feel inside for the hard case. I unclip it, touch the smartphone, and run my thumb over the home button. Peering into the bag, I see the screen is as black and shiny as obsidian.

"Is it working?" Martin whispers.

"Of course not."

"We can't rely on it anymore. We need another plan, Juliet."

"But you saw it turn on last night in my room. You saw Billy's message."

I'd gripped the phone, kicked off the covers, and walked toward the sliding glass door that opened to the back porch of my mother's beach house, facing the ocean. *Where could I run to*, I thought. *Who on this island could help me?* The moon illuminated the busted stalks of cattails in the flooded marsh below the house, where the water was rising, and cast a faint glow across the black dunes in the distance.

Against my better judgment, I slid back the screen, exposing myself to mosquitos and the viruses they carried, pulled it closed, and stepped onto the porch. I moved close to the railing to feel the maximum breeze coming off the ocean. The balmy, briny air seemed to stop time until I looked back at the black screen in my palm, and my pounding heart brought me back to the night. I fondled the phone like a toddler with a toy, as though mere imagination would make it come to life, until a buzzing mosquito drove me back inside.

As I closed the sliding screen behind me, my right thumb stroking the home button, I felt panic spread. An irrational rage gripped me, aimed at Billy for not texting and then Tom and George for their silence. And where was my brother anyway? We grown-ups had been negligent for having no plan despite our big talk, long lists, speeches about responsibility, impending doom, and a changing world. My worry morphed into melancholy as it sometimes did when the boys played with their phones or watched YouTube for too long, or when I checked our Netflix account and saw that someone had binge-watched five mindless episodes on a Sunday morning.

I threw the useless phone on the floor, where it bounced and tumbled across the braided green and purple rug. Instantly, I was on my knees, groping at the device again with a reverence one might have for a crystal ball. I imagined returning with it to the porch and shoving it toward the heavens. It still held promise, after all. As I stood up, intending to head to the bathroom to tuck it into its alloy case on the shelf, it came to life for the first time since the water covered the island. It vibrated and blasted Queen's "We Will Rock You," courtesy of Billy, who liked to change my text tone, his name now flashing across the top of the screen with a message this time:

Mom? Are you—

"Oh, my God," I said to myself, my trembling hand squeezing the phone as if pressure could extract something. "Come on, Billy," I said out loud and then punched out, *?? What's going on?*

I went into settings and turned off Queen. The humor was gone—the anthem now just a raucous soundtrack to a difficult day. As I watched the rolling gray speech bubbles, I tried to block out all the possible bleak scenarios of where he might be and how he might feel. What was Tom telling them? He was practical, intuitive, and quick to act. I knew he'd make the right choices with the boys and their safety. But for God's sake, where were they all? What landscape were they now looking at? Or was I delusional? We were just getting some weather down south; the sporadically defunct cell towers had finally expired, and Martin was mistaken.

The guest bedroom door opened and closed as the screen went black again in my palm. I heard Martin moving in the hallway, rapping lightly at my bedroom door.

"Everything okay, Juliet?"

I stared at the screen and pecked my finger at the glass and home button, trying to get back to Billy. But the portal, so full of promise moments ago, closed, leaving me with a handful of faulty metal and plastic resting in my palm and possibly contaminating me.

Martin wriggled the doorknob.

"Juliet?"

"Come in."

He pushed the door open and looked discreetly around the room.

"What was that noise?"

"I dropped the phone," I replied, holding it up.

"A smartphone?" His whole face beamed confusion. Then he chuckled, "You kept it?"

"I'm a delinquent." I sat down on my bed. "I let Billy keep his, too. And he just texted."

"And said what?" asked Martin, coming over to the bed to sit next to me, his brow constricting, shoulders slumping as he marveled, cautiously, at the phone in my hand as if I held a lump of Kryptonite.

We passed the phone back and forth, flipping it over like primates with a puzzle. Martin in boxers and me in an oversized T-shirt, we failed to maintain any distance as we accessed the screen together, elbow to elbow.

Even though it was past midnight, and we were half-dressed and baffled at being stranded together on an island, it was in our best interest to collaborate. He pressed the home and on/off buttons three times simultaneously. The screen glowed again like the moon, with Billy's previous question hypnotizing us.

Mom? Are you—

Was I what, for God's sake? Alive? Happy? Eating another of my brother's frozen catch from Grandmother's overstuffed freezer?

"What should I say?"

But the screen winked closed, throttling my heart.

Martin stared at the device as though his vision could reverse its failures. "Steph and I should have kept one. Can you reach Tom?"

"No. He rebated with my older son and got flip phones."

"Same," he said, reaching out and putting his hand behind mine to scaffold the phone. "Wait. Let me try something else."

"I know what to do," I said, pulling back.

But he wouldn't let go. I could feel the strength of his grip, his warm palm at the back of my hand, his wedding ring against my knuckles. When I pulled back harder, he looked at me the way George did when he tried to help me troubleshoot, and I lost my patience and demanded my phone back. George would say, "Mom, you are soooooo annoying," before storming up to his room and slamming the door.

Martin smiled at me now. We laughed uncomfortably. He felt his face with his fingers, scratching at his jaw.

When he lowered his hand and our elbows touched, he stood abruptly and started toward the door.

"Don't leave yet," I said. "We have to answer Billy."

"It's full of toxic material. Besides, it doesn't seem to hold power long enough to text."

"But it might if we give it a minute," I said. "Wait here with me. When we're done, I'll put it to rest in the safety box in the bathroom."

He crossed his arms and stared down at me, my telepathy aimed at Billy failing miserably.

"We can try again in the morning, Juliet."

But I didn't want to be alone. My mind feverishly scrolled through hooks to keep him there, to keep the lights on, my mind focused on someone else.

"What would your kids have done today," I blurted out, "if it were a normal day and you were on your business trip?"

He looked at the door behind him, hesitated, and then came toward me and sat back down on the bed.

"Would they be riding their horses?"

"What?" he asked with confusion.

"Can I tell you about Billy?"

Something about how "Billy" came out of my mouth let down my guard, and I burst into tears and sobbed into my hands.

Martin slid himself next to me on the bed, as close as he could get this time, and wrapped his arms around me tenderly, the way Tom or my brother might, so that I could bawl on his shoulder.

After a minute or two, he said, "We won't be here forever."

"Okay," I managed to stutter.

"In the meantime, Juliet, try not to abuse the phone. It's our only connection to home now. To figure out what's going on there."

CHAPTER FIVE

Billy

A supersonic boom wakes me. It rocks the whole house. I can hear it rebounding around me like jet bombers, even though my headphones clamp my ears in a vice grip. I rip them off to get a better sense of why the ground is shaking underneath me like nothing I've ever felt before. Like it wants to suck me into its depths for being sneaky and going down into the Vault after Dad and George fell asleep. After Mom told me not to.

I roll onto my side, grab my phone from the charger to turn on my flashlight, and sit up. My feet hit cold water and sink to the concrete floor, which jolts me awake. I reach for the door of the Vault. When I open it, frigid water rushes at me, rising in the darkness of Dad's workshop.

I scream his name, but I'm drowned out by other distant cries, shouting, and sirens from above, and a roaring in my ears that won't stop: Mother Nature gone berserk. I beam my flashlight at the small rectangular windows near the ceiling, where water pours in from the window wells and soon rises past my thighs. I'm gonna die here in Dad's shop if I can't reach the steel door to the bulkhead that leads to the garden.

As I'm feeling my way through the darkness, terrified by the screaming and shouting outside, what sounds like a bomber plane roars in again and seems to drop all the United States military stockpile on top of my town. A minute later, it's all eerie silence, as if a higher power looking down on my neighborhood just pressed delete. My hand, still batting around, hits something sharp on a metal shelf crammed with tools, shooting a bolt of pain through my palm and wrist. I grab the shelf anyway and pull myself forward until I find the cold doorknob. The thick steel door snaps back, and then water really floods in—cold, suffocating pressure pushing against my hips, like the waves in Gloucester after the hurricane.

I think I've just shit my pants right here, but who cares. I'm clamping the phone between my teeth, the light shining in my eye, desperate cries from my neighbors banging my eardrums as I try to find the goddamned railing I've gripped a million times down here. Eventually, I find the metal bar in the stairwell and pull myself up into the early light of dawn, into our flooded garden, my arms flailing against the pressure of the rising water that has already buried the basement. I'm fighting for my bloody life and the life of my phone wedged between my teeth, keeping my hands free so I don't get swept back into the crypt that used to be Dad's workshop.

Despite the waist-high water, I make it out of the bulkhead and to the front door, which I manage to push open with a lot of effort. If this is a dream, somebody wake me! More water gushes in through broken windows, filling up the first floor. If this isn't a dream, where could all this water have come from? I scream George's name, then Dad's, but no one answers. I'm at the cabinets and fridge now. I grab as many boxes and jars of food as I can and stuff them into one arm while my free hand grips the banister, and I pull myself upstairs. I drop the loot and the phone onto my bed and head for the stairs again. But when I get halfway down, it's like a dock, and I have to wade in. I grab more food, filling my T-shirt with cans of something, cereal, ramen, and a banana. I go down one more time, struggling through chest-high water to find the five-gallon Poland Springs container we keep on the counter in the pantry for camping. Soaking wet, I haul it up the stairs, water surging behind me, reflecting a little light of dawn, a flash of vanishing hope through smashed windows.

"Geoooorge! Daaaaad!" I scream again, placing the food and water container next to my bed. When I see fresh blood smeared on the plastic handle, I realize it's from the deep gash on my left palm, which I can't deal with right now because I'm grabbing the phone with my good hand, trying to make it work. "Fuck-face phone.

Turn on," I shout, poking it with my increasingly numb fingers as my eyes fill with tears, making it impossible to see anything. I wrap my palm with toilet paper to stop the bleeding, change into clean, dry shorts and boxers, and collapse on the bed. I grab a pillow and pull it over my head, wishing all those people screaming outside would shut the fuck up. There's nothing I can do to help them because the water has come in, and it's filling up my house.

I don't know how long I've been asleep. I stand up and walk toward my bedroom window. Through hazy drizzle, I see the sickening sight of my poor neighborhood swallowed by the sea. The screaming, shouting, and sirens have stopped, and all I hear now is a low whistle and a buzzing like millions of bees swarming. Like the water is alive, eating everything in its path.

I watch it through my window as it swells around the houses like a lazy river on steroids, dragging paper and plastic, shoes, mattresses, telephone poles, wood and plaster sections of houses that have collapsed, a body face down, sloshing against a flipped red Jeep. How long can I stay here alone? Where is everyone? Where did George and Dad go? And why can't I reach Mom on the phone?

I go back to my bed to wait for any human sound. Sirens. Helicopters. Megaphones barking instructions.

Where are they all? My house has become a boat; half the staircase is gone. What if it begins to collapse like some of the houses out there, and I'm forced into that sludge outside my window with who knows what floating in it?

CHAPTER SIX

Juliet

The man in orange unlocks the door to the IGA and leads us inside. He gives us a list of basic items two people can purchase: milk, eggs, two sticks of butter, toilet paper, canned meat, cheese, rice, crackers, and two canned vegetables. Martin takes the list and two plastic bags and heads for the aisles. I stand with the man while he logs us into a chart using our last names and my Social Security number, even though I tell him we'll be long gone by the time we're allowed another visit.

He tells me the roads are washed out; the National Guard set up roadblocks to discourage movement in dangerously flooded coastal areas. We shouldn't count on getting too far. Tallahassee is flooded, and very few, if any, flights are going out. He gives me the names of a handful of gas stations that still have fuel between here and the Georgia border. And maybe, I think, vestiges of an otherwise defunct Wi-Fi network, its feeble blockers programmed and installed abruptly after the Ban, with few regulations. A pilot program barely flickering, no one in the cockpit.

"Do you know anything about the Northeast?" I ask.

"Northeast being what, exactly?"

"Boston, New Hampshire, Rhode Island, anything like that."

He raises his hand and pulls back the hood of his raincoat, uncovering a drenched mat of caramel curls that dribble water down his temples and into his face.

"No clue," he says, shaking his head. "Don't even know about Jacksonville or Atlanta, for that matter."

"But surely the people who are bringing in this food have heard something."

"Food is coming from the Walmart warehouse up the road in Crawfordsville. Don't have a plan for when it runs out."

He's watching the aisles now, trying to keep track of Martin and the Daltons as they shuffle past half-empty shelves, looking for basic items on their lists. This isn't the IGA I've always known, with its plots of beach balls and beach gear, flip-flops, all things red, white, and blue, candy, chips, ammunition, and boxes of soda pyramided in front of tidy food aisles.

"But people are still driving around here in their cars, coming in boats. You must have heard something."

"Ma'am, I can't help you," he says as Martin approaches us and stands beside me.

"You've already helped," says Martin, holding up the two plastic bags he's stuffed with food, handing the man thirty bucks, his best estimate.

As the man steps away from us, trying to track the Daltons, I turn to Martin.

"We need answers," I say.

"He just said he doesn't know."

"He has to if he has the keys to this place." I look back at the man. "Are you with FEMA?" I try again.

"I'm just the manager here and town alderman," he replies with a friendly smile.

I hear the faintest ping. Then I'm on my knees, rummaging in my backpack, my arm thrust in, up to my elbow. I unhook the safety case, grab the device, and stare at Billy's words on the glowing screen:

Water everywhere. Can't find anyone. Where are—?

The screen flickers and goes black again.

Martin follows me onto his knees. "Let's make this work, Juliet."

"How?" I plead, shaking the device like a snow globe.

"Give it a minute," he replies, reaching out and steadying my hand with his palm while he pulls the phone closer to his body.

As we wait for Billy's reply, I tell myself that everyone back in Boston is probably carrying on as usual. But the quantity of water rolling into Carrabelle and the news blackouts meddle with my common sense.

Billy???? I text as the screen flickers and glows again, just long enough to hold the message box.

"It's not getting through," says Martin, fondling the black plastic casing as if his touch can engineer miracles.

He tugs the phone slightly. I pull back.

Billy???????? I try again. *Billy??????*

Triplet gray bubbles joggle beneath my query, spitting out his reply:

Where are Dad and George?

"He's alone," I sputter. "Why would they leave him? And why does he think I know where they are?"

Where r u? I text back.

George's room. When r u coming home?

My thoughts begin to spin with lots of questions to gauge his situation. Prioritizing them paralyzes me. The man in orange, assisting the Daltons in one of the aisles, waves at us from behind the cage where a few bright red and blue beach balls linger. He tells us we need to take our provisions and get to the shelter. It will get dark soon, and he has to lock up the market.

"We aren't going to a shelter," says Martin. "We've got a car, and we're heading toward Tallahassee. Just give us two more minutes to answer this text."

"You won't make it to Tallahassee. But, okay." He steps around the cage of balls and looks curiously at us, straining his head to see the screen in my hand. "A smartphone?" he says with amusement. "Looks like you've got service to boot."

Ignoring him, I hover my pointer finger over the screen, trying to sort words of caution and advice for Billy, none of which seem an adequate response to his solitary situation. The truth is, I have no idea what's going on in Boston, or where the rest of my family went. I've waited twenty-four hours for this communication window, and now my thoughts cartwheel, my fingers don't work. Martin leans into me, his chest against my arm. I let the phone slip into his palm and take a deep breath to clear my head while he pokes the keyboard. When I look back, he's written:

Give your mom as much info as you can she's ok here in FL. Who is this?

Martin Featherstone, Lana and Agnes's dad. I'll explain later.

I picture his daughters, for an instant, polite, self-possessed like him, in white jodhpurs and tall black leather boots, saddles, bridles and grooming kits in their arms, marching across their lawn to the car like little soldiers early on a Sunday morning. And just like Martin and their mom, Stephanie, they value schedules and blue ribbons.

Can I talk to my mom? Billy texts back.

I grab the phone firmly enough to remind Martin who it belongs to, and with my pointer finger, type, *It's me. Give us details.* This opens the floodgates because, after a brief burst of text bubbles, he responds:

Explosions of water very strange everything's flooded can't find dad and George everyone's gone houses gone streetlights gone shit floating everywhere dead animals dead rats bodies. Mom? Can you come get me? NOW PLEase I can't—

His words evaporate.

"Goddammit!"

"Juliet, you have to calm down."

"It's really time to go now," says the man in orange. "Sure you don't want to go to the shelter in Danville? They're serving hot food."

"We're heading home. But thanks," I say.

"Can't guarantee the roads to Tallahassee are passable. Why risk it?"

"We're looking for our families," says Martin, standing, grabbing my elbow and pulling me onto my feet. "Her son is alone. I don't know where my daughters are. Or my wife, for that matter. But thanks for your help, buddy."

CHAPTER SEVEN

Billy

My parents think I don't know how to take care of myself. But because the climate is all messed up, there's no more snow, and viruses jump species, not to mention what an ordinary mosquito can do, I decided, several months ago, to find help online in case of a catastrophe. I taped an emergency checklist inside my closet door, and I'm going through it now:

- Store food and water
- Make a first-aid kit
- Shelter in place
- Wait for first responders
- Avoid electrical outlets
- Find help right away

This last guideline is the only one I can't follow because of the flooded streets and collapsed, abandoned houses.

I spend a good part of the morning thinking about whether I should wait for my family or leave somehow. We used to have a small dinghy in the basement that George and I would inflate with a foot pump, but I won't make it down there without scuba gear and a death wish. I imagine breaking apart furniture and making a raft, but the currents outside that run between the houses are strong. And the water is rising, sloshing, and hissing like it's talking to itself. I'm petrified that I'm going to see more bodies from the window. But I don't. Yet.

In the afternoon, I'm still thinking about escape options when I hear my name from somewhere near the driveway. Or rather, what used to be the driveway and is now part of a lake—or the new coastline.

Relieved to hear another human voice, I snatch my phone from the bed and run to George's room. I raise the window and find myself looking directly into Mr. Barrett's eyes. He's only about ten feet away, seated in an aluminum boat, the name *Pequod* written on the hull in fancy black script.

He's my English teacher. His wife left him, which has turned him into a very solitary dude. He's friendly enough but a little neurodivergent in the way he always sticks his nose in my business and can't stop asking questions, especially when Sam and I walk by his house, and he's outside gardening. He'll ask us if we want to pick his raspberries. If we need help with the *Iliad* (God knows it's a tough book). Do we want to check out his restored Karmann Ghia in the garage?

"Hellooo," he calls, sweeping his hand through the air as he sometimes does when he sees us from behind his hedges. His Adam's apple bobs, and wisps of thinning, damp gray hair cling to his temples. "Is your family here, Billy?"

I think about saying: "Yes, we are all inside enjoying a pancake breakfast!" But seriously, I'm as alone as I've ever been, with no idea where George and Dad went and unable to reach Mom on my phone. I don't want to dwell on this with Mr. Barrett. I don't want to explain that it was my fault for going down into the Vault last night to mess around with a phone that's banned while I smoked a fat doobie I stole from George's stash. If he and Dad have been swept out to sea and washed back in like so much else around here, it'll be because they didn't know where I went last night and tried to search for me.

"I don't know where my family is at the moment, Mr. Barrett. I'm hoping my dad and George will come get me."

He leans his bony upper body forward on the seat like he's losing his shit. He tries to stand up in the boat, but it pivots unsteadily despite three white, overstuffed plastic garbage bags at his feet that must help anchor the boat. Now, he's sticking his paddle against the top of one of the columns of our porch, pulling the boat closer to the house and out of the angry currents. But he's going to need to grab the second-story porch railing if he wants to steady the boat in this rough water.

"Come with me, Billy. I've got room." He nods his head enthusiastically toward the empty seat in the front of the boat.

"Should I?"

"Yes!" he says, laughing loudly through the drizzle. "God, yes!"

"But my family. I'm waiting for them."

The instructions on my closet door say that sheltering in place is sometimes better than fleeing without a plan.

"Billy, can't you see?" shouts Mr. Barrett, his chin jerking left and right at the muck everywhere. "The water is rising."

His laugh sounds maniacal now, like all the dampness around us has swollen his brain. It makes me want to slam the window shut and lock the doors. I don't need all this craziness. But he's the only live human being around here, as far as I can tell.

"Where do you think everyone went, Mr. Barrett?"

"Drowned or evacuated," he blurts out, clawing his paddle at the top of the porch until he finally lodges it under a gutter. He catches his breath and asks, "Why didn't you evacuate with your family, Billy?"

"I didn't know. I didn't hear anything until it was too late." I don't feel like explaining my near-death experience in the basement or how I sliced up my palm. I just want him to leave.

He cocks his head, like he thinks I'm lying.

"What about you?" I ask, immediately feeling a tightness swell in my throat, a dampness in the corners of my eyes that could gush out if I don't get away from this sad sack.

"I'm a survivalist at heart, Billy," he shouts, that horrible nervous laughter bursting from his throat again. "Or I thought I was."

I'm not sure what he means. Don't all humans want to survive?

"You can't stay here alone. This is cataclysmic." His Adam's apple bobs again, like it's struggling to climb up his throat and exit when he says that word. He wipes his hand down his wet face and cranks the paddle, trying to hook the gutter.

"I'm going to wait for my brother and father."

I pull my phone out of my back pocket, keep it below the window, out of sight, and look down at a dead screen.

Mr. Barrett begins to shake his head. "Come, now," he calls in a more urgent tone, as though his brain is back to normal.

"I'm good."

There's no way I'm going on a boat ride with this dude.

"Billy, it's a dead zone out here."

I've heard those words before from Ms. Fagan in my environmental science class. She says that Miami is going in that direction. That our government is redirecting federal funds only to cities that actually have a chance. How, I wonder, have we gotten to where the world's best engineers are going to scrap an entire city because of so much rising water?

"Help me tie up my boat somehow, and we can chat." Mr. Barrett looks down over the sides of his boat and frowns. "On second thought, I'll throw you this rope. Secure it to something, and I'll climb through the window."

When he throws me the rope, I let it slide through my fingers. My palm, where I cut it on the basement shelf, begins to throb. I really want to find Dad now. What if he and George don't come back? I try to imagine what George would do, staring into the eyes of someone so highly respected in our town but whose vibe makes you question the judgment of adults.

"Billy? The rope?"

"No, no ... I'm fine, Mr. Barrett. I'm going to wait for George and Dad."

"They can't come back, Billy."

Why would he be so hopeless? Why do grown-ups do that all the time now? When all this shit happening with the weather is their fault. He starts to grunt and curse. He claws at the second-floor porch with his paddle but the current is too strong.

"Where will you go?" I call out, afraid I've made the wrong decision. I look across the street at the Wilsons' yellow house. The entire wraparound porch has collapsed, most of it carried off when the tides first crashed in. The Taylors' house, built on a slight mound and set back from the street, like mine, looks intact, but it's missing clapboards. The water laps at the tops of the first-floor window casings, prying them loose. I look back at Mr. Barrett's boat as it rocks and shifts and begins to slip away.

"Wait! Mr. Barrett!"

He slaps his paddle at the clapboards next to the gutter like he's trying to put something out of its misery.

"Help me, Billy."

"How? Where are you going? It's all water down there," I say, glancing at the milky brown-green channel that used to be my street.

I run into my parents' bedroom, raise the window with my good hand, and watch him below, sailing around our house, between the roof of the garage and the brown abyss where Mom's flower garden and compost were yesterday. The boat tangles in something I can't see; I hope it's not a body. Then, it knocks against the side of the house like a bumper car.

"I guess I'm leaving you, Billy," he shouts.

"Where, though?"

"No idea. Toward Route Nine and hopefully to safety. Hang tight. I'll send someone."

"Okay, Mr. Barrett."

"Remember to ration your food and water," he calls back. "And don't touch electrical outlets."

A wave rolls in from somewhere and raises his boat, hurling it forward into what used to be Saint Paul's Street. For as long as possible, I watch him and the *Pequod* slip away from me, bobbing through the rain, the wood and plastic debris, past demolished homes crushed by what Mr. Barrett, in one of his English poetry lectures, would call either nature's rage or human folly.

CHAPTER EIGHT

Juliet

We say goodbye to the Daltons outside the entrance to the IGA and head toward Martin's rental car, trudging through the rising sea that laps at the rim of our rain boots. I scan the brackish green-brown seawater that rolls back and forth over the normally sandy, dry terrain of Carrabelle. As Martin plods along in my brother's black and yellow steel-toed industrial rain boots, head down, I keep my eyes up, looking for cottonmouths, which love warm water. If one of us got bitten, we'd be hard-pressed to find help, let alone antivenom, which my mother always says has a short shelf-life.

"Goddamned Peterson," Martin mutters, as I'm mentally going through the steps of what we'd do in the event of a snake bite: Run back to the marina? Go to the now bolted IGA? Flag down the occasional person we've seen at a distance, slogging through the same inundation or cautiously driving through it in a vehicle? On the island, Doctor Ackerley always treated my kids' surfing abrasions and my mother's occasional asthma. I have no clue where to find the closest urgent care.

Martin stares at an empty parking space ahead of us in a small lot owned by Dog Island.

"Damn him!" he says again, shaking his head.

"Your friend in the boat this morning? The one who supposedly capsized?"

"Yup, Peterson. He took the car."

"Do you want to tell me what this is all about?"

"I do," he says. "But the sun is going down. We have no car now, no place to stay, and I'm terrified of snakes. Your son's alone, and I don't know where my family is."

"Well, we have a picnic," I say, holding up the plastic bags of crackers and canned ham from the IGA and trying not to crumble.

When Duncan came to tell us to get to Karl's boat as fast as we could, I couldn't find Martin anywhere. I tore out of the house, toward the beach, along the sodden sandy road, through deep puddles that had swelled overnight from the surge. At the end of the elevated sandy path that led over the dunes, someone had dropped a piece of paper. I picked it up, turned it over, and saw Martin's name scribbled at the top of what looked like an invoice. I skimmed it but grew impatient as the drizzle picked up. We had limited time to get to the boat, so I carefully folded the damp paper and slipped it into my pocket to hand it to him later.

As I came up over the dune, I saw him up to his thighs in the rising surf that had swallowed the long stretch of white sand. He was shouting to a man in a small whaler tossed about on the waves. Martin was trying to grab the boat to steady it but gave up as it began to rock and drift.

The man shouted back, gesticulating intensely with his arms while leaning precariously over the edge of his boat in an effort to be heard, one hand securing his wide-brim caned hat.

I waved irritably and shouted, "Karl's waiting. We have to go. Now!" But Martin, not hearing me, turned back to the man in the boat, which only made me slam my feet into the sand and march toward the edge of the flooded dunes. We were wasting precious time, and he was about to be swept away. It began to rain, and big droplets perforated the sand with a pelting sound. The sea and sky seemed to collude just then, lifting the small whaler and causing the man to fall backward. His Panama slipped off, skittered, and tumbled across the white caps as if programmed to get as far away from him as possible. He stood back up, stared for a moment as I marched toward Martin, then started his engine and took off toward the East End, seesawing miserably through the coming storm or whatever was stirring up the tides and engulfing the island.

"Who was that?" I asked Martin, who joined me in a steady sprint back to the house.

"A local guy."

"He's going to have a hard time getting back around the East End in this weather. Locals know better. They know not to let their friends go into surf like that."

"He knows what he's doing, and so do I," he replied, blinking at the rain falling into his eyes. "I'm going to throw my stuff in my bag, and we'll see him down at the dock."

"But who is he?"

"Peterson. A friend. Can we talk about it later?"

"Why is he out here in this weather?"

"He's based in Apalachicola. He wasn't born here, okay? But he knows his boats and weather patterns."

"How do you know him, though?"

"We've worked together over the years."

"Well, he's nuts."

CHAPTER NINE

Billy

When I can't fall asleep at night, George lets me climb into his bed—if I keep my mouth shut and don't joke around. He lifts the comforter, drapes his arm over my stomach, pulls me close, and spoons me. His pillows are fluffier than mine and smell like patchouli, mint vape smoke, and weed.

I miss him now more than I ever imagined. If he were here, we'd make a plan. I'm good at listening to his ideas and making them happen because he has trouble finishing what he's started. On Dog Island, he once found an abandoned all-terrain vehicle near the dock. With my help, we convinced Duncan to tow it out, order parts, and show us how to get it going over the dunes.

I sit down on his bed now and try to ignore the pounding ache in my palm, where I tore it on the metal shelf in the basement during my escape. Rain pummels the side of our house and hits the glass. Something large scrapes alongside the clapboards. The strong currents and crushing debris are horrible, but the silence inside my house is worse because it makes my mind race and picture bad shit happening that I have to push away with a lot of mental effort. I'm probably going to drown soon or get crushed to death, and I wonder how, exactly, it'll happen, about the pain, and who'll find my body.

For some reason, my house, and a few others like it sitting on higher ground, look okay, pretty intact. But how much longer can they hold out from the pressure of the surging water filled with cars, trees, and all kinds of plastic crap?

I remember those Buddhist parables my eighth-grade teacher used to recite about misfortune transformed into opportunity: A man breaks his leg but avoids the draft. It's reversed in my case: Fortunately spared in my house, only to be buried in a matter of hours.

I look at George's green rain jacket and black rugby sweatshirt hanging from a hook on the back of his closet door, next to several banged-up license plates nailed to the wall: Colorado, New Mexico, Utah, Oregon, and Ontario—places he's always wanted to visit. They give me no information about where he's gone across this geography that's shifted overnight, churning and eddying, disappearing before my eyes. I climb into his soft bed, reach for my phone, and push the home button point-lessly over and over with my thumb.

Something scrapes against the house again, near the side of the porch where Mr. Barrett stood in his boat earlier. I wonder where he is right now. *You're an idiot, I tell myself, for not jumping into his boat and trying to move mountains with him because I'm pretty sure George and Dad aren't coming back for me. Only Marvel characters do that shit.*

I wake in a sweat in George's bed, my left hand throbbing, the phone deader than dead. The room is dark. It must be around nine or ten o'clock. I grab the flashlight from George's desk, locate the first aid kit, and take two ibuprofen. Then I eat a banana and a few handfuls of dry frosted corn puffs. I stare at the milky glow coming through the window from a moon somewhere out there, buried behind clouds. As I'm shoving another fistful of cereal into my mouth, the phone pings on George's desk. The screen glows a silvery blue for the first time in twenty-four hours. Nearly spitting out the cereal, I grab the phone and text, *Mom? Are you—*

Bubbles roll along before she replies, *Where r u? What's going on?*

I pound out, *Where r u*, but she's gone again, and I'm jamming my finger against the home button, thinking of Mr. Barrett slipping away in the *Pequod.*

I could really use George's advice right now, however scrambled his brain is sometimes. Maybe he secretly kept his phone, too, and might even text if I keep mine charged with the portable batteries I know won't last forever. As I lie back down on his bed, praying for a miracle, the room begins to spin. My breath takes on an alarming life of its own. Weed would really help right now, but I smoked it all last night in the Vault before the water rushed in.

It's late morning when I see the phone glowing stubbornly on George's desk. I stare at the dark gray sky through my window, above the pointed green peaks of a neighbor's roof, still holding like ours. I get up and change my clothes. Then I stand at the window for a while watching the rain falling onto a mattress and bicycle ensnared in white plastic fencing and lawn furniture—jagged pieces of humanmade chaos that stir up the watery trenches outside, discharging that sickening, putrid, marshy stench again that's creeping me out.

I see another body in the debris. Face down, white hair, loose blue and beige clothing, it bobs in the rippling currents. I have a horrible thought that maybe it's someone I know. Even though I can't see the face, I force myself to stay at the window because someone has to see this. God, it's unbearable. I run to my phone and press the home button several times, trying to get service so I can reach Mom. With no luck here, I unplug the phone from the portable charger and go to my parents' room. When my bare feet touch the wooden floor, it doesn't feel very solid anymore. The big oak bed with the tall headboard looks abandoned, as if my parents jumped ship months ago. I put the phone on a shelf next to a window and beg the heavens for help, for just a sliver of access, thirty seconds please. I glance at a photo of me and George on the back of that ATV behind Grandmother's house on the island. The place where the sun, waves, shells, and even the storms make life worthwhile because they're so real. It's the only place on this planet where I can chill, look out at the sea and sky, and think about who I am without everyone's bullshit pressuring me all the time to snap the perfect photo and craft it into a PR campaign.

CHAPTER TEN

Juliet

From the parking lot in Carrabelle, near the marina, I look out past the harbor toward the island. Normally, on a sunny day, I can see the splinter of land and its bleach-white shore shimmering in the Gulf. There's nothing there now but mist. My mother, on her invisible island, seems as distant as Billy, George, and Tom.

Martin looks wearily at me, his head slightly inclined, exaggerating the violet crescents below his eyes. He looks different now from the spirited neighbor and VERT member who had flown with me on the same Delta flight from Boston to Tallahassee.

I was coming back from the bathroom when I saw him in my seat, facing the window, fixated on the endless gray beyond the two panes of plastic. As I reached out my hand to steady myself on the empty aisle seat, he turned and looked up.

"Hey, Juliet. I saw you from the back of the plane and thought I'd join you."

I laughed nervously and asked where he was going.

"Business in Tallahassee. Are you going to sit, or what?"

"I'd like the window back."

"I can't move right now," he replied with a cool chuckle.

His vulnerability surprised me. He'd always seemed reserved, austere, and invincible in our VERT classes.

"Come on," he pleaded, raising his chin slightly, an urgency in his arched brows that distorted otherwise symmetrical features: high cheekbones, just the right amount of weathered look that modified his urbane manner. I called him the Boy Scout behind his back to the half dozen other VERT members because he came prepared with a notebook, number-two pencils, a recording device, and enough granola bars for all of us.

Reluctantly, I slunk into the aisle seat and buckled in, kicking my backpack under the seat in front. My ears popped as the plane descended. I'd braved a bumpy flight, and now Martin, my neighbor, had confiscated the clear view below cloud cover of tupelo and cypress swamps, rugged pine groves, and a stretch of the undeveloped Emerald Coast.

Sensing my irritation, he turned swiftly, unbuckled, and looked at me.

"Sorry. Let's switch."

"It's fine. Don't bother now."

But he was already on his feet, turning, bracing his hands on my seat and hovering over me.

"I had a bike accident last year," he explained. "Sometimes I get dizzy during take-off and landing."

"Looks like fear of flying," I replied, gazing up at him.

"Possibly," he said, a confident grin blooming as he looked down at me.

I unbuckled, pushed up the armrest between the two seats, and slid over toward the window, our knees bumping awkwardly. He smelled like cloves and eucalyptus or whatever it was he used for that clean shave.

When we broke cloud cover and I could finally see the ground, I relaxed into my seat. Through the window, I watched the trail of scrub brush and the jade expanse of ocean below, laced with white-crested waves in the distance, ferociously consuming and expelling the shore.

"Something's wrong down there," said Martin.

"Where?"

"With the water."

"Killer rip tides on a perfectly sunny day? Sounds like northern Florida."

"I'm talking about the velocity of the currents. Vertical transport and mixing. The salt content." He sighed. "Never mind."

"No. Tell me."

"I just did." He turned to me. An internal tempest thrashing his own shores, his eyes bulging. "Gulf Stream collapse. Past one point five degrees now."

"The tipping point."

"I'm not a scientist. I hardly know. And now the bullshit with the phones."

I wanted more science, more numbers, more proof, but we were on to other calamities.

"Do your kids want them back?"

"Not an option."

"No pushback?" I asked as the landing gear groaned beneath us.

"Nope. And I will say, parents who stall the process are delinquent."

The plane touched ground unsteadily, the reverse thrust joggling us in our seats, rescuing me from a dishonest comeback about Billy, his phone, and my negligence.

The single-story regional Tallahassee airport appeared in my window as the plane taxied a short distance and parked at the gate. Martin unbuckled.

"Nice flying with you, Juliet," he said in that official, self-possessed voice I now knew was different from his more rapid, uneasy mid-air speech and his anxious outburst about the tides. "Are you visiting your mother on that barrier island south of Tallahassee?"

"Yes," I nodded. "Driving her back north."

"Dog Island, right? Snakes and alligators," he said, with a big grin, apparently game to take on the world again.

"Good memory, Martin."

"I do listen," he replied, standing up and reaching for the overhead compartment.

We need to get out of Carrabelle now and head as far north as possible before the sun goes down. I look out at the cars in the lot in front of us and remember that Karl keeps a hidden lockbox with keys secured to the backside of a small wooden gazebo near the dock. He accesses it when he needs to shuffle cars that have sat here for months so he can accommodate new arrivals to the island.

I toss Martin my bag and run, splashing toward the dock, my damp clothes chafing my skin. A light, humid rain falls. The sky turns blue-gray as the late afternoon progresses.

The lockbox, which lost its ability to lock long ago, opens easily. I grab two sets of keys, blindly aim them at the parking lot, and push their buttons.

"This green Nissan sedan," shouts Martin, pointing at the beeping, flashing car closest to him.

As I turn back, I see a cottonmouth on the hood of a sinking car, its thick black-green body curled like a Danish, topped off with a head that's flat and broad like an arrowhead, cat eyes with vertical slits. I skirt around it as it flits its tongue aggressively at me, uncoils with one seamless motion, and disappears into the cloudy jade water.

We get into the car with our bags and the food from the market. I slide the key in, turn the ignition, plug the phone into the charger, and with three-quarters of a tank full of gas, we roll through the muck and out of Carrabelle.

As the town disappears into the periphery, the road ahead rises above the Gulf. On my drives from Tallahassee to the ferry and back, I studied the modest vacation homes along the shore to my right, weathered gray docks jutting into the bay. But the briny, jade ocean has swallowed it all and keeps streaming in over brush that borders the road, across the asphalt, dragging seaweed, dead pelicans, fragments of fishing nets, buoys, fiberglass, and wood. It reaches into farmland to our left, flooding scrub pine and bald cypress tinseled in Spanish moss, inundating the shotgun shacks, the farm stands that sell tupelo honey and boiled peanuts. Slurping at everything in its path, it's creating a new coastline.

"Watch out!" shouts Martin, pointing at a large fragment of window casing rocking in the middle of the road, its glass smashed out.

I press the brakes and carefully maneuver the car around it, looking for sharp objects that could put an end to our journey. And then what would we do?

"I'm going to head up to Woodville, where that guy in the IGA said there's an open gas station. We'll fill up, and I'll try Billy again. You can try your flip phone."

"That sounds good," says Martin, staring ahead intently as the flooded road dips and water creeps another half-foot up the tires. "Maybe we can find a place to stay west of Tallahassee. See if there's a flight out."

I force a smile. But as I survey what's left of the land-scape underneath the surf, my mind drifts north to Boston, to Billy, George, Tom, and my brother and his family. What's bobbing through the streets there? Daylight is limited now, dimmed by the clouds, rain, and mist that press in on all sides of the car.

"There's the tide I was telling you about," Martin says. "It's coming in. It's expanding. And it's going to get us. Pick it up."

"Do you want to drive?"

"No, no, you're doing great, Juliet."

I turn on the headlights and adjust the wipers as the rain falls harder. Neither one of us wants to mention that the gas station may be unreachable. The car slowly moves forward as the road dips once more. I can see the wake we've created, continual swells that bracket the front tires and expand to the buried edges of the road, a constant reminder of the physics we're up against. I think of my mother and Pepper again. Should we turn around? We would never get back over on a boat now. I feel a crushing regret at not having convinced her to leave with us. Her stubbornness is hard to wrangle. And mostly, she wins. I keep reminding myself she's over there with Karl, Duncan, Gypsy, and the doctor. One of them could surely get a Cessna off the drenched fields if it came to that.

"Billy didn't say much back there at the market," says Martin.

"We can try again at the next commercial strip," I say, pressing the gas as the road rises and the water line dips. "Assuming there's a connection."

"Try to get specifics so you can help him."

"I need to know where George and Tom went."

"See if he can leave the house," Martin suggests.

"He retrieved his phone from the basement, didn't he?" It occurs to me that he could have gone into the Vault to grab his phone way before the flooding, which was probably what he'd done as soon as I was on my way to the airport.

Before the Ban officially went into effect, I came home early from the university to find Billy stretched out on the couch in navy flannel pajamas, his black smartphone jammed near his face in a familiar pose that filled me with regret. His entire body was rigid, except for his flittering pupils that raked the screen like a mechanical scanner. When I saw him like this, I always spun time back to a point where I imagined altering the scene that played out in front of me.

It was the spring of sixth grade, and Billy had not made the travel soccer team. On the way home, in a burst of misguided empathy and boosted by an impressive rebate, Tom stopped at the Apple Store and bought Billy a phone. There are some decisions that strain relationships. Our marriage was a good one, but this was what dragged us down for weeks. Every time I saw Billy on his phone, my mind went straight to Tom and his purchase, which I'd prophesied correctly would cause long-lasting issues for all of us. Promising efficiency and connection, it plugged us into a world that demanded more, not less. Its nagging presence, like a needy, narcissistic friend, generated all kinds of misunderstandings.

I dropped my backpack on the dining room table with a bit more energy than normal. Billy didn't move.

"What are you doing home?"

"I don't feel good," he mumbled at the screen, four inches in front of his face.

"Put the phone down and either go to bed or go to school."

"But I called Dad, and he said—"

"I don't care about Dad," I said, marching toward him.

He threw the phone at his feet like a criminal ditching the evidence and gave me his best convalescent look: eyes half closed, a droopy crescent frown.

I nudged him over and sat next to him on the couch. Reaching for his unkempt chocolate curls, I pushed them aside and felt his cool forehead.

"Go get dressed," I said, repulsed by the uncertainty in my own voice. Should I use stern discipline or compassion? How did other parents do it?

"Come on now," I said, dropping the lecture. "I'll drive you to school."

"Mrs. Nardone says the phones are going to kill us," Billy announced in a cautious tone as we passed the fire station in our cherry-red Prius. On the long, empty expanse of road by the reservoir, I pressed my foot to the gas. It was post-morning rush hour, pre-lunchtime, no cars around, and just a few runners circling a track next to an empty dog park. "She says they have an extraordinary rare metal that causes tumors in people's brains. And kids are more susceptible."

"I don't think anyone really knows exactly. I certainly don't think she should go around saying that to your class. What does she know?"

He slid down a bit in his seat, peering over the dashboard. His shoulders convulsed as he chuckled.

"That's what you said when I was in sixth grade. When I told you she couldn't get the condom over the rubber dick in health class."

We both laughed. And I was grateful to Mrs. Nardone for taking on adolescent health education.

Billy sat up in his seat as we pulled up to the high school. He looked down at his feet, flaring his nostrils slightly the way he always did when he wanted to get serious.

"Mom?" he said firmly. "I want you to take my phone. I'm going to use the money I make from Stop and Shop to buy a simple flip phone."

I slowed the car to a stop, pivoted in my seat, and looked into his blue eyes.

"I like that plan."

But later that evening, he had misgivings.

"Why don't you try retiring it for a week or two and see how that feels," I'd suggested, hoping that a break would simply segue into the official federal Ban we all knew was coming.

We went downstairs together, outside and through the bulkhead to the basement workshop, and opened the solid metal door that led to a back room no one ever used. Billy insisted on putting the phone in a toolbox that Tom had bought for him a few years earlier. He locked the box and put it on a shelf next to an antique brass bed along the back wall. It was about as deep into the basement as one could get. This was the Vault.

"If we reach him again, can you ask if he can see my house?" Martin asks as I maneuver the car through more clumps of seaweed, dead pelicans, and mangled white patio furniture.

"Not sure he can from George's room. I could ask him to climb to the apartment on the third floor."

"Could you?"

"Of course," I say, pushing the car against wooden planks bobbing in the rising tide.

"Do you think my house is still there?"

"If mine's there, I'm sure yours is too."

"Billy said everything was gone."

"He's dramatic," I reply, squeezing the wheel as if that will steady the car in the middle of the two lanes.

"He sounded pretty sensible back there."

"He exaggerates. Makes shit up all the time. Who knows what's going on in Boston."

CHAPTER ELEVEN

Billy

Since early afternoon, I've been pretending that Mom, Dad, and George are home in separate rooms, doing what they always do—cooking, working in the office, fixing something in the basement workshop, watching television. I manage like this for a while. As the rain comes and goes, I try not to think too hard about the body stuck in all that shit outside. Dear God, please let it be the last to pass by my window. To keep busy, I play a few games of solitaire, which Grandfather taught me before he died a few years ago. Concentrating on hearts, spades, clubs, and diamonds calms me down.

I'm not hungry, but I eat a can of beans and two rice cakes anyway and play some more solitaire. On my way to check the portable chargers in my room, I pass the stairwell. Emphasis on *well* because water percolates there—dark, dank, and slopping halfway up the stairs. With thumbtacks I find in George's desk and a dark green sheet from his closet, I block the view of the first floor, making it easier to continue pretending that everyone's home and I'm happy to be alone on the second floor. The truth is, though, I really need to speak to Mom.

The cut on my palm is red and infected. Anyone can see that it's not healing. I cover it with more bacitracin and gauze from the first aid kit and hold it up so the blood flows away from the throbbing pain. Now would be a perfect time to watch TV or YouTube or flip through Instagram. Instead, I prop myself up in George's bed and read a couple editions of *Thrasher*, still pretending that Mom is downstairs making chicken soup. But the constant mental pressure of imagining something different from what's really going on is exhausting. I just want Mom to bring me a BLT with avocado and sriracha mayo.

As I'm finishing some saltines in George's bed, trying not to think of that body, how it drowned, and where it came from, my phone pings and lights up on the desk like a small glowing miracle. I move so fast that I slam my sore palm down on the mattress and rip open the wound again. But I don't care. The phone is already in my good hand.

Billy. What's happened?

I'm so relieved at these words. Clearly, Mom is okay on the island. Whatever happened here, although terrible, must not have been as cataclysmic as Mr. Barrett said. Maybe Dad and George are just fine. But as I put my finger on the keyboard, the sounds outside, like thousands of homes running bathwater, invade my brain, and I wonder how an entire town evacuates.

I text, *Water everywhere* with a frenzied energy that seems to shoot from my pointer finger. *Dad and George?*

This question must freak her out, so I hold back the news about my infected palm and the collapsed buildings and stuff scraping against our house. And the smell.

Where r u? she texts.

Does she not know where George and Dad went? Did he not call her on his antique flip phone to say they're on solid ground and about to send someone to rescue me?

I climb back into George's bed, tuck the phone into my sore palm, and type, *In George's room. When r u coming home?*

I watch the gray bubbles pulsate at the bottom of the screen. I hope she'll reply with information about where all this water came from. Why so much destruction. Maybe she'll have some ideas about how to get me out of here and on a plane to Tallahassee or a bus to George and Dad. But then a small text box pops up:

Give your mom as much info as you can she's ok here in FL.

What the fuck, I think.

Who is this?

Martin Featherstone, Lana and Agnes's dad. I'll explain later.

Can I talk to my mom?

It's me. Give us details.

This is really weird. I mean, why is he there? I decide to give it to her: *Explosions of water very strange everything's flooded can't find dad and George everyone's gone houses gone streetlights gone shit floating everywhere dead animals dead rats bodies. Mom? Can you come get me? NOW PLEase I can't—*

The screen freezes, glaring at me with that glossy-silver, ice hockey-rink glow that makes me want to smash it. Goddammit, I want to kill it. I can't stop thinking about Mr. Featherstone. He's one of those dads who's always whizzing through our neighborhood on his bike, trying to dodge old age. His daughters are stuck up and hard to talk to. His wife, on the other hand, is super nice and always volunteers at school, raising money and organizing stuff. Mom once said that Mrs. Featherstone's flower garden had been sprayed on in a matter of minutes by one of those corporate landscaping vans that drive around our neighborhood. And that she probably couldn't identify a daisy if it was staring up at her from her own perennial bed. She's really fit because while Mr. Featherstone rides his bike all over town, she and a bunch of other moms, some with newborns in strollers, run and hop through the park, trying to dodge old age as well. Or, as George used to say when he saw them, trying to get away from their kids as fast as they could. I told George that maybe Mrs. Featherstone was trying to get as far away as she could from Mr. Featherstone, moving her body like that, jamming her sneakers against the pavement to get out all her aggression at him because he's so uptight.

"Yes," George had replied, nodding. "Obviously, that, too."

But why is Mr. Featherstone with Mom now? Does Mrs. Featherstone know that? Maybe she's there, too. Maybe they went on vacation to Florida and bumped into Mom. Although I doubt that because no one vacations in Tallahassee.

As I look out my window at the gray sky, the rain beating static against the glass, I know that Mr. and Mrs. Featherstone aren't in Florida on vacation. Something's up with the weather.

The sinks and toilets don't work anymore, so I have to piss into a bucket in the hallway. Just as I'm finishing up, I feel the house shift under my feet. I stand completely still for several minutes, barely breathing, trying to figure out if the house is about to collapse or if I'm imagining things. I zip up my pants and pace between the bedrooms, folding my clothes, hurling old magazines out the window, and rearranging the furniture in my room.

I go into George's room and look through his desk drawers at a lifetime of his crap: Swiss army knife, vaping supplies, photo of a girl he liked, corny postcards from that same girl, his old phone case decorated with black and white skull stickers, weird rusty coins he collected in fifth grade.

In a side drawer, I find one of the inspirational messages Mom taped to the door last summer, after she went nuts about us being on our phones all the time. I think she was going through menopause, like Sam's mom, because she went crazy when she saw us staring at our screens, especially on the weekends. She'd get agitated in the kitchen, slamming pots and pans on the stove and throwing the silverware into the drawer. Then she'd shuffle fast like she was in a hurry. Only, it was Sunday, so she wasn't. George and I would look up from our phones and glance at each other as she barked out random commands: Make sure the key was in the lockbox. Transfer a big gallon of Tupelo honey into five small jars, which she'd pulled from somewhere and slammed down on the counter. Go to the basement and find whatever. She was like a stand-up comic on uppers, pulling this shit out of nowhere. George and I tried not to laugh. She'd never behaved like this before, and frankly, we were a little concerned.

Once, when we did burst out laughing, she lost it and threatened to turn off our phones for a week. "These so-called smartphones, with all their apps, actually make you dumb," she screamed. Dad interrupted and told her, in a gentle voice, she was going a little overboard. We could hear in his voice that he, too, was a little worried because he just nodded and said: "I understand, Honey, but you're going from zero to sixty." And then she really blew her top. They went into another room, and we could hear muffled arguing.

I think Dad must have set some limits with her because after one pretty bad episode and some yelling behind closed doors, she stopped slamming dishes and enslaving me and George, and instead left inspirational messages in the kitchen, usually in black marker, taped to the fridge.

The one I pull out of George's desk says: "Notice something beautiful in nature today."

No matter how many times I told Mom that the smartphone actually brought people closer to nature by showing them its secrets, promoting conservation, and crowdsourcing species rescue, the more fiercely she'd come back at me about the stupidity of the phone and that we existed in a virtual reality that cut us off from nature. Kids didn't climb trees anymore, lie on their backs to look at stars, or search for lightning bugs because they were duped by algorithms. Didn't I know that tech companies deliberately killed imagination for profit?

"Didn't you get that memo, Billy?" she asked, her face turning red.

I didn't buy it. But George did because, after the inspirational note about nature, he handed over his phone, borrowed camping gear from Jonathan, the grad student who rented our third-floor apartment, and slept in the yard for a week. He read Thoreau, ate vegan, smoked weed, and watched the stars instead of doing his homework until a ferocious lightning storm drove him inside and back onto his phone.

I stare at Mom's sign and feel sad that I didn't really respond to it, didn't acknowledge it at the time, let alone look at her garden or whatever. Then I look out the window at the metallic drizzle, the gray sky, the lagoon in my backyard, where George camped for an entire week. And I feel nauseous.

CHAPTER TWELVE

Juliet

My arms are tired. Rain pounds the windshield. The tide pulls at the car as though it wants me to go anywhere but straight. I begin to worry again about my mother on the island. I should have forced her to come with us. But pressuring her to do anything she even remotely opposes can end conversations. And sometimes friendships.

"Could you ask Billy?" Martin says again. "About my daughters?"

"Yes," I repeat, slowly steering the car around a tight bend in the road, the tires twisting out of my control in the swilling ocean water that lifts us off the asphalt and bounces us down on a rise in the road, nearly slamming us into an old white Dodge pickup stalled on the edge of the oncoming lane.

An older man in the driver's seat, with thinning gray hair and a long, sallow face, rolls down his window and waves at us. I pull up as close to him as I can without sinking the car in the sludge on the shoulder. Rain falls into the cab, soaking his dirty, ribbed, white muscle shirt.

"Don't stall the car. Whatever you do," Martin tells me.

I roll down my window and shout through the drizzle, "Can we help?"

"Truck won't start."

Martin leans forward in the passenger seat. "Come with us," he hollers past me. "We'll take you back up this way."

"That'd be great," replies the man, with a deep smile and sorrowful eyes that flex downward at the corners.

He bounds out of his truck with gratitude. Grabbing a fishing rod and tackle box from the cab, he glides through knee-deep water in thigh-high black rubber waders, pushing through the murky swamp before folding himself and his gear into the back seat of our car.

"We don't really know where we're going," I say as I press the gas.

"Straight ahead is good. I live a mile up on the left."

"Any news about what's going on?"

"Ain't heard nothing. Ain't seen no one either."

"What do you think it is?"

"A whole damn lot of water. This ain't no hurricane."

"What were you doing out here?" asks Martin.

"Gonna fish me a grouper or a Jack, maybe. Didn't realize high tide was running in so fast. Guess I'll have to save it for another day."

"Not the best fishing conditions right now," mutters Martin.

The image of fresh grilled Gulf fish makes me hungry, makes me focus on something ordinary and routine like all the times my boys have fished down here with my brother at dawn, wading into the surf with their rods for hours, coming back with redfish, snapper, or even pompano, if we're lucky. We'd toss it on the grill with butter and salt and pick every last bit of flesh from the bone.

"Ya'll need to get off the road now," says the man, who has introduced himself as Darrell, born and bred in East Point, just west of here.

"Turn left there," he points ahead. "I live up on that little hill. You can stay the night."

The sun is nearly gone. It would be idiocy to continue in the dark with so many unknowns.

"I'm an honest, God-fearing Floridian," says Darrell, ending his sentence with a soft, husky smoker's laugh.

His square, white clapboard house on a knoll at the end of a sandy road perches high on stilts above pastures bordered with scrub brush and spindly southern pines. Our car sheds water as we climb the driveway covered in crushed oyster shells. We park behind a red jeep on an elevated ledge beneath the house, which Darrell reconstructed after Hurricane Michael.

"Swept away my Jeep Cherokee down by the shore," he says.

I get out of the car, stand on solid ground for the first time in two days, and stretch my arms and legs. Low mist engulfs the last bit of daylight, obscuring the flooded, disfigured fields. I look down at the phone in the console but decide against it. Nothing will work out here. Besides, I don't want Martin to see me groping for it every five minutes, in the rain, in the middle of nowhere. We need to be reasonable about where and when to try Billy and when to resist the urge if it isn't productive. We've already failed to reach a gas station, a simple goal that, under normal circumstances, takes twenty minutes from the Carrabelle dock. If Martin and I can't achieve even the most basic leg of our journey, how will we fare through the next obstacle, the next disappointment, the next swollen lake on Route 319?

He tugs at my arm, sensing where my mind is going.

"We'll try it later, Juliet. Grab your things, and let's get inside. That fish talk back there made me hungry."

From the back seat, he pulls out the two gray plastic bags from the IGA.

"What's for dinner?" I ask.

"Canned corned beef hash."

"With saltines?"

"I'll see what I can do," he replies, his uncomplicated smile eclipsing my worries for a moment.

Darrell waves us toward the back of his house.

"This way," he says. "Watch out for snakes."

"Good God! Now snakes," says Martin, finding a flashlight in his rain jacket pocket and casting light on the crushed shells beneath our feet.

As Darrell climbs a rickety set of wooden stairs with open risers, he pauses for a moment and reaches his hand into green shrubs that poke through the balusters and seem to want to follow him up to the second floor. He stirs his arm around gently, like a vet helping birth a calf, and then presents us with the most beautiful red tomato resting in his open palm.

"Let's hope these babies survive the storm," he says. "Or whatever it is."

"How do you pull that off in sandy soil?" I ask as Martin and I wrestle with our boots and wet socks and leave them on the second-floor landing.

"Round Up Ready and lots of fertilizer," he replies with a wheezy laugh while removing his black waders.

Darrell is the manager of the Franklin County Water Treatment Plant. Isolated this far up a hill, away from town, he tells us, bragging, he's dug his own well. He lives here with his wife, Evelyn, who happened to be driving over to her sister's house in East Point when the water came in. Darrell has created a large vegetable garden behind his house with what he proudly calls a boost from Monsanto. He also harvests tupelo honey, which we sample on toast to complement the salty corned beef hash, saltines, and the best beefsteak tomato I've ever eaten.

"Didn't notice much the other night when everything flooded," he says from his kitchen table, where we sit illuminated by candlelight. "Didn't think much about the rumbling. Eglin is over the hill. They break the sound barrier all the time."

Fighter jets are a ridiculous assumption. He must know that. He must have seen and felt what we did.

During dinner, my mother had commented on the sound of the ocean pounding the tide line so hard we could feel it reaching the ground beneath us. It had been calm in the late morning when we swam, collected shells on the beach, and planned our return journey back East in a rental car, three nights on the road in Red Roof Inns that accepted dogs. But as we ate our shrimp dinner and watched the sunset from the porch, we began to hear the surf swilling like a continually flushed toilet. It flogged the shore as if it wanted to demolish the island. I wondered if we were in for one of those storms I'd seen so many times before, when wind from the east ripped siding from beach homes on stilts and scattered it across the sandy roads, and the thunder and lightning competed in chaotic energy that drove everyone inside, away from windows and outlets. But the wind wasn't blowing that hard. The surf, however, kept striking, pausing our conversation, pulling our gaze toward the crashing pulse beyond the dunes.

"I'm going to bed," I finally said, slowly rising out of my chair, convinced that any minute, gumball-sized drops of rain would fall with fury from the night sky, soaking everything instantaneously.

"Don't be silly," said my mother, her warm fingers brushing my elbow. "Sit here with me for a few more minutes."

I smiled at her affection and sat down again. But when I hit the seat, the ground shifted beneath us, and a large flash of blue and white light, singed orange at its edges, arched over the dunes on the east end of the island. It was as if all the electrical transformers along the Eastern Seaboard had succumbed to acute failure, igniting a silent explosion of crushing force that devoured the night sky and all its stars for an instant, momentarily blinding me. My jittery heart seemed to want to race somewhere and leave me behind. I blinked back my sight and thought of my kids and the fastest, most direct route to them.

"What was that?" I asked.

"No idea," she replied, staring in the direction of the roaring ocean, the shifting shore that seethed and rose like black molten glass.

Below the glow of a nearly full moon, the ocean had breached the dunes. It began to crawl toward the house, hissing and sizzling as it careened over the sandy road, infiltrating the weeds in the brackish pond behind my mother's house. I'd seen flooding before once or twice, but not instantaneously like this.

"Who else is on this end of the island?" I asked, wondering how we'd evacuate if the water didn't stop.

"Not sure."

"We should call someone."

I looked at the McKinley house perched on stilts. But the lights were off, and the driveway was empty.

"I'm going inside," I said in full flight mode as seawater fizzled around the base of the stilt house, walling us in.

"I suppose it doesn't matter where we go," she replied, looking at me in the moonlight, her judgment muddled by the surf chafing the dry reeds in the marsh below, making them crackle against each other.

The frogs and birds were quiet, the bugs gone, which seemed to confuse my mother since those were the predictable sounds of life that accompanied her when she was alone on the island.

"There's a lot of water coming in, Mom. We need to do something. I'm going to call Duncan on my flip phone. Tom, too."

"I'll get the news," she replied, following me into the house as the rain began to fall.

"What are you getting at?" asks Darrell, staring at me through the candlelight with slight mockery or cynicism in his wincing eyes. He inserts an entire saltine, topped with a wedge of tomato, into his mouth. "An explosion? A tsunami?" he sputters through crumbs. "I don't get it."

"More like a catastrophic sudden rise in sea level, unclear why," says Martin.

"You're one of those climate people who worry all the time," says Darrell, with a slight guffaw. "I'm just too old for that stuff."

"What *stuff*?" asks Martin, trying to stay calm and maintain his gratitude for the hospitality while making the point that greed and miscalculations might have to do with what's going on outside.

"You know. That it's our fault the weather is weird." The playful jauntiness evaporates from Darrell's face, replaced by a belligerent stare. I can't figure this guy out, but I'm not sure I care. I do wonder about the woman he shares this home with and if he's worried about her over in East Point, which is close enough to say "around the bend" if you're a local but, in fact, requires a good part of the morning to drive there and back, especially on a stormy day.

"Blaming hard-working Americans is insulting, frankly, to both flag and church, which, by the way, keep this country honest. Maybe this is God's plan."

"Science says burning fossil fuels changes the weather," replies Martin.

"I wouldn't want to be a part of that," says Darrell, a big smile and sunshine eyes clamoring across his ruddy face again. "You all believe it's really that bad?"

"I'm in touch with my son in Boston," I reply. "Something's wrong." I regret my words instantly because I have no idea what's going on in Boston. Darrell stares at me with his mouth slightly open, waiting for details. I have so few that they aren't worth mentioning. But now my mind begins to spin the few threads Billy's given me into images of him, alone in a sinking house, waiting for me, George, and Tom. I think of Martin's family, too, because they're on my radar now. Two adolescent girls and their mom.

"So, what's the story?" asks Darrell, his jaw hanging lazily.

"Ice loss," says Martin. "Feedback loop of open ocean and heat absorption, thermosteric change, too much salt. It's complicated."

"He means collapse of ice shelves," I say as Darrell shoves another stack of saltines dipped in honey into his mouth.

The gnashing seems to malfunction as if the edible mortar has clogged his gears. A quick swig of water loosens everything, and he's all smiles again.

"Well, Boston's on the coast. You'd expect some flooding now and again. We get flooding here all the time."

"It's glacial," snaps Martin.

"But we're in Florida."

"Temperature changes around the globe are unstable now."

"So, what's an old fart like me supposed to do?"

"You're not the problem," says Martin. "We've known about this and had the tools to stop it, but we've done next to nothing."

My arms feel too heavy to lift the fragrant honey cracker from the plate to my mouth despite my appetite. Martin has stopped eating, worn out by his own sermon. I suspect that mentioning Billy all the time reminds him that we aren't mentioning his daughters, Lana and Agnes, and his wife, Stephanie.

"Well, I hope your son's okay," says Darrell, standing and clearing our plates from the table. "Do you just have one kid?"

"We actually aren't married," I say, glancing at Martin, who is lost in a thought. "I mean, we are married. Just not to each other."

Darrell comes back to the table. He nods slowly and looks into my eyes. "Okay by me," he says, grabbing a candle and carrying it over to some cabinets, where he rummages for a moment, clinking glasses.

Back at the table, he places the candle and three shot glasses down, uncorks an unmarked bottle of yellow syrup, and pours what turns out to be homemade honey and elderflower mead. It's intensely sweet with a scorching kick-back that burns my throat.

"We met down here, accidentally, sort of."

"I was here on business," adds Martin, sipping the mead, looking at Darrell, and then down at the shot glass. "Do you mind if I pour myself some more of that?"

"Please!" he replies, his penchant for fermented honey chronicled across his flushed cheeks and capillaried nose in the flickering light.

"We're from the same town," I say. "We have kids the same age."

"And you're driving back home together?"

"Hoping to get a flight out somehow," says Martin.

"You got a plan B?"

"Not really."

"Well, then, safe travels," he says, raising his glass, throwing the liquid down, and washing away the absurdity of his statement.

Martin raises his shot glass, pausing at his mouth before swallowing it all. He isn't in the mood to be deterred by a stranger's half-baked well-wishes that contradict the empirical signs outside.

"We're going to take the road back toward Tallahassee. I came down that way after the initial flooding. Some of the roads were impassable from water and roadblocks. If we strategize, we'll be okay."

Darrell shakes his head.

"You're going to have to go by Wakulla Springs. All sinkholes. I've seen it reverse course with my own eyes, pulling salt water from the ocean through the cave system and spitting it out on land. I imagine that's some of what you saw. If I were you, I'd bypass that area, including Tallahassee, avoid the crowds, go straight north across state lines, and hit the regional airport in Macon. You might be pleasantly surprised."

"If we can even get across the border," I say, sipping the mead, comforted by its numbing effect that burns away my worries and warms my whole upper body.

"I heard Georgia has some passible roads inland," says Darrell, coming around now to the reality outside the window.

"We aren't going to Georgia," I say. "We're going to try Tallahassee."

"Where did you hear about road closures in Georgia?" asks Martin.

"On my radio. Before I bumped into you."

"Can we listen?"

"It's just a list of open and closed routes that won't mean much if you're not from around here."

He puts his large hands on the edge of the table and pushes himself out of his seat, tired, stiff, a little tipsy or maybe just bracing himself for more disruptions to a routine he's perfected for himself over the years.

At the wooden countertop next to the stove, he gropes in near darkness, scratches a matchstick across the side of a box, and lights a propane gas lamp. It illuminates a toaster, a bowl of ripe cherry tomatoes, peppers, and cucumbers, and boxes of tea—Lapsang Souchong, Jasmine, Prince of Wales. Through the shadow of the lamplight that reaches into an adjoining room, I see a gray couch, a coffee table, and some chairs, with a small bay window looking out at the darkness and the rain and a coast that's disappearing. I feel my heart pounding in my limbs as wave after wave of that bright yellow and orange light of crushed infrastructure along the coast ricochets in my memory, the rush of water, the ringing in my ears, and now an overwhelming urge to get out of here, to get in the car and drive all night through the flood because something has happened to the weather and no one knows what to do.

CHAPTER THIRTEEN

Juliet

I bolted out of bed, stepped onto the porch, and surveyed the flooded landscape under a gray quilt of clouds hovering low over the ocean. The swollen surf roiled but had receded enough to show a lunar landscape of deep puddles pitted in the dunes flecked with seagrass and severed cattails, their perforated brown catkins releasing silky beige fuzz everywhere.

Back inside, I stared at the bathroom door as though I could see where the smartphone sat on the shelf in its protective alloy case, far from my brain. I thought about bringing it into bed. But after the initial Ban, I kept my distance, unless covertly sending a silly emoji to Billy, telling him: "Time's up. Vault the phone."

The lights turned on midmorning as I was sorting through old linens in a closet and organizing drawers. I ran into the bathroom and grabbed the phone, full of guilt for thinking maybe Billy would grab his phone, too, maybe only for the sake of telling me about the surge of water last night, the ground shifting, the light crackling along the distant coast to the north.

I fumbled with the case, the firm clip that snapped open, enabling contact between rare, allegedly tainted metals and human tissue. I pressed the home button, trying to be gentle but feeling rage at the glowing screen that stared at me like a failing third eye. I squeezed it and knocked it against the side of the sink. "Come on, Billy. Text something."

The television projected a static crackle when I walked into my mother's living room.

"Does this ever happen with your TV?" I asked her as she rinsed dishes in the sink.

"Storms kill the power, but the generator just kicked on. No connection, I guess."

I pecked at the TV remote just as I'd done with the phone keyboard, as though aggressive pressure would fix everything. I dropped to my knees and poked at the buttons on the monitor below the TV screen until my mother yelled at me to stop.

"Don't mess with that, please! I spent hours programming it. Breaking it won't help us."

I continued to push buttons anyway.

"It's the satellites, the towers, not the television itself, Juliet. Stand up."

"Maybe I can find a local station."

"I don't have that set up. Just cable. Crappy cable."

"But maybe they'll broadcast a message. The Emergency Alert System or something."

"Stop it, Juliet," she said, walking toward me.

She grabbed my wrist and pulled me up with a forcefulness I'd seen only once or twice in my life, initiating a mutual silent treatment in the sinking indigo beach house that seemed to shrink-wrap itself around us, sucking out oxygen.

I was sick of this place now, of the silence I thought I wanted for a few days away from Boston, a break from the family. And of the water that percolated outside, humidity coating the surfaces, the screens, my skin. Any appetite for breakfast or a second cup of coffee vanished as the morning wore on. I was ready to throw everything in the car and leave. But anyone looking out the window would know that the ferry couldn't make it through the choppy, swollen surf with blustery white caps consuming the dunes in front of our porch.

I turned and bounded out of the house, hit the stairs, reached the landing, and looked across the bottom deck at the jumble of blue, white, and orange flip-flops, the boogie boards tipped against a yellow kayak as if my kids had just raucously dropped it all there before heading to the outdoor shower and then onto to the porch to devour a whole party-size bag of corn chips and a large jar of hot salsa. But I wasn't feeling festive. The ocean, as black as lava under the pewter sky, was unfamiliar, ominous. Like a domesticated rodent you'd played with all your life that, without warning, spun in your palm and sunk its teeth into you.

At the end of my mother's driveway, I turned toward the beach and walked briskly, barefoot, down the flooded sandy path, splashing through deep puddles, looking in vain for frogs, cranes, herons, butterflies, vipers, even. Anything to grasp normalcy and prune the distance I felt between me and my family. My feet, covered in sand and pine needles, were soaking wet from pools of ocean water everywhere and the marshes annexing the roads with their brackish oolong hue.

I couldn't climb the dunes as most of them had been swallowed by the surge, creating a new coastline that lapped at the road. The roiling sea had spit out onto the sand oysters, sinewy blue-green seaweed, rotting fishnets and orange buoys, jellyfish, skates, sand dollars, starfish, corals, sponges, sea slugs, mermaid's purses, horseshoe crabs and gelatinous creatures I simply didn't recognize. Some twitched with life, but there wasn't much I could do apart from grabbing a piece of driftwood and flinging the animals back toward the ocean.

A dead seahorse with a broken snout brought me around to the futility of my task and made me think of

Billy and all the questions he'd ask had he been here: How did it break its nose? Can you tell if it's male or female? I thought of all the times we fished here at dawn, a picnic at sunset. But the beach was collapsing into the sea as waves battered the shore, winding up with a great wheezing inhale, exploding with a ferocious crack and swirling froth of energy. If my kids had been with me, they would have climbed what was left of the dunes, their abstract empathy for dying marine life spilling out, and me letting them go for once without trying to smooth the edges of their disorder. We would have rescued what we could and then triumphantly headed home for a big breakfast. But not today.

The wind picked up as I stood there, a jade ocean expanding for miles. With no ferry running, there was no place to go. There would be no visitors on the island today or tomorrow. The water turned the color of molasses as clouds dimmed to a slate gray, and the rain began to fall.

My mother was standing on the porch when I got back, shaking sand from her blue doormat.

"Beach is gone," I shouted from the driveway. "Crap all over the dunes."

"Plastic?"

"Mostly organic."

As I reached the top of the stairs, she whispered, "There's someone inside."

"Captain Karl?" I asked, hoping he had some answers and a magic carpet ride off the island. She shook her head as she knocked the mat against the railings, oblivious to the falling rain.

Maybe it was Duncan, the island manager. Maybe he'd have information, I thought, as my damp arm grazed my mother's in front of her door.

But it wasn't Duncan because my mother added, "I found him this morning on the beach at the East End," which was what she always said when she found a drifter looking for a meal or a disoriented birder needing directions.

The person staring back at me from her couch, however, with a cup of coffee in hand and a lopsided smile, was Martin. I heard myself gasp then, like someone who comes back to life in a movie.

"What's going on?" I asked, crossing the living room on wobbly legs and embracing him. We had role-played so many disasters in our VERT classes, and now this; it was hard to equate our friendship with pleasure.

"Tallahassee is flooded."

"How flooded?"

"Underwater flooded."

"How did you get here? Karl, our boat captain, isn't running anything."

"A friend brought me over."

"That must have been unpleasant."

I looked at his shorts and faded navy cotton T-shirt, imagining he'd dressed at dawn to come down here for reasons I was having difficulty comprehending.

"You're not here to boogie board and look for shells," I said, taking a seat at the kitchen table.

"They've barricaded the roads north."

"What about the airport?"

"No flights."

I wished he'd stop shaking his head.

"The surge flooded highways, smashed homes, swept away cars and telephone poles." He sipped from his coffee, gripped in both hands as if it helped keep him upright. "I knew you were here. The road south was open, so I took it."

My mother came in from the front porch.

"Well?" she asked, her fist resting on the counter. "What's the plan?"

"Can we find that friend of yours?" I asked.

"Long gone," said Martin. "Besides, the water is rising."

I thought of my children, and my heartbeat thudded in my throat. "Where's your family?" I asked.

"Not sure. Flip phone's dead. No one picks up."

He reached for his black bag, pulled the phone from a side pocket, flipped it open, and pressed buttons futilely.

"You can charge it over there near the sink."

"Not sure I'll get an answer," he replied.

"This is insane," I said, standing up from the table. I walked to the porch and looked through the rain, through threads of mist hanging low over the steel-gray ocean. "How do we get out?"

Despite the endless horizon and miles of undeveloped beaches, I felt hemmed in. We were wasting time. I turned to my mother.

"Where's Karl? Where's Duncan? Why haven't you gotten any answers?"

"They have no answers, Juliet."

"I want to be clear about this," said Martin. "Tallahassee is underwater. Homes are gone. People have fled. The National Guard is everywhere." He ran his hand through his brown curls, a little scruffier than what I remembered, and stared at his lap, looking mildly seasick. "We may be safer here until we figure out what's going on."

"I'm not staying here," I said.

"You might not have a choice," said my mother as she pointlessly skimmed the hand-typed island phone book. Her turquoise reading glasses perched crookedly on her nose because she was always sitting on them. "Karl is trying to reach the mainland on the radio, but it's too rough to go over right now. I'm going to see if Gypsy will take us over."

"Who's that?" asked Martin.

"Leonard's son. And a good friend," she answered, standing, shifting on her feet, grabbing the coffee pot and refilling Martin's cup.

She offered him a corn muffin.

"What are you doing?" I asked. "We can't drink two cups of coffee now and have midday snacks. We have to conserve what we have. You, yourself, said we might be stranded."

Sometimes her hospitality was superfluous.

"I want to get off the island now and drive north. Let's pack our bags and go. We'll pay someone at the dock to take us across—Gypsy or whoever. We'll get in Martin's rental car and drive."

"I just came from the mainland, Juliet."

He looked exhausted, lids heavy, despite the coffee. I was glad he was here, relieved to strategize with someone else. But I couldn't shake the mild repulsion I felt at our incompetence. Sitting around doing nothing. If Tom or my brother were here, our bags would be down at the dock by now for a one-way trip over on anything that floated.

"We may not be able to go home today. Or tomorrow, for that matter," said Martin. "I'm pretty sure something catastrophic happened along the Eastern Seaboard."

CHAPTER FOURTEEN

Juliet

Darrell grabs a black radio from the corner of the counter and begins to twist its antenna.

"Solar powered," he says proudly. "Everything in this home can run off wood and sun. You might think I'm a nut, but I'm prepared. I can flush the toilet, pull up water with the solar pump, and cook a hot dog without relying on anyone."

He wiggles the antenna and jams it into the top of the radio.

"Can I help with that?" Martin asks, standing up and focusing on the black box in Darrell's hands.

"I got it," Darrell answers, pushing a switch and aiming the antenna in some magical direction he discerns, a divining rod for electromagnetic frequency.

The static crackles. He turns the knob. Martin freezes, his ear angled in the direction of the sputtering radio. But after a minute or so, Darrell purses his lips and shakes his head.

"Too many clouds. Too much rain."

Martin stares at me with expectation. He knows my phone is in my backpack at the top of the stairs that descends to the parked cars below the house. Now is not the time for the smartphone, for more technological failure. We both know it.

"Well, I'm going to bed," Darrell announces, grabbing the lantern. "There's a double bed in the guest room downstairs on ground level. Annette, my good woman, keeps it tidy for guests. You should be dry down there."

When he gets to the kitchen doorway, the lantern in his fist casts light into the living room again, across the couch and chairs, barely reaching the small bay window. He turns sluggishly, clearly fatigued, and tells us to watch out for snakes at the bottom of the stairs.

"You be real careful," he says. "And use your flashlight."

"I hate snakes," mutters Martin. "Especially pit vipers."

We make it down the stairs, past our car and the Jeep, and over the driveway of crushed oyster shells. Martin vigilantly sweeps his flashlight across the driveway until we reach the small side room below the kitchen. He opens the door, and I enter. Rather than feeling awkward or irritated by his silence and distance, I feel oddly drawn to it, placated in a way. Nervous chatter can say a whole lot of nothing. There's serenity in our lack of words, the way we move with intention, and the dialect of adversity and emergency when the body does the talking. At least until my next round of fear and prattle bubbles over.

We pull back the sheets and fall into bed with our clothes on. The room smells like any musty southern home inundated with excess humidity and mold. I think of the laundry room below my mother's house on Dog Island, the squalor of empty Tide bottles, single socks, and rusty hinges that no one ever bothers to sort. And my grandparents' beach house near Destin, the turquoise cabinets in the pantry crammed with pots, pans, and an inexpungable mildewy smell that never faded.

The rain batters the window and keeps us awake. I ask Martin if he thinks we'll get swept away because that's what it feels like. He reminds me that we are up on a hill. I tell him that I miss my family, and I can't stand this anymore. Can't we find someone with a helicopter and pay whatever it costs to get us back home? He laughs, more bewildered than amused. Then he slips his arm under my pillow and pulls me close. He props himself up on his elbow with what seems like his last bit of energy, leans in, and puts his lips against mine with the same certainty he had on the boat when he lunged for the rope. He kisses me deeply, tenderly, with a distant abandonment I imagine is meant only to delay the inevitable solitude that will soon descend as the dark, wet night wears on.

We kiss for a long time, with the mead on our lips and tongue, and our bodies drained, fearful to let go or acknowledge that we've crossed a line. He finally pulls away, puts his head on my shoulder, and burrows his face into my ear.

"I am so fucking sorry, Juliet," he whispers.

"Don't worry about it."

I reach for his hand and hold it as he rolls onto his back and sighs. I'm not sorry, though. It feels like the dead weight of my entire body has liquified into the mattress, my thinking brain left to throb. Goddamned the endless rain. When will it stop? He can do anything he wants, as far as I'm concerned, just to spite it and everything else colluding against us. I just want to sleep. So, if I can get there by connecting with him in some primitive and comforting way, then so be it. Anything, I think, to abbreviate this confinement, to interrupt the rain pelting the window, to pause the lashing waves of regret I feel at leaving my kids and husband in Boston and ditching my mother on an island.

I lean toward him and against his body, scissoring my legs and linking them with his, hoping that his warmth and embrace can dilute the jumble of games my own mind is playing with me. But it feels careless, the cues are tangled, and besides, he's elsewhere. So I slowly roll onto my back, blink away thoughts of Billy and his solitude, Tom and George and their disappearance. What if they've been washed out to sea like the houses, docks, cars, and pelicans?

CHAPTER FIFTEEN

Billy

For the first time since the flooding, I climb the stairs to Jonathan's apartment on the third floor. I need more food and water and pots and pans that I can put on the roof deck to collect rainwater now that the plumbing is gone.

I reach the small rectangular nook on the landing between the second and third floors. It's like a recessed bench in the wall, with headroom, six feet off the ground, with a little window that looks out on our side yard and the hedges, now buried under water. When I was in middle school, before I got a phone, I used to climb up here onto the lime-green cushion and pillows to read graphic novels.

I grab the small wooden ladder that Dad built, climb the few rungs, squeeze myself into the space, and lie down for a while, for old times' sake. The pillows smell smoky and spicy, like the kitchen when Mom cooks Indian food. I watch the dull yellow light fade and wonder where the rest of my family is. A bird begins to screech. But as I listen closer, I realize that it might be some other wingless animal in trouble because the noise is full of panic, like it's stuck somewhere nearby, losing its footing. There's nothing I can do but repeat, "Shut the fuck up, please," over and over until the shrieking stops. I climb back down the ladder and head to Jonathan's room before night comes.

Jonathan disappeared about eight weeks ago, stiffing my parents rent and leaving a bunch of junk Mom had boxed but not yet donated: food, clothes, and camping gear, including a small propane stove with a couple of gas canisters. Last year, he invited me up here to smoke weed; I even slept in his bed one weekend when he climbed Mount Katahdin. He talked a lot of shit about Everest but didn't have the funds or the nerve because grad school had robbed him of all his money and ambition.

As I boil ramen on his stove and slide two protein bars into my back pocket for later, I look around at the Everest poster, a flashlight, an empty beer bottle on the bookshelf, and an old pair of running shoes on a white wicker chair. I have no interest anymore in staying up here. I can't worry about more damp rooms on top of everything else I have to deal with.

The ramen is delicious, so I make myself another bowl and then pack the rest of the food into a cardboard box. I put three gallons of water, the stove, and the propane canisters near the door. My sore palm is killing me, so

I take it slow, in three runs, down to the second-floor hallway, nabbing Jonathan's thick blue and orange climbing ropes on my last run.

Instead of going into George's room, I climb back into the nook with Jonathan's flashlight. I have to bend my knees and crouch because the space isn't long enough to lie flat anymore or spacious enough to sit up completely. I lean my head on a pillow and eat a protein bar. A silver mist blurs the dark sky, blocking moonlight behind clouds. I feel something under my right hip and pull out an old crossword puzzle book, a pencil case, and a candle and matches from the days of yore when I spent my free time turning pages. I turn off the flashlight, light the candle, and carefully place it on the window ledge at my elbow. The booklet feels light in my hands, the old yellow pages crisp. They smell like glue and elementary school as I turn them gently, the tip of my pointer finger finding the top edge, sliding down the back, and sounding a little like someone whispering. I look at the letters I wrote in boxes to form words. Turns out I was pretty good at it. I find a clean page, open another protein bar, and get to work with the pencil.

By the time I get to "Central American Canal and Roosevelt," I feel my eyes closing, my focus sliding off the page and out through the window into oblivion. I blow out the candle and face my very lonely, dark neighborhood. Across the way, past the hissing currents and shadowy outlines of drowning hedges and telephone poles, a tiny light flickers like one lone star in deep space. At first, I'm sure my eyes are playing tricks on me, or a sliver of escaped moonlight has hit a piece of metal some-where. I prop myself up on my elbow, nearly bumping my head on the ceiling of the nook, and stare hard at the light shining inside a window across the way. I watch it for as long as I can until a warmth overtakes me.

The light from my phone wakes me.

Billy? What's going on?

Why is Mom awake at this hour?

Doing crosswords, I text back to calm her down because she's probably going out of her mind. *Are you almost home?*

I stare at the text bubbles for what feels like twenty minutes until she replies:

Can you get help?

Is she kidding? Is she still on the island? Does she have any idea what's going on here?

Too much water. Still rising. Found food in Jonathan's apartment.

Does she not know that the water has probably wiped Boston off the map? Obliterated the Freedom Trail and JFK's house? It dawns on me that she either can't get the news or is trying to tone it down because she thinks I'm going to panic and jump out the window.

Mom????? I punch out.

Lana and Agnes's house? Is it there?

Mr. Featherstone is at it again, which really bugs me. I don't give two shits about him or his daughters. I need to find Dad and George.

???????????????

Go look, reads the next text.

At what?

Their house.

I look into the black void. The flickering light in the window across the way is gone. It might have come from their house, although it seemed more in the direction of the Taylors.

I text back anyway, *Yes, it's there.* I pause. My finger dangles uselessly over the keyboard, making me feel like an idiot until I get up enough nerve to type back. *Is this my mom or Mr. Featherstone?*

It's me now. Where are Dad and George?

No idea. She wants the truth? *Slept in basement. Woke to water pouring in. Hurry up!*

I think Mr. Featherstone has the phone again because the next message reads: *L and A in their house?*

Can you give my mother back her phone?

CHAPTER SIXTEEN

Juliet

I wake up in the dark, disoriented in Darrell's musty guest bed. Martin is awake, too.

"Listen," he says. "I think the rain is letting up."

I laugh with disbelief. Sure, the rain can stop momentarily, only to pelt Darrell's home ten minutes later with tropical ferocity.

"Let's try Billy," he says.

He sounds wide awake now, self-assured in a way that makes me feel as though I alone concocted our physical contact in a moment of weakness.

"Down here?"

"We can go back upstairs and point it toward the window, like Darrell did with the radio."

"That didn't work."

"I need to find my kids. And Stephanie."

Hoping for a breach in cloud cover is a gamble. If there is no hot spot, as is likely, we'll have to crawl back down here into the dark, the mold, the unfamiliar bedding, the two of us alone.

"Come on. What's to lose?" he says.

"Our minds."

He finds my hand in the dark and pulls me up, steering me toward our bags with a firm grip, his flashlight searching. His blustery movements are off-kilter like one of those tottering hazard buoys in the bay signaling bad weather to come. But I understand his drive, his hope. I felt the same thing last night when I saw Billy's words on the screen and imagined, for a moment, that he would walk through Darrell's door and that my worries would dwindle to a more manageable pitch aimed at finding George and Tom. My texts with Billy have always been temporarily resuscitative, a spritz of dopamine for both of us, until the next bit of mischief or misunderstanding that's too complicated for messaging and has to be dealt with head-on.

I let go of Martin's hand, reach into my backpack, and burrow for the protective phone case. I feel the folded, damp land deed instead and pause.

"Who was the man who *drowned* in his boat, by the way? Who brought you to the island and then stole your rental car?"

"I told you his name is Peterson."

I pull out the folded, damp paper and put it as close to his flashlight as I can.

"And you cosigned a purchase and sales in his name?"

It had felt like a rainy Sunday from my childhood, except there were no puzzles or board games or binge-watching TV. Every hour that ticked by in the sinking beach house, every inch of rain that fell, slowly closed our escape hatch, our Yellow Brick Road back to Boston.

The generator was spotty toward early afternoon, which motivated us to gather candles and matches in a pile on the counter. My mother had a good supply, but gathering these provisions drove home the fact that food, beverages, and candles wouldn't last forever. And furthermore, had I stockpiled these items at home? Had Tom ever put aside an emergency kit and told the boys how to use it? Was that even necessary?

I found it hard to sit at the table, looking at torn paper maps and speculating about rising water. When Martin and my mother debated heading west toward the Pensacola Air Force Base, I slipped into the bathroom to check the phone. The screen glowed ice blue, but there was no connection. Like the TV, it was now a mute inverse of its former self: No information, no way to access its extensive menu by pressing buttons. I went back into the kitchen and sat on the couch next to Martin while he and my mother schemed. I just wanted to blow out of there on Karl's boat. I imagined him circumnavigating the peninsula, racing us up the coast in his cruiser until we hit Cape Cod and breeze through the canal, past Plymouth, Quincy, Dorchester, and right into Boston Harbor.

I made a pitcher of sun tea midafternoon. Martin, who liked strong, black coffee, courteously accepted a glass and took it out to the porch to watch the rain pound the sinking dunes, as it had been all day, as though it would never stop. I regretted that I'd been irritated with him on the beach earlier and distant here at the house. We'd all been boxed in by our own worries, by the news blackout, the mutinous water, the glowing screens that gave us nothing.

I brought the glass of tea to my lips. Through the sliding screen door, I watched him slip one hand into the pocket of his shorts and stare at the storm, presumably thinking about his wife and daughters, how to get to them as fast as possible, even if it meant blowing us off and risking his life to launch a rogue boat with the help of Peterson, his fisherman-friend in Apalachicola.

I joined Martin on the porch, where drizzle from the storm floated through the screen and spritzed our faces.

"I'm out of solutions," he said.

"We'll try again tomorrow when the rain eases up."

"When the rainbow comes out?"

"When the water subsides, and Karl agrees to take us over."

"I should have driven north, through the roadblocks. Or slept at the airport."

"Probably good intuition that you didn't."

"I thought of you and took the road to Carrabelle. Once I got past Wakulla, it was wide open."

"That's good to know for when we get off the island and try to find an airport."

He looked at me. I had no clue what he was thinking. I raised the glass of tea to my lips again and drank, grateful for a prop. Below us, over the porch railings, the pond inundated by high surf engulfed my mother's property and the base of her house, which was now like an island on an island, her former yard teeming with cottonmouths, ocean, and loads of mosquitoes.

"It's not like we're castaways, and they don't know our coordinates," he said. "They aren't coming for us because they can't."

We heard someone climbing the stairs. The front door swung open, and Duncan stepped inside with all his unbound energy.

"This is a storm from hell," he hollered, water dripping down his face, over the surface of his oversized rain jacket, forming puddles on the floor. "What'd we do to make Mother Nature so upset?"

I had my suspicions but kept quiet because Duncan didn't like to talk science.

"Any news?" I asked as Martin and I came back into the kitchen. "Did the Coast Guard radio back?

"No, dear, nothing. Karl is still trying."

He accepted the towel I grabbed from the coat rack by the door, sloppily wiped his face with it, and threw it on a chair.

"There was a man overboard," he said. "Karl thinks he drowned around the bend, probably coming off the ocean side."

I looked at Martin and thought about mentioning the slip of paper I'd found on my way to the beach, but Duncan was agitated.

"Not very smart to take a whaler out in this weather," he continued. "Must have had a good reason to be over there. Wasn't a local boy, though, to pull a stunt like that."

"I know who that was," said Martin. "He's based in Apalachicola, and I doubt he's drowned."

I slipped away and went to my room to search for the piece of paper I'd found on the beach earlier. I pulled it from my damp shorts slung over a chair, unfolded it carefully, and saw Martin's name at the top. It looked like an invoice or plot plan of sorts: $75,000 for an isolated strip of land on Dog Island, facing the Atlantic. Surely, the transaction hadn't taken place within the last forty-eight hours. It wasn't uncommon for visitors to see the wonders of this barrier island and impulsively buy a plot, only to have it sit undeveloped for months or sometimes years. But even if the last two days had been normal, unwavering sunshine and a sublime sea breeze, that kind of whim wasn't Martin's style. As I folded the paper and delicately tucked it into the front pocket of my backpack, Martin rapped on my door.

"Karl wants us at the dock," he said. "Duncan's waiting in the pickup. It's now or never."

Martin sits down on the bed in Darrell's basement, shoulders hunched.

"Peterson and I bought a piece of property together on Dog Island four months ago."

I sit back down on the bed. This time, as far from him as I can get.

"To mass produce bicycles?" I quip.

"He's my business partner. A geologist. Please don't look so alarmed. We own a surveillance company based in Tallahassee. A start-up that monitors changes in the East Coast's weather and shoreline. We needed a base on the Gulf, in the hurricane corridor, with warming ocean temps."

"And Duncan agreed? And the trustees?"

"We didn't get that far."

"Have you been here before?"

"No."

"Did you hear about Dog Island from me?"

"I did."

"Were you planning on telling me at some point? On the airplane, perhaps, when you took my seat?"

"I saw you at the park in our neighborhood a couple of times. I tried to bring it up, but you turned and took off the way you do sometimes."

"Really."

He smiles, just one corner of his mouth retracting in the shadow.

"Do I ever cross your mind, Juliet? Outside of VERT classes?"

"I—. Yes. I don't know. Maybe."

I'm not prepared for this. Left to think of perfect answers in hindsight, in a stranger's basement guest room, while the East Coast sinks before our eyes. I do admire his commitment to VERT, his confidence, his kindness in class. The way he volunteers before anyone else, holds the door, and pours coffee at break. It's natural, with him, to exchange a smile, a nod, a glance. And yes, I admit to myself, his profile is easy to look at.

"What about you?" I deflect.

"I'm drawn to your mystery," he says without wavering. "You walk around sometimes like you've got things swirling around in your head. I want to know what they are."

He holds up the deed, redirecting us because we've gone too far with our words.

"I don't like to talk about this start-up. We're still looking for venture capital. There's a lot of unknowns, from Newfoundland to Cape Hatteras down to Brownsville, not to mention what's happening globally with the weather."

"So, what's this?" I gesture at the window.

"Bad news," he replies, looking toward the rain-spattered glass, the darkness beyond, where seawater crawls inland.

"Like, seismic?"

"Glacial. The Thwaites, maybe. Hell, the entire Western Antarctic Ice Shelf, for all I know. Except it wasn't supposed to happen this fast."

"I've never heard of the Thwaites."

"Well, in the last twenty years, you've definitely felt it falling from the clouds onto your face."

"Maybe you should have bought a surveillance plot on the Vineyard," I say, thinking of Billy's disturbing descriptions. "Kept an eye on New England?"

"WHOI. NOAA. They're all over it. But there are variables in the models. Uncertainties."

"Let me know what's happened to our neighborhood when you figure it out." I try to lean back onto the pillows, but he reaches out and grabs my elbow. Tender? Tactical? I can't tell.

"Let's try Billy," he says.

I follow Martin back up the stairs, through Darrell's kitchen, and into the living room. The flashlight in Martin's hand casts a glow over the gray couch with two matching plush armchairs. At the bay window, I raise the phone screen in my palm. It might be weather patterns, an electromagnetic anomaly, or a remote transition tower coming online. Something opens the portal, and I send a text:

What's going on?

Three dots joggle in the oval gray bubble, and Billy's name appears at the top of the screen. I exhale as though it's my last rattled breath. My next inhalation brings condensed hope, rekindling my soul. I could blast out the door right now without my bags, jump into the car, with Martin by my side, if we were blind to the raging nature around us, had our common sense been suspended, as it was earlier, in the bed in Darrell's basement.

Martin slips his hand behind mine, scaffolding my palm, as we wait for Billy's text.

Doing crosswords.

Jumbled days and nights, I think.

Are you almost home?

I pull my hand away and let the phone slide into Martin's.

"How do I answer that? How do I tell him I'm practically still on the island?"

"We could still be there. Be positive," he replies, feverishly typing into my phone until I pull it from his grip, hesitant to comfort Billy even virtually. It's always been our disrupter, our enabler; I never get it right.

Can you get help? I hammer out.

Too much water. Still rising.

"Shit!" I say as Martin leans in close, our cheeks nearly touching.

"Can he go to the roof and just see if my house is still there?"

I understand his desperation. But for God's sake, I have possibly only seconds to figure out where Tom and George went. If there's anyone in our neighborhood who can help Billy. And how high the water actually is.

Found food in Jonathan's apartment.

"Northeastern grad student who rented our in-law apartment," I tell Martin. "Stiffed us rent and disappeared."

Mom?????

Martin turns from Billy's text and stares through the gaping darkness of Darrell's window as though he can see for miles, over highways, across borders, and into our neighborhood.

I give in and text, *Lana and Agnes's house? Is it there? ???????????????*

Martin looks back at the screen. He puts his hand to his head, sighs, and rubs his scalp repeatedly. God, I wish he'd stop.

Go look, I text.

At what?

I'm wasting precious time.

Their house.

Martin and I stand very still, watching the bubbles.

Yes, it's there.

"Fucking hell. Thank God," says Martin.

Is this my mom or Mr. Featherstone?

I put my finger on the screen and frantically swipe upward to find Martin's confession to Billy that we are together. I forgot that he'd inserted that bit of information at the IGA when I let him have the phone for an instant.

It's me now. Where are Dad and George?

No idea. Slept in basement. Woke to water pouring in. Hurry up!

"I knew he was in the Vault," I tell Martin. "It's like a bunker behind a big solid door. He could have drowned down there."

"He didn't hear a whole town evacuating?"

"Maybe the water swept everything away."

"Except for Billy?"

He looks back down at the phone.

"Can you please ask if my girls are in my house? And Stephanie, too."

Using the last few seconds that a miraculous breach in the clouds has allotted, I try again:

L and A in their house?

But Billy doesn't answer.

I pass Martin the phone. He grabs it and, without missing a beat, begins to type. I figure I owe him this. I've benefitted in a way he hasn't, from being savvy or stupid enough to maintain secret communication with Billy through the Ban. I resent the phone so much that I've refused to comply with the rules: condemning it when it was legal, keeping it when it was condemned, in my own petty act of rebellion.

Martin drums the home button repeatedly with his thumb as we lose the connection.

"Don't break it!"

"I have to reach Stephanie. She isn't going to do very well in this."

"She'll do the best she can like the rest of us. We'll have another chance later on the road," I try to reassure him. "Somewhere closer to Tallahassee, maybe. We need sleep now."

But instead of going back down to the bedroom, we turn and grab each other and crush our bodies in a tight embrace, as if to give the impression to ourselves and the weather that together we are bigger than we really are. Over his shoulder, through the bay window, I glimpse the hazy, jaundiced dawn breaking through a charcoal sky that threatens more water. I can make out the faint winding ribbon of a flooded road past sand pines on the edge of Darrell's property. What are the conditions like down the hill, beyond the tree line? Will the water sweep our car away?

Martin's heart thumps in his chest. His body feels warm, familiar but not, faint aftershave and perspiration, and a tenderness that clutters our intentions.

"Let's go now," I say. "We'll drive over obstacles in the road if we have to."

"We'll move them with our bare hands."

CHAPTER SEVENTEEN

Juliet

In the same dirty muscle shirt he'd worn the night before and oversized green polyester shorts that sweep over his doughy knees, Darrell bids us farewell from the staircase below his house. Holding onto the railing, his bare feet anchored on the rough-sawn boards, he hands me a small cardboard box full of tomatoes and peppers from his garden.

"Stay away from the coast," he says. "The radio transmissions are warning people."

"More flooding?" I ask, desperately wanting facts as I throw my bag into the car and carefully place the vegetable box against the back seat.

"The weather stuff you mentioned," he replies, his eyebrows pulsing with ambiguity, a slightly illegible smile.

He turns, climbs the stairs, and disappears into his stilt house. I get into the passenger seat, pull the charger from my backpack, and plug in the phone.

"I heard those transmissions in the kitchen this morning," says Martin. "They're just a barely audible litany of road closings."

He presses his foot to the gas as we try to make time. We pick up speed when we can see the blacktop under the surface, poking through like a giant sea slug, and slow down when the water, nearly consuming the tires, seems as though it wants to guzzle the entire car. The day is not exactly clear, but the sun does shine momentarily through the dark gray cloud cover. Then, it retreats for good about a half hour into our drive, replaced by alternating drizzle and pounding rain. All we can do is keep our eyes on the road for objects that can puncture tires or cause more serious damage. I check the phone a few times, where it sits in the console charging, no service. And Martin doesn't even bother with his flip phone because no one answers his calls.

When I point out what looks like soybeans or cotton fluttering through the foggy haze in a distant field to our right, as if under a serene breeze, Martin tells me to look closer. It's a Panhandle mirage of seawater rolling in over the crops and burying them.

"Catastrophic sea level rise," he says. "Warming is supercharging the rainfall. Cold water's hitting the Gulf Stream, which probably isn't moving much anymore."

"We need to go inland."

We have no GPS, no paper maps.

"Darrell gave me this," says Martin, reaching into the pocket of his rain jacket and pulling out a paper napkin scarred with squiggly lines of ink and route numbers.

"Good luck with that."

He veers left on a route that rises away from the Gulf. But soon, the road dips again, hits more surf, and devours our tires. I wonder if water pounces like this through the streets at home, reaching its sopping paws at everything. What are Tom and George looking at wherever they've gone? Together and strategizing a way to get back to Billy, I can only hope.

As we rise on a slight plateau above sea level, water recedes just below the wheel rims. The rain subsides to a drizzle, and Martin guns it.

"If we can keep this up," he says, "we can get to Macon in a couple of hours."

"Just don't sink us in the soup on the shoulder."

As we go around a corner and glide into a tide that rushes in from the field to our right, we have no choice but to crawl the car through jade muck, creating a continual wake that fans out from the tires. Rain pelts the windshield. The wipers swing back and forth, back and forth, back and forth across the glass endlessly, rhythmically, numbingly.

Martin spins the wheel to navigate a sharp bend and nearly slams into a black Toyota Corolla spun out on the road, its trunk extending toward swollen swamp waters at the edge.

"What the…," says Martin, pulling up behind it. "I think that's my rental." He opens his door before we've even come to a full stop.

"Don't turn off the car, whatever you do."

He searches for firm footing before getting out.

"And shut your door!" I shout as water splashes in and covers the floor mats.

He wades toward the rental, murky water almost crowning the top of his rubber boots.

"Peterson?" he calls out. "What's wrong?"

The panic in his voice tells me to get out cautiously and follow him. I drag my legs through the swampy green water, keeping an eye out for cottonmouths, which are as plentiful here on this stretch of the Panhandle as robins on the Boston Common in springtime.

Before Martin reaches the left rear door of the rental, I've already spotted Peterson through the window, slumped in back against the right door, legs stretched out on the seat. Martin opens the door resolutely, then cautiously, crouches over, pulls one knee in and onto the back seat, and reaches his hands to the front and back headrests for support.

"What happened, Petes?"

His friend has just enough breath to tell us that he'd pulled the car over onto the shoulder of the road to relieve himself around eleven pm. When he turned around in the rising water, high beams glaring, a water snake bit him.

"Thick. Brown. Green," he slurs.

"Your calf is really swollen, dude. I can see the punctures."

"Burns like fucking fire," Peterson winces.

Martin reaches for Peterson's limp wrist at his hip.

"Pulse is fast."

"Anaphylaxis?"

"Let's hope not."

"I think we went over every scenario in VERT, but this."

"Not a lot of vipers in Boston."

"Grab our bags. We're switching cars."

I slosh back to the Nissan, scanning the watery path for snakes. After stuffing my phone and charger into my backpack, I grab my small red bag, swing Martin's black gym bag over my shoulder, and kill the motor. I leave Darrell's blue-ribbon vegetables in the back seat.

"Throw me my navy sweatshirt," shouts Martin as I'm tossing our luggage into the back of the rental.

He catches the wad of blue cotton and stuffs it under Peterson's leg to keep it elevated. While he raises a plastic water bottle to Peterson's parched lips, I unzip the pocket of my backpack and pull the phone from its case, wondering if anyone would even answer 911 if I were to get through. I unlatch it and look at the screen. There's no service, but I can see Billy's texts. I swipe up for an instant to see his previous chatter, scan a few texts from yesterday, and then read Martin's private one, which he wrote at Darrell's house in the early morning when a brief break in the rain or some other celestial chemistry, brought the phone to life.

Can you see my house? Looking for my daughters.

Hasn't collapsed yet like some of the others.

Martin calls my name now.

"How can I help?" I reply, stuffing the phone back in the backpack.

"Get in the car."

With our belongings in the trunk of the rental and Martin's friend slumped in the back, we roll away through the water as fast as we possibly can with nearly a full tank of gas.

We're on a county road somewhere west of Wakulla Springs. The abandoned scattered homes will surely soon give way to a commercial center, the gas station Darrell promised, a hot spot, and medical services for Peterson. Despite all the practice that Martin and I went through on Sundays in the school gymnasium, checking for a pulse, pumping plastic torsos, and staunching imaginary blood flow, there's nothing we can do for Peterson except keep him as still as possible and make sure he's comfortable. He needs antivenom, and he needs it now.

I pivot in my seat and look down at his pale face, features pinched in agony, buffered by moist tufts of sandy brown hair. I remember very little of him from the windy day at the beach when his boat rocked violently in the waves, and he lost his hat to storm gusts.

"Hold on, buddy," I say, staring down at his swollen calf, where two clear puncture wounds weep blood onto the sweatshirt that Martin placed under his knee.

He trembles as he tries to tell me something through labored breath, gulping for air, saliva dripping from the corners of his mouth.

"Don't talk. We're getting you help."

I flip myself onto my knees and hug the back of my seat as Martin steps on the gas. Reaching out to Peterson, I touch his hand on the seat's edge next to his thigh and then work my fingers under his clammy wrist and feel his racing pulse.

"My fucking leg is burning off," he manages to slur before falling silent and closing his eyes.

"Peterson, you fuck. Hang on," shouts Martin.

"We need to get him somewhere fast."

"You absolute dick," says Martin, gunning it a little recklessly. "Why did you take the car?"

"Game over if we slide off the road," I remind him.

Peterson begins to vomit. The gagging echoes in his throat and tumbles out of his mouth with his last meal. Martin attempts to look over his shoulder but thinks better of it. Knees firmly planted on the front seat, I hug my headrest with my right arm and reach my left hand behind Peterson's head to help him lean toward the floor, littered with McDonald's bags and other junk paper. He moans and pukes again. I try to keep his airways open, but the car begins to slide underneath us as Martin pushes the limits to get help.

"Here it is," he says a few minutes later, slowing down and turning into a gas station mini-mart surrounded by a half dozen pickup trucks steeping up to their axles in water. Martin stops the car, and I step out.

I can see a couple of people through the long rectangular windows of the one-story brick building and begin to slog through the water toward the door. But a middle-aged man in jeans and a T-shirt must have sensed our urgency because he comes out of the gas station and splashes toward me. He rubs his ashen beard with one hand, the other jammed in his front pocket, as he tries to explain the route to a hospital closer to Tallahassee.

"I don't think we have that kind of time," I interrupt.

He reroutes us to a fire station two blocks away. I thank him, get back in the car, and we speed off.

Behind us, the water swirls in a wake over the two-lane paved road, careening into the small mini-malls that sail past my periphery. The landscape that sheds itself through the back window could pass for the aftermath of a bad rainstorm if it weren't for the fields, overgrown trees and shrubs, livestock pens, and a trailer all seemingly sinking around us.

We pull into a small parking lot in front of the brick fire station, where a dozen or so people wait in line. Several others file out through a small side door—a mother with a baby in her arms, a middle-aged man pushing an elderly man in a wheelchair through the water, and a young guy dragging his stiff leg. A man in black firefighter boots with a yellow rim, like my brother's pair that Martin wears now, tries to wave us into a side lot as we pull up. Ignoring him, Martin puts the car in park, and we get out.

"Snakebite," Martin shouts at the man, who then seamlessly barks orders to a middle-aged couple at the station entrance.

The doors burst open, and half a dozen people in civilian clothes, rain boots, windbreakers, and baseball caps approach us. Two men follow through the station door with a stretcher and join the group that swarms the back door of our rental car. Within minutes, they get Peterson onto the stretcher and into the station with little conversation and a lot of efficiency, as though they've done this kind of thing dozens of times. It's the videos we saw in our VERT classes in the school gym in real-time.

A woman comes out of the door of the building. She's short with an athletic body, dark brown skin, and strong biceps that swell from the short sleeves of her pink polo shirt. She wears tortoiseshell glasses, and her many black braids, gathered loosely with a thick orange and pink hair elastic, spill down her back.

"Ma'am," she calls to me, beckoning with one of her hands clad in a powder blue rubber glove. "Please come with me."

But I don't want to help anymore. I want to leave Peterson here, in good hands, keep driving to Billy, and find the rest of my family. Martin won't go for that. So, reluctantly, I leave the car and follow the woman into the station behind the group carrying Peterson. I stand on a waterlogged carpet and watch as they place him on a long aluminum table. Looking past him for an instant through a big glass window, I see the engine room, devoid now of firetrucks. Medical equipment covers a long table next to a pile of drenched orange and yellow firefighter uniforms on the flooded concrete floor.

Peterson still has enough life in him to groan as they carefully adjust him and cushion his leg on a folded gray fleece blanket. I scan the walls for dry outlets that can charge a phone faster than a car. But there are no signs of functioning electricity, no lights on anywhere.

Peterson moans and vomits again. I step toward him to hold his hand, but I'm blocked by three people who hook him to an IV and take his vitals. They discuss the dates on vials that one of them removed from a small foam box.

"Is he going to make it?" I ask the woman with the many braids.

"Probably. He's had a severe reaction. When did he get bitten?"

"Around midnight. We found him this morning."

"Any idea what the snake looked like?"

I shake my head as I picture the thick, black, and green water snakes I've seen around my mother's house. I try to keep focused on the woman and her questions, but my thoughts drift to Billy again. I hope to God there are competent people somewhere in the vicinity of our house if he gets into any kind of trouble.

"Ma'am, the snake?"

"Not sure. It got him in the water."

"Not a lot of dry land right now."

Peterson moans again and says everything burns. I glance toward him and see a monitor on a stand behind the table, plugged into a portable generator with several outlets. He wretches again, but nothing comes out, and then he sputters: "Big, green, thick."

"Moccasin," says one of the men tending to him. "Let's go with that. We're running out of time."

"Start the drip," says another.

"Let's get a second IV line going. Fifty to ninety MLs."

"You'll need five vials."

"Date … November 15th, 2026."

"That's good enough. Slow drip."

"TT vaccine. Epinephrine."

"Got it."

"Doc," says a man, turning to the woman with the braids. "Should we go with corticosteroids?"

"Don't have any," she replies.

She turns to me, "How old is your friend?"

"No idea. I don't really know him." I look around for Martin. "My friend will have better answers," I tell her.

Martin steps into the office just then. Looking down at his feet, he pauses for a moment as his boots sink into the beige rug that feels like a mossy Maine forest floor. He looks up at everyone, a glint of faith in his smile. He believes in something that moves in the opposite direction of despair, and I'm grateful for it, for his companionship, too, despite the awkwardness at times, our burst of tangled intimacy. He takes my place next to Peterson and the doctor, and I go outside to grab my backpack and charger from the rental so I can try the phone again.

The line of people has grown by a dozen or so, I note as I head toward our car, which is parked in a space on the side of the station next to two black SUVs. The fact that I'm here and not on the road, heading toward New England, begins to eat away at my patience. Peterson is a stranger, surrounded by numerous competent emergency medical personnel who will probably save his life. Billy, on the other hand, is alone, as far as I can tell, with no one to help if he gets into trouble, runs out of food and water, or needs some reassurance after dark. We can't hang around here for much longer.

I open the car door. My backpack is gone from the front seat. I look back at the line of people. Two guys in their mid-twenties talking in low southern drawls stare at me. The taller of the two, half his face consumed by curly red facial hair, jams his hands deep in the pockets of his denim shorts. The other guy, in a maroon baseball cap with Florida State on the front, splays his legs, his arms pretzeled in front of him, propping up his slumped shoulders. They watch me as I splash around the car, peering into the back window. I think I hear them laughing, mocking my edginess, my nervous darting from one side of the car to the other. I try to keep a lid on my reactions despite the tension that hums around us all, despite Peterson, the crying baby, the interminable gray of what feels like an endless delay.

I'm afraid that if I can't text Billy soon, he might think I've drowned and do something stupid. My anxiety for his anxiety balloons, and I resent Tom and George for their absence, though I miss them desperately. I resent Peterson for being in the wrong place at the wrong time. And I resent Martin for bringing us here to tend to his business partner, for coming down to *my* island in the first place and underhandedly cosigning a purchase and sales, sight unseen, with not even a courtesy call. I close my eyes, my mind tamping down on the rising ball of heat in my throat and the tightness at my temples.

When I fully open them, my gaze lands on drowning cattails bobbing in a swampy marsh, just like the one in front of my mother's beach house. Soon, the soft brown seed parcels will succumb to the sludge and join forces with the ocean, like so much of the farmland we've passed on the road.

We need to get out of here.

I open the passenger door again and glance inside. Maybe my bag has been shoved under the seat. With no luck there, I slam the door, wade to the trunk, and open it with a little too much force as it rebounds in my face. I curse loudly and then realize that the people still waiting in line for medical help, most of whom arrived here before we did, stare in my direction.

The guy with the Florida State hat asks if everything's okay.

"I need my phone," I reply.

He glances at his friend with the red hair.

"You think we took it?"

"Naw, ma'am, we don't do that around here," says the redhead.

"Y'all let it go," says a young woman, a listless baby with a croupy cough in her arms.

I step toward the infant, swaddled in a yellow blanket, and look down at her flushed face.

"You need to get to the front of the line," I tell the woman. "You shouldn't have to wait."

"She's got a fever," she says, chewing at her bottom lip.

"Let's get you up there." I put my hand on her shoulder. "I know the doctor inside."

"They know I'm here. We're waiting for fluids."

"In the drizzle?"

"There are sick people inside. Humidity's good for her lungs."

The guy with the red hair grins at me with contempt.

"We can take care of her," he says. "Take your Toyota rental and your fancy phone and go home."

"Look. My son is stuck in the flood, far from here. I'm just trying to reach him, okay?" Martin appears in the doorway and calls me over.

"What are you doing?"

"My bag's gone. With the phone!"

"Your bag's in here. Someone thought it was Peterson's and brought it in." He puts his hand on my shoulder.

"You can't act like that here, Juliet."

"You're right. I'm sorry. There's a woman with a sick baby over there. Jesus, why aren't they helping her?"

He pulls me close and gives me a bear hug as if to reset my mood. I stiffen in his arms but then give in and embrace him. When we let go of each other, he stares into my eyes.

"I'm fine," I say, stepping back. "I'm going to get someone to help that baby."

"They know what they're doing in there. Don't piss people off."

There's some commotion in the line, splashing and swearing.

"We got our own fucking problems," shouts one of the guys at the back of the line. "We don't need her shit, too."

"Amen," says someone else.

"I can't find my diabetic mother," shouts another.

"My grandpa drowned last night."

"End Times, people."

I turn my back. With his hand on my shoulder, Martin gently prods me through the doorway into the makeshift triage, where the doctor with the braids stands over Peterson. His eyes are closed, a dash of color on his cheeks glaze his otherwise pallid expression. I find my bag, grab the phone, and plug it into the portable generator.

"Where'd you get that?" asks the doctor.

"I kept it."

"Don't those cases cost like five hundred dollars?"

"Not that much, but, yeah, a lot."

"Those phones have made a lot of people sick."

I nod my head and start to defend myself but think better of it after what just happened outside.

"Why'd you keep it?"

"It's complicated. I keep in touch with my son."

"He's got one, too?" she asks, her nostrils flaring with disapproval. "I've seen kids sick from those devices."

"Yeah, you said that. My son's alone up north. I'm just going to plug this in for ten minutes."

She looks at it like it's radioactive.

"Yeah, okay. Go for it. I hope you find him."

"I plan on it," I reply, placing the phone on a small shelf above the generator, as far from us as I can.

"Be careful," she says. "The Eastern Seaboard is inundated." I can feel Martin looking at me, but I don't return the gaze. I can't risk our entangled worries derailing my push to get us out of here, keep us going north. I'm relieved when he leaves momentarily with an attendant to search for fluids and antibiotics in another room.

"How do you know that?" I ask the doctor as she prods Peterson's wrist like a pro, checking his pulse again.

"Chatter around here. People connected to the air force base near Panama City. That's all I heard, just chatter."

"My son in Boston answers me through texts. I'm going to find him," I say. "Add that to the chatter."

She smiles sympathetically.

"Your husband seems devoted to his friend."

"They're business partners. And he's not my husband." She winces at the sudden ping, audible through the protective case perched on the aluminum shelf above the makeshift bed supporting Peterson. I lean toward the generator, grab the phone case, pull out the phone, and hold it close to my face while the doctor and two attendants step away from me and stare with distrust.

Neighborhood smells rotten. Losing my appetite. Can you hurry?

"Shit," I say loudly.

Should I try to leave? Running out of eggs and beans. Some ramen left. An orange.

The doctor looks at me; trained to act, she's waiting for a cue.

"He's alone," I tell her. "In Boston."

"I have a son. I understand."

I look back down at the screen.

Are there other houses? I text. *Food there, maybe?*

Not sure.

Can you look?

I'll try.

Be careful.

A ridiculous directive, considering the circumstances. Gray bubbles roll on. Another ping in my palm.

Houses got swept away.

I blink away images of my neighborhood imploding into an invading ocean. I've seen footage of tsunamis guzzling cities, coastal floods surging and creating rivers out of roads, but this notion in my own neighborhood lacks logic. I need to ring meaning out of Martin when we get back into the car because he seems to know something about the weather that the rest of us don't.

You need to leave, I text.

And go where?

Inland, is all I can manage because I'm desperate to find Martin now.

He needs to read the description of our neighborhood and feel the same desperation to blow out of this place despite Peterson, who is in good hands. But Martin has disappeared again.

The soppy floor, the swampy odor, the strangers outside, standing around waiting in increasingly fetid water like cattle in a manure lagoon, send my mind spinning. What is Billy looking at? What does he smell, exactly, as the hours drag on inside our flooded, sinking home? As he runs out of food, waiting for nighttime to come? I picture retreating to Dog Island and my mother, summoning my family there, living off Gulf shrimp, bay oysters, and kelp.

I glance at the doctor dressing the punctures on Peterson's swollen purple calf that ooze watery pus. She loops adhesive tape around a sterile gauze pad slathered with antibiotic ointment while Peterson knots his face in agony. If Martin and I leave now, we can take turns driving through the night. If we can get through the water and past the roadblocks, maybe we'll be home in twenty-four hours.

I look back at the phone and text.

Hang in there. Be there soon.

Just as I press send, there's a ping and Billy texts:

Girls are in house. Candlelight in window at night. Stuff hanging on porch. Pretty sure it's them.

I catch sight of Martin now through the glass windows, heading toward us with some boxes in his arms. He glides through the foot-high waterline, steady and swift on his feet, like a hockey player, like nothing can tip him over. Striding up to us, he squeezes himself past Peterson and hands the boxes to the doctor.

"Has he gotten back?" he asks, turning to me and looking down at the phone in my palm.

"Not yet," I reply for some reason, immediately wanting to take back my words and tell him what Billy has just texted about his daughters. But I've already lied. And that lie feels powerful.

"We should get going," I say.

"Yes, we should."

He looks curiously down at the phone in my hand.

"Like now," I repeat.

CHAPTER EIGHTEEN

Billy

I wake up in George's bed and squint at his window. There's a sun out there somewhere trying so hard to shine through clouds and constant drizzle, reminding me a little of my screen when the power is on and it glows, but there's no connection. I take a whiff of the air, and it's more than a little off. Something's rotting, and I need to let someone know, preferably George or Sam Carmichael, but we've been out of touch lately.

I grab the phone from the portable charger on George's desk. I jam my thumb against the home button over and over until I'm sure I've broken it. Anger isn't going to get me anywhere, as George likes to say.

I get out of bed, put on a pair of his long gray cotton shorts and long-sleeve black and white rugby shirt, and go about my morning because Dad always says that sticking to a routine can be therapeutic. But when I raise the bathroom window to grab some water from the buckets and pans on the roof deck, that rotting stench wafts in, making it very unpleasant to wash my face, brush my teeth, and dress my palm with bacitracin and clean gauze.

To distract myself, I boil water on the propane stove in my bedroom to make a cup of Jonathan's Turbo-Charged Echinacea Tea because, as the box says, "It's a powerful immune system booster with antibacterial and anti-infection properties." Unfortunately, it doesn't treat extreme anxiety, loneliness, and absolute hopelessness due to cataclysmic, sci-fi-scale weather events in your neighborhood. In any case, I try to read an old *National Geographic* about Russia taking over the melting Arctic.

Since I can't concentrate, I invent a bunch of conversations in my head aimed at George:

"You're a real dick for leaving me alone."

"Where were you, little brother, when we got swept away with the rest of humanity?"

"You know damn well where I was."

"I don't know about the Vault, if that's what you mean."

"Fuck off, George. You should have found me. You should have looked harder."

"That's your secret with Mom? Well, Dad and I have a little secret, too. And you'll never find out."

"George, you've left me alone, and now I'm going to drown."

"Buck up, bud. Time to be an adult."

I doze off. When I wake, I try to read again, but that rancid smell hits me like a punch to the gut, killing my appetite for lunch, which I've been looking forward to. My focus glides off the page and toward the open window. I know what it is. Why pretend any longer? It's dead flesh; it's coming from outside, and it makes me very, very, very upset.

I'm not sure how much longer I can lie here on George's bed. I feel more and more agitated, like I do when I have way too much homework, basketball practice, ultimate Frisbee, model UN, and midterms. Only now, the stress comes from loads of time with nothing to do but wait it out and push away the thoughts that rush into my head and spin like Sam's pet gerbil on its exercise wheel.

I finally force myself onto my feet, go right to the nook, and climb in. I look out at the house where I saw the candle burning last night. I'm pretty sure that this is the first time I've seen colorful panties and T-shirts draped over a second-story porch railing. Girls wear electric colors like that for the same reason certain birds, fish, and insects have florescent trumpets, bioluminescent antenna, and plumes sticking off the top of their heads.

When I look back at the window, I see a gray shape move across the pane. And then another. I stare for a long time through the hazy, overcast glow and drizzle at the back and forth of two figures moving through the room, avoiding the rest of the house, it seems. The two houses bookending the one with the drying panties have caved in on themselves, exposing whole rooms, open now to the elements. A white curtain hangs limply in a broken window frame; an exposed crumbling chimney rises from a yawning hole in the roof.

I hear the scratchy echo of a screen opening out there and gaze back at the window with the moving figures. An arm up to the elbow appears and drops several cans and a wad of paper towels out the window. Under normal circumstances, that behavior would have made all the moms and dads around here lose their shit and talk about it nonstop at dog parks and soccer fields. The next time Mr. Featherstone texts, pretending to be Mom, I'm going to tell him that his daughters are trashing the neighborhood.

As I stare at their window, looking for their shapes again, I wonder if they smell the same foul air that I do. I reach toward George's desk and grab the phone. There are no apps or settings anymore. Just the message box, as blue-gray as the lining of an old, moldy swimming pool, that pops up for fuck knows why or how inviting me in and getting my heart rate up.

Neighborhood smells rotten, I manage to text, hoping to God that Mom has service wherever she is. *Losing my appetite. Can you hurry? Should I try to leave? Running out of eggs and beans. Some ramen left. An orange.*

I smile down at the gray bubbles marching along, grateful for the phone despite the cancer, which has always seemed half-baked to me, a conspiracy or a New World Order.

Are there other houses? she texts back. *Food there, maybe?* She clearly doesn't get it.

Not sure.

Can you look?

I'll try.

Be careful.

I want to laugh like Mr. Barrett at her cluelessness, but text instead, *Houses got swept away.*

You need to leave.

And go where?

Inland.

She needs a dose of reality, but I don't want her to lose her mind and have a panic attack in front of Mr. Featherstone.

Hang in there. Be there soon.

Be there soon? Is she shitting me? It's like she still thinks I'm five years old. Gray bubbles circle around, trying to deliver her message through crashed electromagnetic waves. Maybe if Mr. Featherstone knows that his kids are still here, he'll make a better effort to get Mom home. So I text:

Girls are in house. Candlelight in window at night. Stuff hanging on porch. Pretty sure it's them.

I'm tired of waiting for her texts. Why does it take so long to answer? The skin of my arms and legs begins to tingle as if I've been swimming in salt water for too long and need to dry off.

What's going on? Mom? Mom? Mom?

CHAPTER NINETEEN

Juliet

Standing over Peterson in the firehouse, I look at Billy's words again. If I convey them to Martin in the right way, I can get a quick departure with no strings attached to poor Peterson. But I've just lied to Martin, so I'll have to backtrack somehow. If I tell him everything Billy texted, Martin might ask for the phone and attempt a back-and-forth with Billy, causing more delay and maybe resentment from Billy since he knows now that Martin is with me and his own father has gone missing.

I swallow hard. The girls' names seem slow to exit my mouth, even though I know how happy Martin would be to hear the news that they might be home, alive, maybe with their mom. I want to shout them out because I'm thrilled for him. But for self-preservation and Billy's welfare, I want to stuff this information deep into storage where I can get to it if Martin needs persuasion, as dishonest as it sounds because he isn't hearing the urgency in my voice when I say we need to leave now. He's been helpful and comforting up to this point. That Lana and Agnes are two doors down, diagonally across from Billy, in a somewhat intact house, is a burst of hope, proof of the resiliency of young people, which could change Martin's reality. Our reality. I open my mouth to say their names, but nothing comes out, and I'm both ashamed and pleased with myself.

He's turned his back and begins helping the nurse pack a small black bag with sports drinks and protein bars. I glance down again at the phone in my palm and then over at Martin, his muscular forearms working efficiently to make sure we have supplies on the ride back. The strength and no-nonsense of his efforts, grabbing a tub of peanut butter and a box of protein bars and stuffing them into the bag, get me thinking about his determination.

What if this news about his girls causes him to find whatever means he can to bolt out of here without me? People do that for their kids, regardless of how nice and fair they seem. Peterson has caused delay. But maybe I do, too, when I question what we're doing or unrealistically think out loud about retrieving my mother from the island. Or when I hesitate to share the phone. His unflappability, the deep concern he often shows, putting others first, could morph into self-preservation if the circumstances favor it, to save what he values most. I understand that impulse now better than anyone as I stare down at the screen and rapidly tap a message back to Billy:

Are you sure it's Lana and Agnes? What do you see exactly?

As I wait for his reply, I say to Martin, his back still turned, "Peterson will be in good hands here. This way, you and I can go straight to Macon and try the airport there, like Darrell said we should."

Martin zips up the bag of food and turns to me.

"Peterson is coming with us."

"That's insane," I say, looking down at Peterson, still connected to the drip, resting underneath the gray fleece the nurse threw over his upper body.

I stare at his swollen calf wrapped in gauze and think what absolute madness it is to put a guy in this condition into a sedan and drive him, zigzagging in a flood, across borders. It's also more delay at the expense of Billy. And besides, where are we taking Peterson? How in the world, in his condition, could he handle a car ride even under normal circumstances?

"We have no choice," says Martin. "They're closing this place in an hour. More water's coming in."

"And into New England."

"Probably," he nods.

"Then why delay?"

I look at the doctor as if she'll back me up. She has a son. Doesn't she understand what's at stake? Ignoring my plea, she sweeps by me, grabbing a blanket and a gallon of water from a cabinet and an armful of meds from various drawers and placing them on a desk.

"I'm going to walk you both through dressing the wound," she says. "Keep it clean with an antimicrobial. We have no intravenous antibiotics, so he'll have to take these."

She shakes a bottle of ampicillin at me.

"This is nuts," I say. "Take him to a shelter or another facility where there's medical personnel." I feel the pestering tug of my conscience, but for Billy's sake, smother it. "How can we possibly take care of Peterson in the back of a rental car? It's not fair to him."

"We got a man with a heart attack, two dialysis patients, and a baby who's showing signs of meningitis. There's only so much I can do. He got the antivenom. It's up to him now."

I look down at the phone in my palm, squeezing it as if that will extract Billy's reply—the affirmation I need from him to press my point with Martin: that it's definitely his girls in their house. Just like Billy, they're alive and waiting for us, possibly without a mother. It's time to find a hospital for Peterson. Then Martin and I can leave, unhindered by someone as severely injured as his business partner. But before I can even form words, Martin comes over to me.

"We can't leave him alone. That's basically a death sentence. This is the world we're in now, Juliet."

Two volunteers, who entered the room a moment ago, are already lifting Peterson onto the stretcher. Seeing no response from Billy, but pretty sure those two girls are

Martin's, I pack my phone into its case and into my backpack and follow Martin toward the door. My thoughts dash between the doctor's instructions—do I have any question for her about Peterson's care?—the news of more water, and how and when to tell Martin that his girls are probably still at home. And maybe his wife, too.

The people waiting outside for medical care have broken the line. Some wander along the side of the road, kicking their rain boots aimlessly through the brown-green water. Others stand in it, cursing at the station. An older couple in baggy denim shorts and oversized T-shirts with Looney Tunes characters don't seem to understand. They watch the line of people disperse and look left and right until a volunteer escorts them toward a curb and huddles with them to break the news.

The two volunteers carrying Peterson maneuver him into the back seat like an oversized package. They prop him up with a blanket and pillow and wire a bag of fluids to the handle above the back window.

"This isn't right," I say to the doctor who has followed us out.

"We go with what we have," she replies. "Now listen." She points toward Peterson in the back seat. "Let the bag drip until it runs out. There's another one packed with the medicine to administer this evening. Antibiotics every twelve hours."

"Okay," I nod.

"Watch for dangerous swelling."

"Edema." I want her to know I'm not clueless. Just impatient.

"You'll see it. Taut, shiny skin. The wound will weep profusely." She pushes her glasses up the bridge of her nose and winces to help them climb. "There's a small chance he could have an allergic reaction to the antivenom."

"Anaphylaxis."

"Well, a milder serum sickness. It can happen later, down the road."

"Thanks for your help."

"Sure thing, and best of luck. I hope you find your son."

I turn to the car door and pause for a moment, looking beyond flooded fields and sinking pine forests toward a coast that's mutating rapidly. Is Dog Island still there? I fear the worst and miss my mother. But there's only one path now, and it's north.

"Get in, Juliet," shouts Martin, climbing into the front seat of the rental.

Out of habit, I grab my phone from my backpack. I glance down as my other hand reaches for the passenger door. Service is gone again; my conversation with Billy about Lana and Agnes is inaccessible. I could tell Martin now that Billy thinks he's seen his daughters. I could raise his spirits and, by proximity, mine. For a while, at least. But half a dozen people, including the two men I'd skirmished with earlier, congregate around our car. Perhaps they've taken an interest in Peterson. Poisonous snakes are common around here, but it isn't often that one bites.

As I open the car door, the weight of rising water against my boots slowing me down, the man with the red beard scoffs, "Looks like you found your phone."

"Didn't get the memo from the feds?" shouts his pal.

"She's got privileges," says a woman in a purple spandex running bra and bike shorts.

"Okay, guys, enough," orders one of the volunteers, who started back toward the station but pivots now to address us. "Let's break it up. Water's coming."

"She's bombarding us with toxic metals and radiation," warns the woman in spandex.

"Just what we need," calls someone from the back of the small crowd.

"Give her a break," says the woman with the baby in her arms. "She's lost her son."

I slide into the car, close the door, and look over at Martin, who's assessing the rearview and side mirrors. As I roll down my window to defog the windshield, Martin takes his foot off the brake and begins to slowly reverse the car so as not to threaten anyone and cause more rage. I lock the door and listen to Peterson's labored breathing, the car now moving forward and away from the fire station.

We head toward the regional airport in Macon on a narrow county road, avoiding Route 75 and the possibility of unpredictable crowds, few resources, and no emergency personnel to keep the peace. Muddy water sloshes across our path—six inches, two feet, and everything in between, depending on our elevation. Our front bumper repels driftwood, soda bottles, flip-flops and sneakers, weeds and branches, an old doll, thick, tawny, snake-like hemp rope, and colored bits of plastic. Every so often, a car passes by, vying for the shallowest space in the center of the road; it's a game of yielding and dominating with the steering wheel and foot pads, and Martin might be better at it than I am.

I'm distracted now, anyway, by kids, babies, teens, and old folks, whose bewildered expressions behind glass we probably project right back. A couple on the side of the road tries to salvage belongings from a flooded home. They seem to lack the strength to heave it all into their pickup. A mile or so on, a young man trudges along the shoulder, leading a black horse through two feet of water, going God knows where for shelter.

Late morning turns to early afternoon as we slog on. Peterson, with his eyes closed, moaning every so often. Someone, Martin, I imagine, removed the McDonald's bags covered in vomit from the floor below the back seat, but I can still smell it. Regardless, I try to feed Peterson a corner of one of the protein bars they gave us at the fire station. But he just wants to sleep.

We trail behind a big black pickup that carves us a passage in the floodwaters until Martin is forced to slow because of heavy rain blasting the windshield. The wipers scrub the glass, and he holds the steering wheel firm. I pivot and kneel on the seat again to cover Peterson's shivering body with the gray fleece blanket and adjust the hydration drip. Mostly, I feel ineffectual, as fluid from the wound leaks through the gauze binding his swollen calf.

When I try the radio, all I get is static, a litany of closures, routes I can't identify, and a list of open shelters in unfamiliar towns.

"Should we go to one of these places?" I ask.

"You want to unload him."

"It's not fair to put him through this."

"We need to reach the airport. Just an hour or so more, and we'll get him emergency services."

"Is that where they are?"

Martin cracks a feeble smile, but his lips are clamped with regret for a business trip that was upended, for his split-second decision to flee to the island, and for Peterson, who, no doubt, will further delay our journey home.

Out of habit, I reach toward the phone in the console, thinking of Google Maps, which disappeared around six weeks ago, shortly after the Ban.

"Can we not do that now, Juliet? Too much going on. I need to focus on the road."

But I want to reach Billy to see if he got my last text. It is Agnes and Lana, isn't it?

"Please," says Martin, as I clutch the phone in my palm. "I just can't take it. The conditions out here are awful."

I take a deep breath. "I have something to tell you."

"Go ahead, then."

I can't quite get the words out. It's like the fib that you tell when you're little, when the truth becomes more difficult to divulge for the sheer length of time that you've held it in. What if Billy is mistaken and saw a reflection in the girls' window rather than candlelight? It wouldn't be the first time he's confused facts or expressed wishful thinking. Or said something he thinks will please me.

"Well? The car is sliding all over the road. Say it."

"It can wait," I say, putting the phone back in the console.

"Good," he replies, his hands seesawing on the unstable wheel. "Not sure I can keep this up much longer."

I hold onto the door handle as the car swerves and shimmies. Peterson moans. If we can just get to the airport and find him help, I can take a minute to confirm with Billy what, exactly, he saw in the house across the way. Then I'll tell Martin the truth. One way or the other, I'll have to console him. It's terrifying not knowing the whereabouts of people you love. But then, when you do locate them, their situation conjures a new set of alarming scenarios.

"Okay," says Martin, as we rise on an incline. "It's a little better here. What were you going to say?"

But before I can answer, Peterson gurgles urgently in the back seat. I unbuckle, flip myself over onto my knees, hug my seat again, and look down at him.

"What is it, buddy? What do you need?"

Maybe he's cold, I think, grabbing the fleece again and pulling it up toward his chin, tucking it around his shoulders. He somehow curls himself over onto his side. What's left of the bag of IV fluids plunges to the floor of the car.

"Pull over," I say to Martin. "Something's wrong."

"Where? We'll sink."

He swerves to avoid junk on the road.

Peterson moans again and rolls onto his back, and then whispers, "I'm going to shit my pants."

Martin slows the car and stops in the middle of the road, a milky green tea up to the axles.

"Give me the goddamned phone," he says. "I've had enough." He reaches toward the console and grabs the device.

"No, no, no!" I shout, sitting back against the seat.

He glances at me, his eyes flashing with confusion. I grab the phone out of his hand with such force that he pivots in his seat for an instant, his whole upper body interrogating me.

"Look," I say, furiously poking the home button. "You said it yourself—there's no service out here. No 911."

"What the hell, Juliet."

He leans back against the seat and exhales hard, peers at Peterson in the rearview, and looks left through the foggy, sweating window, searching for counsel in the saturated fields and falling rain. The only thing predictable out here are the windshield wipers thumping and scouring the glass.

I grab my phone and throw it into my backpack.

"We need to find higher ground now," he says, steering the car back into the lane. "Get him out so he can relieve himself. Or we're going to have a real problem."

As we slow around a corner, looking desperately for a patch of road where we can pull over, Martin slams the brakes. The black Ford pickup we trailed a while ago is stalled in the middle of the road. Five men in baby blue, V-necked, short-sleeved shirts and matching baggy pants are climbing out of the vehicle. They slam their doors a bit too hard and look back at us.

The smell of lingering vomit mixes now with an even more repugnant odor. I can't open the door fast enough. I step into the water, where the drizzle, humidity, and unsoiled air compress the chaos of the moment. But Martin grabs my arm and pulls me back.

"Those are convicts," he says, in a calm tone that understates the potential risk we're now confronting. I duck back in, slam the door, and lock it.

"I wouldn't get out again if I were you."

"I'm shitting my pants," gurgles Peterson.

"Fuck this," I say, unlocking my door and opening it again. "We've got to get him cleaned up despite our new comrades."

In blue scrubs, water stains up to their knees and sodden-leather work boots barely laced, the group of five splashes toward me.

"Miss!" they shout, dragging themselves through the water. "Do you have anything to eat? We're starving."

The shortest one, with a dirty-blond buzz cut and patchy, puffy, sun-damaged skin, pushes the tall man in front of him, who careens forward while maintaining a disarmingly cheerful expression. His long, muscular brown arms futilely paddle at his sides, and his legs extend into a sprint position but ultimately give out as the velocity of the push propels him toward the water onto his knees. He's on all fours in the water for a split second before bouncing back on his feet, laughing and slapping his soaking thighs.

"You're dinner, Rogers."

"I'm in," shouts one of them. "Can't live on this crate of oranges."

"Ma'am, can you help?" says the blond who pushed his buddy. They all turn and stare at me.

"Where are you going?" one of them asks.

"Our friend in the back of the car has a snakebite and isn't doing so well." I feel a certain security in what I've just said, as if any temptation to antagonize us might be thwarted by Peterson's crisis within the larger one we all share out here on rural Route 155.

"Cottonmouth?"

I nod. "And a bad reaction."

"That's not good," says the tall man in soaking scrubs.

"He got the antivenom. We're just waiting now."

A guy with straight black hair falling over his ears and into his unshaven face asks again if we have any food. If that's all they want, we can negotiate.

"Protein bars and peanut butter," says Martin, getting out of the car reluctantly and coming up behind me. "You're welcome to have some."

"No hamburgers?" asks an older, muscular bald guy with toffee-colored skin and a short white goatee that meagerly shrouds deep ruts at the corners of his mouth.

"I wish," says Martin, as he turns and heads back to the trunk of our car to get the food.

The bald man pulls his muscular legs through cloudy, green water that reaches just below his knees. Grabbing the back of the pickup, he nimbly pulls himself onto the rear bumper and steps one leg into the flatbed; the other stays firmly grounded on the tailgate. He bends forward and begins to fill his shirt with oranges that glow florescent against the early afternoon gray haze of this corner of pastoral Panhandle.

Cradling the fruit like a newborn puppy guarded tightly against his chest, he climbs off the truck and moves back toward me. Martin is at my side again, clutching the tub of peanut butter and a six-pack of protein bars. No sooner have we made the exchange, the oranges now in our trunk, when the men eagerly rush the bald guy as he places the peanut butter and protein bars in the bed of the pickup.

"Stand down," he tells them.

They fall in line and stare silently as he now wades toward the back door of our car. He opens it and withdraws his body from the vehicle.

"Fuck, that stinks," he says, frowning.

I hear Peterson's faint voice, but I can't make out his words.

"Let's go, boys," says the bald man. "Get our amigo out of the car."

"Wait ... what are you ... " I attempt, but Martin grabs my elbow and squeezes it as the four men swarm the vehicle, each straining to peer inside.

The passenger doors open, and two men kneel on the back seat and fold themselves into the car, griping and laughing.

"Gently," says the bald guy.

"Dang, he reeks."

"Time to feed the warden."

They laugh gruffly but harmoniously, as giddy and familiar with each other as siblings, collectively efficient, like workers on an assembly line or bartenders in a cramped pub. Careful not to knock against Peterson or each other, they slip their hands under his back and legs, avoiding the soiled seat of his pants, and birth him out of the back as if he were a delicate sea creature and the mere air could soon dry him out.

I stand back, keeping my eyes on my backpack in the front seat as Peterson is transported to the pickup bed. The bald guy swings himself onto the tailgate again, grabs a gray tarp from the back, and unfolds it.

They lay Peterson down on the tarp in front of the crate of oranges, tenderly elevating his festering calf. A task made easier by the paramedics at the fire station, who cut off his pant leg with scissors. No one acknowledges the smell as his pants are carefully peeled off, leaving him naked from the waist down. The tall guy discreetly uses Peterson's blue plaid boxers and jeans to clean him and then flings the soiled clothing far into the swampy brush. Peterson is back in their arms, hammocked in the gray tarp, heading toward the reedy, boggy water at the edge of the road.

The blond guy has found an old paint can in the muck. He scoops up flood water and pours it between Peterson's legs while the bald man carefully elevates Peterson's calf to keep the gauze dry. Water cascades from the corner of the tarp into the currents below Peterson. The men move him several strides upstream, repeat the process with the paint can, and then discard the tarp. Peterson, eyes half closed, brow puckered, seems to surrender to the circumstances, which we can only hope don't conclude with a blood infection. Watching him, I'm uneasy at how unprepared Martin and I are despite the VERT course and the goodwill from strangers.

I think of my family again, how far we are from each other, from the simple Sunday mornings with coffee, bagels, and a walk to the Arboretum. Or sunning ourselves on the beach at Gloucester. I feel that jittery pull again to sprint away from everyone, jump in the car, and step on the gas. But there's no interrupting this humanitarian mission. It has to get done. I look at Martin, a little too far away to hear my plea. I put my pointer fingers together and make a wheel motion: time to go. But he's fixated on Peterson, who wobbles in the arms of the prisoners.

They've pulled him now into a culvert where deep water runs in gullies, the bald man still supporting Peterson's elevated bandaged calf. Ripples of water rebound and push against the reeds, making them chafe and whistle. Peterson moans, but the intonation is sweeter, a rattling in his chest that seems more pleasurable than the despair he warbled earlier. The moaning coalesces into a plural baritone melody as the men begin to sing, their voices deep and celestial, from another time in this country when people broke out in song to communally savor joy or sorrow.

Shall we gather at the river ... With its crystal tide forever ...

Martin pulls off his rain boots, stuffs his black socks inside, and glides through the water toward me.

"What the hell are you doing?" I stammer as he shoves his boots—my brother's boots—at me.

He marches past into the deeper water, gliding at times through the swampy tide, his stride extended like a modern dancer's. I can see that he's singing now; he knows the words of the hymn. Submerged to his thighs, water soaking the bottoms of his navy shorts, his mouth open, the words pour out.

When we reach the shining river ... Lay our every burden down ...

What about the snakes? No one seems to care about that danger anymore. He pushes through the circle, finds his place, and slips his flat palms under Peterson's lower back. They carry him out of the water, over the bank, and back along the flooded asphalt road, shedding water and remorse as they chant their canticle about a better world beyond ours, as if what we've been gifted in the here and now—pomegranates, elms, honey bees and cicadas, waterfalls, rainbows, pine forests, frost crystals, tropical coral reefs, deep canyons, and sunsets—just doesn't measure up and we need something else to placate our hungry, frail souls.

I squeeze my brother's rain boots against my chest, wishing I could teleport him and his horse sense down here because my path home might have been shorter. Standing idle in the water and drizzle, I begin to really miss him, to pray for his safety, while I watch Martin and the men place Peterson on the bed of the truck, someone's shirt under his head.

"What'd he do to get a pair of these?" asks the blond prisoner, holding up blue prison trousers someone has grabbed from the cab. He slashes at the pant leg with a hunting knife to accommodate the wound.

"DWI."

"Insurance fraud."

"Naw, dogs," says the older bald guy. "With a baby face like that, manslaughter. Now give me the knife."

I'm watching the long, thick blade, hoping the knife gets tucked back where it came from. But the blond doesn't want to give it up. To buy time, he slices an orange in half, lifts Peterson's head, and brings the orange toward his face and over his mouth, crushing the fruit and all its shortcomings to a pulp in his palm. Peterson parts his lips, and with a desperation that shows he still has life, sucks at the air and the weak thread of juice like a fish stranded on a riverbank.

"Weapons down," says the bald guy.

The prisoners belt out laughter, and I try to play along with a big smile, telling myself that bolting for the car and leaving them all here, including Martin, might not be the best solution.

"Where did you learn to sing like that, Martin?" I whisper as he pulls himself toward me in a slow-motion sashay, as though musical notes still flow through his brain, buoying him in the otherwise dreary peril of Franklin County.

"My mother was a Sunday school teacher," he replies, taking the boots from my arms and heading toward the car. "Played organ for funeral services, too."

"Can we please pack Peterson back in now?"

He opens the car door, sits on the seat, his feet and calves steeping in the marshy water, and slips on his socks and boots.

"I'm just going to grab the bacitracin to dress the wound, and then we're out of here. I promise."

"It's really time to go."

I look back at the five men. I'm glad for their manpower. But what do they want in return? Perhaps a six-pack of protein bars isn't going to do it. I need to check in with Billy again, and that requires getting closer to a cell phone tower or whatever alchemy is needed to connect us.

Martin is crawling through the car now, kneeling on the front seat.

"What are you doing?" I call out. "The antibiotics are in the back."

"Nope," he says, holding up a plastic sandwich bag of medicine. "They're right here."

With the first aid baggie in hand, he dresses Peterson's wound on the bed of the truck. I refrain from telling him to hurry up again; my patience is spent. Now that Peterson is clean, dry, and hydrated, we need to thank these guys and blow out of here before dusk. Martin knows that, but I can see that he's drawn to their fraternity, as though he can play a role in their promising rehabilitation.

As I eat a fragment of a protein bar that one of the prisoners gave me, I watch Peterson, a stranger, a ball and chain with every minute that ticks by, reminding me that the longer we delay, the more likely something will go wrong at home. No one is tending to Billy, or the girls for that matter, feeding them, singing hymns at their side. Maybe we can leave Peterson with these guys, and they can get reduced time for their heroic act.

It's time to tell Martin that his girls are probably there in the house. Presumably, Billy has seen them with his very own eyes. But before I can slosh over to Martin, the tall guy speaks up.

"You gotta get him somewhere," he says, staring down at Peterson. "He don't look so good."

"There ain't no *somewhere*," says the prisoner who has been silent up to this point. He avoids eye contact, which makes it easier to glance at the red and black skull tattoos on his neck.

"Where are you all headed anyway?" asks Martin.

"The Cañaveral," answers the tattooed guy.

"Ain't no more cane on the Brazos," says the blond.

"Jodón, suck my dick."

Some of the other prisoners laugh and tell us not to take the tattooed guy seriously.

"He's missing part of his brain."

"That's so wrong, dog."

"Well, good luck with wherever you land," says Martin, looking down at Peterson.

The men lift him from the bed of the truck and carry him to the car. They slide him in the back seat with a surreal precision and gentleness that interrogates their communal blue pajamas. Backing away from the car, they seem to have a bit more bounce to their step.

"Thank you," I stammer as I get to the car and reach for the door handle.

I turn and look at the bunch of them staring at us. The bald guy steps forward and stands very close to Martin, who braces his hand on the top of the driver's door. I can see the drowning fields, the overgrown reeds behind them, and the water rolling over what was once asphalt on the winding road that leads north. I feel the seclusion of the moment. Despite the long view through inundated pastures, I feel confined.

I get into the car slowly, close the door, and slide my hand toward the lock but hold back. Martin has wedged himself in the crook of the half-opened driver's door, which he wears like armor, as he thanks the men. I hope none of them saw me crawling my fingers toward the lock after all they've done for us. No sooner has Martin slid in beside me, felt the ignition and the console, than he ejects himself back out into the drizzle and floodwaters. I can't see his expression, but I hear him say calmly:

"I can't get help for my friend without my keys."

The water around us seems to pick up speed; through Martin's open door, I watch it swirl around his boots and threaten the already slick floormats. When I look back up, the wall of men is staring not at Martin, but at me, and I freeze.

I think Martin senses my panic, infused by his own growing anxiety because he asks them if they want money. Looking down at my lap seems the weakest act of disrespect, the customary suspicion they know so well, despite their assistance, their visceral kindness, an attempt at second chances. I put my chin up, meet the bald man's gaze, and smile. He's now standing very close to Martin. He reaches into his back pocket, pulls back his arm, and thrusts it back toward Martin. My heart flip-flops.

"You left these on the back of the truck."

"Right. Thank you," replies Martin, taking his keys.

And then they embrace.

"Better go take care of your buddy."

"Thanks for your help, man."

Martin slips him a bill, insisting that he take it.

"We can't exactly show our faces at Walmart."

"Take it anyway," says Martin. "Buy yourself that hamburger if you can find an open drive-thru."

"Amen!" says the blond guy, with a big smile.

During the slog toward Macon, with Peterson subdued in the back, we vary our speed, braking when the rising waters call for caution, speeding up as much as we can when the road climbs.

By early afternoon, we reach a small commercial district. We roll slowly behind other cars, through an intersection with broken traffic lights, past people trudging along the side of the road carrying bags of clothing and supplies, water jugs, and red plastic gasoline tubs. A line of people threads through the flooded parking lot of a market, some shuffling in, others lumbering out, embracing a single brown paper bag stuffed with groceries.

I reach into my backpack for the phone, my mind cycling through possible, contradictory, and ridiculous combinations of words I could text to Billy: *leave to find help*—if that's even possible—*sit tight until we get there, until Tom and George return, or I can send someone. Find something to float in.*

I claw my hand into the depths of the backpack until the theater of it all sinks in: the Good Samaritan game, the gospel hymn. My mind roils as my hand thrashes pointlessly in the bag once more and then at the console, under the plastic baggie of medicine, the charger, the protein bar wrapper. Where is it?

"Oh, my God. They took it."

Martin stares ahead calmly, silently. He just saw me plunge my hand into my backpack, rummage around, and swear under my breath. Hunched over, elbows in his lap, palms cradling the bottom of the wheel, he steers underhand, eyes tilling the watery road ahead. His composure can be maddening. Why the silence? The inattention to this loss that impacts us both? I try to remember when the men might have taken my phone. Wasn't I vigilant the whole time? Except maybe when they were wiping shit from Peterson's ass with his own boxers.

"No. It was when they were pulling him out of the car," I say loudly. "Martin. Did you hear me?"

I want to reach for his hand and hold it tightly, shake him out of his calm. I need acknowledgment, sympathy, and guidance. What now?

"It's gone," I exclaim.

He takes my hand and briefly squeezes it so hard that I flinch and shake him loose. Then I sit dumfounded at the violence of his gesture. He reaches for my hand again and holds it tenderly this time. I can't make sense of our reliance on each other, our physical connection that plays out at the worst moments; neither of us is very well equipped, under the circumstances, to interpret our feelings or make the best decisions.

"Did you hear me?" I say again, turning in my seat. "Why the silent treatment?"

"I'm navigating."

"Should we turn around and try to find them? I had my eye on my bag the whole time they were near our car."

"I saw that."

We pass another strip of abandoned stores with broken windows, discarded chairs, a couch, a bicycle, a bed frame soaking in three feet of water in a side lot. Plastic bags and bottles and palm fronds swirl in a large vortex and then unwind, releasing the debris into the currents, where it merges again and repeats the process, the sickening mundane physics of our unraveling world.

"We might have had service here," I continue.

"So you can communicate with Billy?"

"Yes. And maybe emergency services in Macon. Maybe the airport."

"I don't even know where my flip phone is," he says distractedly, followed by a dismal chuckle.

"I need that phone. *We* need that phone."

"You'd do anything to reach him, wouldn't you?"

I look at his face. Square jaw clenched, his high cheekbones turning red.

"I know the feeling, Juliet. You'd kill yourself just to text home. Just for a morsel that might shed light on the situation there."

He turns his face and stares right through me. I know now that he has my phone. That when he fetched the bacitracin to dress Peterson's wound, he also read Billy's earlier ambiguous texts about the candlelight in the window.

He turns back to the water in front of us as I try to come up with something in self-defense. Peterson shifts in the back seat. One quick glance over my shoulder tells me he's almost asleep, exhausted by the ablutions on the side of the road.

"I'm sorry," I say. "I should have mentioned it."

I run my hand through my dirty, tangled, damp hair.

"Yeah. You should have. Why would you leave me in the dark? They're my kids."

"I don't know if Billy is describing your kids or someone else's. If he's even seeing anything real."

"You should have told me, Juliet."

"Yes. I should have."

He pulls my phone out of his pocket and hands it to me. I press the home button, compressing my guilt, which doesn't have much time to consume me because the soft-blue electric screen glows, causing us both to glare down at it.

"See if that's my house, and those really are my kids," Martin commands in a monotone. "Ask if he can see my wife."

Who's in that house? Lana and Agnes?????? Their mom?

"Tell him to go over and help them," says Martin. "And tell them I'm on my way." Gray cycling bubbles pop up on the screen.

Mom is this you?

Hitting airport soon, I text. *Trying to fly out of Georgia. Find the girls. Stay together.*

Martin starts to shift in his seat. Twice now, he's gotten awfully close to the deep, sooty green-gray channels flanking the road.

"Do you want me to drive?"

"I'm good," he says, steadying the car over the blurry, parallel white lines separating what used to be two lanes.

"Did you press send?"

"I did. I promise," I reply, hoping to repair the trust, trying to be thankful that we've gotten this far together and knowing that I might not have crossed this unstable landscape without him.

"And make sure Peterson's still alive back there."

"Sleeping."

I look down at the screen and try one more time:

Lana and Agnes?????? Their mom?

I have a dog now. I'm fine. Hurry.

Martin looks over at me and then down at the screen as its glow begins to flicker.

"What did he say, Juliet?"

CHAPTER TWENTY

Billy

Up here in the nook, on my back, I'm bothered again by the rotting smell. It rises from somewhere on the side of the house and drifts through my window, like the smoke from the strong spliff my neighbor used to light on his back porch every afternoon. But instead of awakening my bad habit, this particular stench makes me wish I'd never lied or disobeyed my parents by going into the Vault.

I can't avoid looking down at the current forever because the smell pulls my vision toward what used to be Mom's garden but is now a slow, swirling whirlpool of plastic, metal, and wood. A gyre, as my physics teacher would say. At the edge bobs a large mass of brown, blond, and black fur, some of it sloshing awfully close to our house. Paws, tails, floppy ears, and stiff frames of animals that used to bark and fetch sticks and make people happy. It's as if someone opened the gates of the kennel over on Huntington Avenue, hoping to give the dogs a fighting chance to cling to pieces of wood, cars, telephone poles, and fencing that rush into the suburbs with an unstoppable tide. But then, what were the dogs supposed to do with their newfound freedom?

I push my face up against the window, which my parents bolted years ago. My nose goes flat against the cool glass as I strain my eyes painfully to the lower right, searching for the dead animals stirred by the water below. It's disgusting, sickening, and sad. There's nothing I can do now but stare at the furry clump of pups, which I smell from all the way up here, wafting in through George's window, into the hallway, and spiraling halfway up the stairs. I can just make out a pink tongue dangling through exposed teeth, the rigid grimace of a puppy-dog face plastered to apricot fur framed in branches, plastic bags, and plaster stuck to two-by-fours that snare the other carcasses. I try to look away, but something stirs my curiosity—a frantic, exhausted mechanical paddle, like a wind-up toy that won't stop.

I leap from the nook, missing most of the ladder, land hard on the floor, and charge down the stairs into George's room. I lean out of his open window and get a face full of that putrid smell that makes me want to heave what little breakfast I've eaten. But I stay at the window because I'm pretty sure there's something alive down there.

Holding my breath, I lean my upper body further out the window and stare toward the floating dead-dog carpet at a small black thing with bulging eyes so full of sadness and desperation. It has hooked its front paws to the body of its dead pals and beats its back legs to keep afloat. I take a gulp of air and feel a wave of nausea that soon melts away, making room for a burst of hope and then fear that if I don't move fast, that poor dog will sail down the same channel as Mr. Barrett.

I bolt out of George's room and into mine for the climbing ropes in the box of Jonathan's crap that I brought down yesterday and then run halfway up the stairs to grab the ladder from the nook with my good hand. No way am I going to plunge my bad hand into that water and risk more infection. I've seen what's fermenting there.

I tie a couple of tight square knots around the ladder, drop it out the window, and secure the other ends to George's bedposts. I work the ladder like a marionette, bouncing it against the side of the house until it hovers just above the dogs. The island of fur swabs the clapboards and swirls in that gyre of junk.

A couple of carcasses slip away from the pack and twirl in the angry current that's about to send the live pup off to bump against the next partially submerged structure entwined with urban wreckage. So I wrap my injured hand in a rice cake bag, which I secure around my wrist with a rubber band, throw a towel over my shoulder, and crawl out the window feet first, the aluminum window casing scraping against my stomach. I slowly let my weight sink, finding the top rung of the ladder with my bare feet, making sure that my knots will hold. As the ladder wobbles and scrapes the clapboards, I remind myself to disinfect with the bottle of hydrogen peroxide under the bathroom sink if I fall in.

There's no time to think it through, though, because the live dog drifts from the mass of furry bodies and glides toward me. I loop my bad hand through the third-to-last rung of the ladder, hook it with my elbow, reach down with my good hand, and grab the black dog by the skin of its neck. I throw it onto the towel over my shoulder, like moms do with newborns who have no muscle control. I'm wearing this poor thing like a pelt.

When I reach the windowsill, I push the dog through the opening. I hear it flop to the floor motionless. Then I pull myself up with all my strength and climb back in, trying to block out the smell.

As I turn to grab the ropes to pull the ladder back in through the window, I look up and see the figure of one of the girls at the window across the way. I can't see her features very well behind the screen, but I can make out long dark hair framing a face and the shadow of eyes that are watching me. I decide not to pull the ladder in just yet.

The smell of bleach rises from the dog as I rub her coat with a blue towel in my good hand, my left one elevated and freshly bandaged. I'm not taking any risks with infection.

We lie down together on George's bed. I rub her tummy and wonder if I saw a girl or a ghost behind the screen in that house across the way and how I might get over there without drowning. But I'd have to be a Bear Grylls, the outdoor-psycho dude who eats spiders and drinks piss and knows how to lasso branches and swing from one out-cropping to the next. And that's just not going to happen. So I get up, grab what's left of my breakfast, and shake it from the pan onto a scrap of newspaper. I whistle softly, and the dog lifts her head, hops off the bed, and eats the bits of scrambled egg. Clearly, she's an old lady, given the salt and pepper around her muzzle. She's also a fighter. I decide to call her Salty. If she ever meets Grandmother's dog, Pepper, on Dog Island, George and I will have fun calling them over the dunes and along the shore.

"How am I going to feed you?" I ask as I kneel beside her.

I'm stroking her bristly black coat and scratching her head when my phone pings. For a split second, I imagine that the two girls are texting to ask about the dog. But surely, they, of all people, don't have phones anymore.

It's my mother, of course, or maybe Mr. Featherstone.

Are you sure it's Lana and Agnes? What do you see exactly?

It's times like this that the phone aggravates me. When people, including my own family, don't answer questions and then repeat nonsense and waste time. If she's going to ask about anyone, it should be George and Dad, not those two girls. I put the phone back down and join Salty, who's resting on the bed again, and press my cheek against her muzzle.

"Good girl," I whisper, stroking her. "You're perfect."

At the second ping, I sit up, grab the phone, and pull it close to my face.

Who's in that house?

Why is she obsessing about these girls?

Lana and Agnes??????? Their mom?

Mom is this you?

Hitting airport soon. Trying to fly out of Georgia.

How did she get from Grandma's island to Georgia? This seems nuts. I wish I could email Grandma, as I do sometimes when Mom, Dad, and George drive me crazy. She's super critical of everything I do, especially with the phone. But it's because she cares about my future. She can smell bullshit a mile away and compliments me only when I truly deserve it.

Ping.

Find the girls. Stay together.

Maybe I should try harder to get over there. But the water's too high and filthy, and my hand still throbs. I can't swim through the currents. Or could I? Not to mention that those girls are just weird. I mean, what would we talk about?

Lana and Agnes?????? Their mom?

I have a dog now. I'm fine. Hurry.

CHAPTER TWENTY-ONE

Juliet

We enter the outskirts of Macon, pushing swells of backwash as we roll past small brick-and-wood postwar houses suffering varying degrees of damage. Curtains flutter through smashed windows, and ripped screens flap solemnly against wooden porches that withstood the initial surge before the water retreated toward the coast and then blasted in again, an aftershock ripple, according to Martin and his recently acquired scientific expertise. I look away from the disfigured dog and cat carcasses poaching in the swampy terrain, the flipped cars and trucks, and the deserted landscape.

The few people we see on flooded streets are industrious in their efforts, repairing a staircase or front door, or waiting in line at a church for food or medicine. Like us, they try to make sense of so much water, of their Sisyphean task of dumping buckets of it from their inundated houses into a street where the tide line is rising again.

"He rescued a dog," I say.

"Billy?" asks Martin. "How resourceful."

"He's not alone anymore."

Martin looks at me with a slim smile, a glint in his eyes that feels curative, maybe forgiving or hopeful. We hold hands as we cross the border until Peterson begins to moan, and Martin lets go of me, sinking my boosted spirits just slightly. I know it isn't anything against me. It's Peterson this time, whose condition destabilizes everything because no matter what we do or say, we can't make him comfortable, can't seem to get him the help he needs. And this feels like failure on top of our bungled, extended journey home. I look over my shoulder at Peterson's sallow face, at the swollen wound that weeps syrupy rosé liquid through the gauze that needs changing. We should have hooked up the second bag of fluids. But what he really needs are intravenous antibiotics to stem infection. His decline in the back seat compels us to speed it up carelessly and against our better judgment.

Mostly, though, we dread the possibility of an upended flight north. That detour would be barely tolerable if our children were safely at home with our spouses. But neither Martin nor I know the whereabouts of those adults, which begins to abrade our cooperative spirit.

We hear a sudden rumble. A small plane rises from behind a saturated grassy embankment. Drowning ornamental shrubs and trees wreathe the periphery of scattered low-lying buildings and the small concrete air traffic control tower that looks like an art deco chess piece.

As we take a sharp right along a chain-link fence, looking for the entrance, my phone pings and flashes.

It's them. Can you hurry?

I frantically poke at the keyboard, *Their mom too? ???*

I'm with their father. He can't reach them.

WTF???

Can you get to them? Help each other?

I can almost hear him say, "Fuck no," with no apology because of the upheaval.

Where's dad? he texts again.

Where would they go?

??????

Do you see anyone else?

Not alive.

Martin glances at me as I try to fathom Billy's words.

What do you mean?

I'm fine. Can you just get here?

I can't help myself and text, *How many bodies?* And then immediately regret it, like all the other times I've pressed Send after an upsetting exchange with him.

I squeeze the mute phone.

"Come on, Billy."

Martin looks over at me again and then back at the slippery road, looking for the airport entrance. He might benefit from a better grasp of Billy's grim snapshots, but I don't want to go there with him right now.

Sorry you're alone. My hand trembles. *Go find the girls,* I manage to type out, wondering why he'd choose to be alone in this when there were other kids just a few houses away. Is it his online identity that's preventing him from trying to get to Martin's house in person? Billy's turquoise sea-glass eyes and his gaze that used to radiate wonderment when he looked at people have dulled over the past two years. Sometimes, he focuses downward as if the muscles in his neck have become accustomed to that angle. If he had an online relationship with these girls before the Ban, maybe staring at their house now and seeing them through a rectangular window feels perfectly detached, distantly present in their lives. No need to talk face-to-face.

My mother summed it up imaginatively the day I got to the island. No sooner had we entered her kitchen after a short walk from the dock, my bag still slung over my shoulder, than she passed me a glass of homemade lemonade and asked about Billy and George.

"They're okay," I answered.

"What a fantastic course of events with the phones. To prevent a whole generation from going down the tubes."

"People are sick. Don't be heartless."

"Nonsense," she said, staring hard, her eyes the deepest blue, shiny and cobalt like the glaze on a pottery piece. "Do you really believe that?"

"No one knows, including you."

"There's an awful lot of not knowing going around."

We went out to the screened porch facing the ocean to look at the strip of emerald etched with swirls of white cresting waves beyond the dunes.

"I listen to the scientists," I said.

"How does one listen to smokescreens?"

"I talk to people, Mom. At the university. In my neighborhood. Not everyone's in denial."

"Talk all you want. Through the hysteria, the fake news, and conspiracy. Scientists included."

"Then I guess we're fucked, and what's the point in continuing this discussion?"

"Your kids, for one."

"Hospitals, researchers, the health department, and schools in my town are throwing everything they have at this. They're going to make a public statement at the end of the month. Hopefully backed up with facts."

"Whose?" she asked. "No one is any closer to finding out what's going on, regardless of zip codes."

In the silence that followed, I leaned back in my chair and felt the warm breeze blowing off the water across my skin and slowing my heart rate despite my mother's lecture. She'd made herself a shandy by pouring a Dos

Equis into her lemonade, topping off mine as well. Thus began the process of my worries and responsibilities fading into the green hues of seagrass along the rugged Gulf shore dunes in front of us.

"You know what?" she asked, raising her glass and knocking it against the side of mine. "Smartphone sales were plateauing even before the Ban. The Third Industrial Revolution did nothing for us. Time to introduce a shiny new bobble to start the cycle of consumption again."

"I can roll with that."

"Whoever brought us the smartphone wants to replace it with something more sinister and lucrative. Maybe an AI implant in our brains."

"Now you just sound nuts. And a little drunk."

"I'm drinking mostly lemonade, darling."

My mother didn't tilt toward conspiracy. She was just trying to fight the good fight, as she saw it.

"Those phones make people dumb. And for kids like yours and your brother's, they are mostly bad."

"For mine?" I said, annoyed with her at first, then wrestling with images flooding my mind of Billy lying on the couch on a sunny Sunday morning in July, the phone jammed in his face until I lost it and threatened to cancel driving lessons, club soccer, and his allowance. And George, sitting in the public library, his finger endlessly looping in front of his nose as he shuffled through hundreds of images of young people continually reinventing themselves.

"What in the world could possibly be the benefit of a fifteen-year-old, a twelve-year-old, even, with around-the-clock access to a mini-computer in his back pocket?

"Autonomy in a highly supervised world."

She scoffed.

"Connection."

"There are lots of other ways to connect, my dear."

I thought about Martin's girls, Lana and Agnes, phone-free, posting and cantering their weekends away in formal, constricting white gloves and jodhpurs, tall, tight black leather boots, and velvet hats. They seemed happy and nice, like their mother. Did they have their pretty faces stuck to social media before the Ban? Was there conflict in their home over phone use? Or just old-fashioned, ruthless determination to be number one?

"Don't give me some baloney about the phone as an essential tool for future generations, the great equalizer, or some other such blather," she continued. "The plural voice is not democratic anymore. It's bonkers."

"You just can't say it was all bad."

"Fake worlds to promote materialism? It's rather underwhelming. None of it has solved the big problems plaguing us."

"What about activism?"

"What about abuse, brainwashing, and manipulation?" she fired back. "And eons of wasted time. Jesus, girl, get a clue. Do you even know what your kids look at?"

I sipped from my shandy, washing down the shame that surfaced when I least expected it. Long before the Ban, I'd wished that Tom and I could have started over with the kids: a clean slate, a clean screen, a scrubbed brain.

"I don't hover," was all I could manage to say.

"Well, maybe you should have. I've seen their posts."

"Why would you look?"

"Why wouldn't you?"

I stared in the direction of the water and blinked away the sun's late afternoon glare.

"Do you know what they look at?" she repeated.

"I know I want to finish my shandy. It's been a long day of travel."

I took a good swig and closed my eyes as another warm breeze blew over my skin. But my mother pushed harder.

"Your entire generation seems to have a problem with basic rules."

"You're generalizing again. There was a component of the phone that provided independence, secrecy, connection, mystery, and mischief. You know, the eternal things that all teenagers seek."

I told her how Billy liked to quote from online stories, even dubious ones. Like the time he walked into the kitchen, staring at his phone, and said: "You can now be cryogenically frozen when you die and brought back to life." I told him to get his facts straight, which launched a discussion about sources and fake news. Other times, I just let him run with a story, yak on without the constraints of fact-checking, the rubrics, the outlines that defined his days. But I felt uneasy about the phone and wondered why parents and school officials didn't band together in a more constructive and aggressive way to address the misinformation, the bullying, the porn.

"Okay, okay," I said, trying to shift the conversation to the logistics of packing, closing the house, and leaving the island. "They were pretty bad. And yes, it was all for the profit of a few. Which route are we driving home?"

She put the glass to her lips and drained it, gearing up for the last word.

"Past generations have had their difficulties," she said. "War, plague, dust bowls. For your kids' generation, the phone will be their trauma. You'll see."

Martin spots the entrance to the airport and steps on the gas. The message bubbles on my phone belch out Billy's text, *Can't leave.*

I'm agitated now as I imagine him shrinking from the logical next step and me unable to help from a distance.

"Ask Billy about the neighborhood," says Martin.

"I thought you already did."

"The water."

How deep is the water? I text.

Second floor. Gooey.

I stare silently at the screen.

"What did he say?" asks Martin.

"It's risen to the second floor."

"How can that be?"

Gooey? I text back.

Dead stuff.

Martin asks, with restrained impatience, if I can fill him in.

"Just a sec," I tell him as I tap at the keys, trying to be as efficient as possible.

Billy?

I stare at the churning gray bubbles, unsure how to respond until they spit out another message:

People corpses animals bloated and disgusting smell is unbearable i'm not leaving the house how can i?

"Oh, God," I gasp as Martin turns into the airport.

"Jesus. What is it, Juliet?"

I drop the phone in my lap, put my palms up to my face and lose it. I simply can't stand the slow back and forth that's failing to help Billy in any concrete way. All the absurdity of my pecking finger, feeling as though I'm making progress, while anemic hope balls up inside me and pressure to fix everything crushes my temples. For a split second, I imagine rolling down the window and chucking the phone. Who cares where it lands?

Martin sighs deeply, pulls the car against the curb, reaches out, and puts his hand on my back as I sob.

"What else did he say?" he asks gently.

I don't want to repeat what Billy said. Can't I keep just a little portion of my connection private, or do I have to share every last detail with Martin in this dank car, with Peterson groaning and puking in the back? My whole body starts to shake, but I don't care. I need to meditate on this awfulness on my own and take a minute to process it without parsing it out for someone else. These devices are so public sometimes. I just want a moment to myself with my son.

"Juliet?"

"That's it. That's all he said," I say, as Martin turns the wheel and slowly drives toward a line of cars at the front entrance to the Macon Regional Airport.

We pull up to the front door, along the drop-off curb submerged in a foot and a half of water. I've caught my breath and now wipe the back of my hand across my eyes, trying to rally for the final push. But I'm exhausted and defeated, having done next to nothing for Billy yet so much for the stranger in the back of this rental car.

"We're here, Peterson," says Martin, looking over his shoulder to the back seat. "Gonna get you to a hospital, buddy. Gonna fly your ass back to Boston."

I know his enthusiasm is meant to give me hope, too, so that I don't sink into despair and pull him down with me. But as our journey progresses, it's clear to both of us that it's getting harder to bounce back.

Airport agents, police officers, and military are helping people park, exit their cars, and enter the airport. I stare at a young couple and an older man who come out through the permanently opened automatic doors, paying no attention to the green sludge that streams in over their boots, lapping at the glass.

"We can't wait here any longer," I say, rebooting myself as best I can. "I'm going up to the front of the line."

Just as I open the door, a guy with a three-inch Afro, dark brown skin, and wearing khaki shorts, a navy shirt, and a bulletproof vest approaches Martin's window. Despite the rifle over his shoulder and a pistol at his hip, he has a kindness about him. Sad eyes, a soft voice, and a five o'clock shadow that hints at a break in protocol.

"Where are you going?" he asks.

"Boston," replies Martin.

"Take this," says the man, slipping him a piece of paper with the number thirty-two written in black marker.

"Our buddy back here got bitten by a water moccasin, and he's in pretty rough shape. He got the antivenom, but the wound is infected."

"In and out of consciousness," I add.

The man stares through the open window, past Martin, to Peterson—awake or comatose; who can tell? The officer makes no effort at triage.

"Boston's definitely not going to happen. Burlington, Vermont, maybe, or Albany." He looks down at a clipboard. "Um ... Ottawa, you'd still need a passport, though. Never mind, they're closing their borders."

"Too far," I reply. "Anything in western Mass? Southern New Hampshire?"

"Nothing in Massachusetts. No service there."

"Meaning?"

"No flights are going in, ma'am."

I look into his large brown eyes for an honest answer.

"Too much water," he says.

"Like, how much?"

"Like, I have no more information."

"Our friend needs an emergency room," says Martin. "I don't think he should fly."

"I wouldn't leave him here. Hospitals are crowded and low on staff. Unless you plan to stay by his side."

Martin and I look at each other. The man stares at our expressions and then pulls out a walkie-talkie and speaks into it.

"Urgent situation. Snake bite. Three people heading north of New York." A scrambled, scratchy message bounces back. I hear *Burlington* and some codes and numbers I don't understand. We wait while the man banters back and forth with someone. Martin asks if I think Billy has checked on his house again to see if there are signs of his family.

"I told him to go over."

"Is my wife there?"

"I don't know, Martin. I just don't know."

I'm pretty sure Billy hasn't said anything about Martin's wife.

Some more back and forth into the walkie-talkie produces three young men in shorts and T-shirts carrying a stretcher.

"You can take one small bag," says the man in khaki. "Leave the keys in the car and follow them."

I grab the phone and the baggie of antibiotics from the console and close the door. I shove the medicine into my backpack, look down at the screen, and text a quick message.

At airport. Getting on a plane.

There's a quick scramble to get Peterson out as painlessly as possible. He moans. His eyes flitter. Despite my fatigue, I feel for him. Martin opens the trunk. We take our bags and follow the two young guys carrying Peterson, the third following behind us.

CHAPTER TWENTY-TWO

Billy

I leave Salty curled asleep on George's bed and raise myself slowly onto my knees, turning toward the window to look out. No sign of the girls in their window. No colorful panties and T-shirts hanging from the porch railing anymore. But it's definitely them. I go to George's other window, next to his bookshelf, and look around at the back side of my abandoned neighborhood, at the Andersons' brown house, sinking in the rising sea. Next door, where the Hintons live, I think, or maybe the Guptas, the clapboards and walls of the light blue house have caved in on themselves, exposing furniture, curtains, and part of a stairwell. A fallen tree crushes the roof, squeezing out drywall and tufts of yellow insulation.

I've tried to avoid looking down, but curiosity gets the best of me, and I stare at the brown-green stew in front of the Andersons' house that's on the verge of buckling. Off to the left, caught in a tangle of shrubs and small trees, I see an orb. Face down, tiny limbs, elbows bent, fists tight like it's having a tantrum. *Look away, Billy,* I say to myself. But I can't. It's all pale pink and wrinkled like a newborn puppy or piglet, and it's rocking in the currents, spared the abyss below that I've been looking at for three days now. It's just a doll, I tell myself. One of the many toys, cushions, shoes, cars, couches, books, and papers I've seen swirling through the canals that used to be streets. Who in this neighborhood, anyway, would lose a baby like that? I bet my neighbors got out, and the bodies I've seen have drifted in from somewhere right along the coast. It's my fault I'm here for barricading myself in the Vault behind those two heavy doors, headphones plugged in, pleasantly comatose from the roach I smoked at midnight.

I step back from the damp window and slam it down. I feel sad for the doll, or whatever it is. Someone either lost it, dropped it, or maybe ended up the same way. I miss Mom now and Dad, George, and Grandma on her island. I used to like islands and water and waves.

I pull my phone out of my back pocket, put it on the bed, and lie down again next to Salty. I rub her belly with my good hand and then just hug her tightly against my chest, her fur tickling my face. Unlike that doll-thing outside, she's breathing. I wonder if the girls across the way have seen the doll and all the other shit bobbing in the water. Do they avoid looking down when they stare at the rain out their window? I gotta go over there soon to tell them about their father. To make sure they aren't going crazy from loneliness, the smell in the air, and the things that float by.

It's them. I tap out with my pointer finger, still cuddling Salty on George's bed. *Can you hurry?*

Their mom too?

How should I know? I say out loud, one quick jab at the keyboard: ???

I'm with their father. He can't reach them.

WTF???

She's with a man, a father no less. And she doesn't know where mine is?

Can you get to them? Help each other?

They're dorks. And why isn't she worried about the rest of our family?

Where's dad?

Where would they go?

??????

Do you see anyone else?

Not alive.

What do you mean?

I'm fine. Can you just get here?

How many bodies?

How do you tell your mother that there might be a dead baby floating in the brambles in front of what used to be the Guptas' house?

Sorry you're alone. Go find the girls.
Can't leave.
How deep is the water?
Second floor. Gooey.
Gooey?
Dead stuff.
Billy?

I watch the gray bubbles rotate around and around as though she's writing a short story. In the end, nothing more appears, so I type:

People corpses animals bloated and disgusting smell is unbearable i'm not leaving the house how can i?

And then I regret what I've just texted because, surely, she's freaking out. And what is Mr. Featherstone doing to help?

Salty sits up nervously, knocking her head against my chin, ears cocked at a rattling sound outside the window. I imagine the water's rising, and something in the current has caught the ladder while scraping against the siding. I dread looking but crawl onto my knees anyway, grab the ledge, and stand to open the window as far as I can. Leaning out, I find myself looking down into the eyes of a girl slightly older than me, gripping the ladder while sitting in an orange rubber rescue dinghy.

"Hello," she says, in a pinched voice that people use when they're about to burst into tears. But instead of crying, she gives me a blank stare, one hand squeezing the second rung of the ladder, the other holding a black rope on the side of the dinghy as it tosses her about. "I'm Agnes."

"I'm Billy."

"I know."

Mom told me once that Mrs. Featherstone's motto was "kill 'em with kindness," but that underneath it all, she was a condescending pit bull. Even Dad, who never gossips, jumped in to say that Mrs. Featherstone had turned motherhood into an elite sport. I don't see any of that in Agnes's disoriented gaze.

"I have dog food," she says, looking down at the five-pound bag of Purina at her feet.

Her face is wet from the drizzle. Oily dark brown hair clings to her temples and cheeks. Apart from dark circles under her eyes, she's prettier than I remember from Calc II. A cute nose that's a little round at the tip and big brown eyes with long lashes.

"Can you take this?" She points at clothing wrapped in a white sheet and two green garbage bags knotted shut. "Our house is about to go."

"Throw me that rope first," I say, pointing at the floor of the dinghy.

She tosses it at me. I pull it through the window and secure it to the bedpost. Still holding the ladder with one hand, her legs splayed, feet anchored to the boat as it rocks her, she lifts one of the plastic bags and pushes it into my arms. We empty the boat like this with real team spirit until I remember the baby doll, which seems to have disappeared with everything else drifting by.

I'm pulling the dog food through the window when Agnes thanks me several times. I want to jump into the boat and paddle her back safely to what's left of her house so that we can pick up her sister. I imagine putting them in my parents' spacious room with the comfortable bed. There isn't much I can do for so many of the things I've seen pass by my house. But maybe I can save these girls' lives and mine and Salty's and get us the hell out of here.

As I grip the climbing ropes that pin the ladder against the house, I realize I should have snapped some photos of everything going on because the topography is changing so fast. People's whole lives wash through our town, and nobody knows what has been lost. Isn't someone supposed to record this kind of stuff for future generations? Or write about it beforehand so humanity can minimize the damage?

"Is your mother over there, too?" I ask.

"Just Lana."

She turns her back and stares at the second-story porch that's disappearing into the currents, leaving a gaping hole in the room with the window where I'd first seen both girls.

"Do you want me to go over and get her?"

"I'm going back now."

"Let me go."

"Well, I'm in the boat already."

"True," I say, unknotting the rope from the bedpost and tossing it back in the dinghy.

She lets go of the ladder and begins to paddle away with desperate jerking motions.

"But come back," I call out.

"I'll try."

If I had a raft or a paddleboard, I could go over with her. Apparently, it isn't easy crossing. Having listened to the commotion from a safe distance, Salty now comes to my side and looks up. As I rub my fingers through the swirl of bristly curls on top of her head, I keep an eagles eye on Agnes, holding her own in the currents and paddling hard. She crosses over the middle of what used to be our street. Looking at her house, I see Lana sitting on the ledge of a window to the right of the collapsed porch. Agnes steers the dinghy under the window and steadies it and herself by grabbing loose siding while her sister lowers herself on sheets knotted together.

I watch them paddle toward me and hope the current doesn't sweep them away. As the dinghy twists and rocks with no apparent logic, they begin to argue. I can't quite hear what they're saying, but it clearly isn't very nice because Agnes bursts into tears, puts her hands to her face, and sobs. I get that we're in an emergency, but this seems extreme. I'd liked to say something comforting to Agnes, but she's too far away. They begin to drift dangerously away from my house, toward the center of the current, where rough water sucks things into its depths.

"Agnes," I shout as loud as I can.

She drops her hands from her face and looks at me.

"Paddle or you won't make it."

She finds the paddle at her feet and, along with Lana, who holds the other paddle, begins smacking the water like mad to get to the ladder.

I lean as far out of the window as I can. With the ropes in both hands, I swing the ladder away from the house several times until Lana grabs it and pulls the dinghy in. As she passes me the dinghy's rope, and I secure it to the top rung, I notice that both girls' eyes are red and puffy. I'm sorry they've lost their home.

Agnes holds the bottom of the ladder, and Lana stands up. As she's testing the bottom rung with her right foot, my screen on the desk pings. I reach for it with my good hand.

At airport. Getting on a plane.

This news, along with the fact that I'm not alone anymore, makes me hopeful. I put the phone down and reach out to Lana as she stands on the top rung in her yellow rain jacket, Capri jeans, and black Vans. Her features are bumpier than Agnes's, but she has the same big brown eyes.

"Can you pull me up?"

I grab her by the arms while she climbs onto the sill. She smells like those sweet, hard, green-apple candies but a little sour and sweaty, too. She crawls through the window and into the room. Sinking her hands into the pockets of her rain jacket, she looks around George's room at the wall of license plates and at his bookshelf.

Agnes follows after Lana, and we make sure the rope is tightly secured to the top rung of the ladder one last time in case we need the dinghy again. They tell me they saw it drifting by and spent half of yesterday retrieving it from what was left of a tangle of small trees and shrubs behind their home. I want to ask what else they've seen floating by, but they looked exhausted and sad, so I give them towels instead. I make them each a packet of ramen, and they devour the noodles and broth in silence.

CHAPTER TWENTY-THREE

Juliet

Eight inches or so of dirty water slosh across the floor of the airport. Paper napkins, discarded plastic bottles, and disposable coffee cups bob in the murk and knock against benches and stainless steel stanchions. People wait in lines that don't seem to move, and there's a strange silence as if talking will contribute to the delay. Even the toddlers look stunned, staring wide-eyed at the liquified surface their parents are standing in, at the airport personnel, and the state police who herd people back and forth, doing their best to answer questions.

As we hustle down a staircase and out to the flooded tarmac, some of my anxiety unfurls, flaps madly like the windsock at the end of the runway, and blows off. We've finally reached our destination. We'll be somewhere near home in a few hours. But we aren't actually on the plane yet. We never bought a ticket. Our hectic, back-route, preboarding adventure feels anything but guaranteed. And then I remember my mother. On the drive around Tallahassee and even toward the Georgia border, it seemed she was somewhere in the vicinity, over there on the coast, or just south of us. But now, the looming flight to a rural landlocked town in the Green Mountains of Vermont will push her out of reach, off our radar, way down on the Panhandle for who knows how long. Unless the island has disappeared and she's already relocated.

We plod across the tarmac, our boots slapping the water, following the stretcher through the drizzle. A balmy wind picks up and rustles my hair. I think of Dog Island, the sea breeze and emerald waves, my mother bent over shells and broken sand dollars, looking for treasures in soft white sand.

Martin, behind me, reaches his hand out and squeezes my shoulder. I slow down, put my hand up to his, which he burrows in my shirt under my damp hair, and we link fingers for a few seconds. We both manage a brief smile as we near the plane. Instead of my usual apprehension before boarding, I can't wait to bound up the stairs, buckle in, and lift off.

If I had the chance, I'd text Billy one last time before casketing my phone into its box, *Almost boarding*. I'd punch out a colon and the end parenthesis to convey the lightness I feel as I approach the plane, splashing my boots almost playfully for a moment through the flood-water. All the obstacles we struggled with are beginning to fade. I glance at the young guys grunting under the weight of Peterson, whom they transport with selfless concentration, and I feel lucky to be here, surrounded by resources and people who are going all out for us.

Peterson is awake now, sensing, perhaps, the commotion as we make small talk on the tarmac about the amount of time a small commuter plane will take to get to Burlington. Peterson stares upward, his eyes riveted on the pale gray sky, his hands clutching as best he can the sides of the stretcher, his wounded leg slightly bent as it rests on the small fleece blanket that the two young men carefully adjusted under his knee.

"Hang in there, Petes," says Martin, grinning down at him. "We're going home."

"Straight flight," I blurt out. "Shouldn't take more than three hours."

A man and woman, presumably the pilots, are waiting for us at the foot of the metal portable stairs, its first rung submerged. They wear civilian clothes, jeans tucked into rubber boots, and yellow rain jackets. The man wears a baseball cap that says Eglin over his cropped gray hair. As we approach, I see a painstaking grimace on his face. He removes his cap, scratches his scalp, and looks away at a vanishing runway. The woman with him turns and starts up the stairs. Perhaps to guide us up with Peterson on the stretcher? But instead of stopping and turning at the top to help us navigate, she disappears into the tiny cockpit. I look up at the windows of the plane and see passengers in every window, staring down at us.

Why is the pilot shaking his head like that? Where is the friendly expression that says: "You made it. Welcome aboard!" I turn toward Martin, who has slowed his enthusiastic approach to the stairs and shifts on his feet as he, too, tries to read the pilot's expression.

"We don't have room for three," the pilot calls out through the drizzle. "I just can't risk it. I can barely fit one more, and I think it should be him. We've got a nurse and doc on board."

I grab the aluminum railing to steady myself and hold back tears and explosive rage.

But how can anyone dispute taking Peterson over two healthy adults?

"I'm sorry," says the pilot. "I really am."

Fury boils in me. My throat constricts, hampering any rational response or gratitude for getting one of us out. My son is waiting for me and expecting me. Haven't I worked so hard to get us to this spot on the tarmac? Peterson's done nothing but sleep, vomit, and shit his pants. And now what?

"I'll try and get you two on the next flight," says the pilot. "Maybe in a day or two, as we're on triage at this point."

CHAPTER TWENTY-FOUR

Billy

The girls unpack food and clothing from two green garbage bags. When I ask if they'd like to stay in my parents' king bed, they look at each other expressionless. Lana finally says that she'd rather stay wherever the dog is sleeping, so I drag my mattress into George's room.

"The plumbing doesn't work anymore," I tell them. "There are pans and a bucket full of rainwater on the ledge outside the window. You can climb out there if you need to. The Poland Springs is for drinking only. As you can see, it's not going to last forever."

I go up to Jonathan's apartment and grab the L.L.Bean electric lantern and batteries and a box of powdered milk for the Cheerios that Lana and Agnes brought with them.

Salty takes a liking to Agnes, who seems slow to answer my questions. She's a little dreamy like some of the girls in my English class, Individuals and Institutions. But everyone knows she got perfect PSAT scores. She stretches out on her back on George's rug, head on the mattress I've just dragged in, ankles crossed. She stares at the ceiling while she strokes Salty. When Salty gets up to eat some kibble off the newspaper, Lana, sitting backward on George's swivel chair, tells us that dog food is mainly flour, chemicals, and water disguised as meat-flavored kibble.

"Glad I don't have to eat that," I reply.

"You eat ramen, don't you?"

We laugh for a moment, but their smiles soon fade. Agnes sits up on the edge of the mattress and, like her sister, stares coldly at the wall ahead, pent up inside. I'm not sure how long I can take this awkward silence inside one bedroom, with shifting fake smiles and eyes scanning surfaces while we avoid what's outside the window.

"Do you know where your dad is?"

They shake their heads.

"He's with my mom in Georgia."

They frown at each other.

"They're about to get on a plane. In fact, they're probably up in the air now."

"That's weird," says Agnes.

"Obviously, they ran into each other at the airport," says Lana, brushing back strands of her brown hair that fell into her face from her loose ponytail. "Dad was on a business trip."

"Does he go to Tallahassee?"

"Probably. He goes everywhere for his start-ups. He has a new one that looks at weather."

Agnes chews nervously at her bottom lip. But instead of asking how I know all this, she says, "So, you know your mom's alive then."

"I just said she's with your dad."

She looks at me with a dazed expression, as though she doesn't understand a thing I've said. I flip onto my knees, crawl toward Salty, and pick up some of the dried kibble she's licked off the newspaper.

"Where's your mom?" I ask as Salty eats kibble from my palm.

"We don't really know," replies Lana. She places an opened box of Cheerios and a can of black beans on George's desk and then freezes. "Is that your phone?"

I nod.

"Can I call my dad?"

"It only texts. But there isn't any service right now. Believe me, I'm trying to reach them all the time."

"Don't those phones kill people?"

Lana straddles George's desk chair with her arms folded and propped on the backrest.

"I'm not sure about that."

"Why would your parents let you keep it?"

"It was my mom."

"Why, though?" she asks, swiping her brown hair out of her face again.

"Most of the time, I keep it in my basement. Which is where I was when the water came in."

I can see from Agnes's distant gaze that she's not really listening to the conversation. Her high cheekbones are flushed in tandem with her sadness, which gives her a natural beauty that doesn't need makeup. I imagine that it probably wouldn't have occurred to either girl to try to keep a phone. Their parents would have none of that. She finally looks at me.

"If nobody else has one, what's the point?"

"Of course, other kids have them," says Lana, rolling her eyes. "I mean, not a lot, but some. Alex Graves kept his because his parents are idiots. Delia Sommers, too."

"My friend Sam kept his and gave his parents a decoy."

"But there are no apps and stuff," says Agnes, looking confused. "So why bother?"

"Because sometimes I can text. To my mother and your father."

Lana fixes her eyes firmly on mine, "If you're smart, like Alex, you can get shit on the dark web." She smiles as though she's been there before. "He's a demon with technology."

"Do you do that?" Agnes asks me, her brow so rumpled that I feel a little sorry for her.

"Sam and I play a game he can access somehow, and we text. Or used to before all this."

"*CyberTrenches*?" asks Lana, smiling again, her round cheeks filling out; she's a little heavier than Agnes.

I know she wants to say, "That game's for ten-year-olds," but instead, she gives me the silent treatment, which is worse because, I mean, I can't even debate her. End of conversation. And I'm left to think about my own infantile behavior.

She rests her chin on the back of her stacked hands and starts to swivel back and forth in the chair.

"Can you stop?" Agnes whispers, staring at her as her hand tickles Salty's stomach. "It's distracting."

"You're annoying," replies Lana.

I try to smile at Agnes, but she's staring off at nothing, her eyes half-closed.

"So, what else do you do with an archived smartphone?" Lana continues, cross-examining me.

"I told you. I just play that game with Sam."

"Aren't you supposed to have one of those super expensive cases, too? But the phone still radiates something through it, no?"

"Maybe."

"You don't believe what they say?" She laughs for a split second, peels off her yellow rain jacket, and tosses it onto the desk behind her. "Well, neither do I."

"What's certain is that without it, I wouldn't know where my mom is. Or your dad."

Lana mashes her lips together and grins uncomfortably. I sense she has lots to say, but for whatever reason, doesn't feel like sharing right now.

"I'm not sure what I believe anymore," I reply. "It's complicated, you know?"

But she won't take the bait.

We hear a distant low rumble. Agnes, chewing on her thumbnail, rises instantly and goes to the window. She stands there looking out, in a red T-shirt with Allendale Farm inscribed on the back and skintight black leggings that disappear into white Converse high tops. Her head dips slightly left, then right, as she stares at our neighborhood through George's window.

"Holy fuck," she says softly, as the rumbling accelerates. "There goes our house. The couch. Oh, my God, I think that was my parents' bedroom."

Lana springs off the chair and joins her at the window. Their fingers link at the last thud, followed by silence. I feel like an idiot with nothing to say as I watch them witness the collapse of their home, their history vanishing before their eyes.

Lana turns from the window and looks at me. "We can't stay here much longer, Billy. Your house might be next."

She's not very tactful.

"We need a plan, Billy."

"I'm not leaving yet. It's holding out just fine."

"We've all seen what the water can do."

"We've felt it under our feet," adds Agnes.

"I understand that. But it's not time yet."

The thought of leaving this place I've lived in all my life, just turning my back and abandoning the memories and the objects is deranged.

Agnes finally turns from the window.

"Lana is right," she says. "Unfortunately, nature will decide when it's time."

"Okay, maybe so. But not today. Not right now."

Agnes moves away from the window, kneels, and grabs Salty. She burrows her face into the dog's neck.

"Good girl," she says over and over, her voice slip-sliding in all different tones, kind of freaking me out.

Thank God for Salty, I say to myself, and then, trying to fill the awkward silence, I ask, "Do you guys have a dog?"

Agnes squeezes Salty harder and faintly convulses into the dog's neck. I dread what I've just asked, even before Lana stares at me and mouths: "Good one," her lips gnarled in disgust.

"Why else would we bring you half a bag of kibble?"

Embarrassed and kind of confused, I stand up and go to the window. What I see there tugs at the knot in my chest. Their sagging dusty blue house slowly slides into the current, like an ice cream cake on a very hot day. There's something tragic about what I'm witnessing, and I wonder: Will my house be next? Will my bed and walls, George's desk and closet, our books, posters, and my grandfather's oil paintings slip away, too?

That evening the rain falls hard, pummeling the house and bombarding the water outside. The spooky shadow of Agnes and Lana's crumbling home causes me to seriously second guess the integrity of my own. Maybe Lana was right about making a plan sooner rather than later. I begin to worry as I boil pasta on Jonathan's stove in my room. I think about the emergency checklist on my closet door: #3. Seek higher ground. But where? And how?

After dinner, Lana announces that she needs to be alone for a while and leaves George's room for another part of the second floor. What could she possibly be doing in my parents' room, the guest room, the bathroom, or maybe Jonathan's apartment? She doesn't ask permission or seem to care what we think.

Agnes watches her leave and stares at the door as it closes. She wrinkles her nose, drawing her puckered top lip slightly over her gums, as though either super offended or flipped out that her younger sister snubs her and leaves her alone with me.

"What's her problem?" she murmurs. She looks at me and then down at my bandaged hand. "What happened?"

"I cut my palm when I was escaping from the basement." She kneels in front of where I'm sitting on George's bed, elbows bent at her sides, head tilted with curiosity.

"Can I see?"

"It's kind of gross."

"Go on. Take off the bandage."

I laugh at her weirdness. She's shy, but I know she has a golden confidence. I've seen it shine in chem class. She's one of those girls who asks questions that even Mr. Bresnick can't answer.

"I'm going to be a surgeon, so I better get used to it."

"Of course you are."

She smiles, reaches for my hand, flips it over in hers, and looks down like she's reading my palm. Her fingers are soft and tickle the skin around the bandage until she applies pressure.

"Ouch!"

I try to pull my hand away, but she holds on firmly and smiles harder. For a moment, I think I see wisdom in her big brown eyes. Maybe even a little mischief. But not the mind-fucking games Lana knows how to play.

"It looks infected under there. I better change the bandage."

"You don't have to," I say, although keeping her busy might help both of us forget what's going on outside the window.

"This could present problems," she says, unwinding the gauze from my hand.

"I smear it with antibiotics twice a day."

"Topical antibiotics can only do so much. What if it's entered your bloodstream?"

"Wouldn't I have a fever?"

She tips her head left and shrugs, her brown shoulder-length hair brushing against her T-shirt. As I look into her bleary eyes, I realize I've been desperate to keep a lid on the drama that's bubbling over in my house with the arrival of these two sisters. Before I can ask what's going on with the simmering anger and tears, she's on her feet.

"Don't go anywhere."

I can't help but laugh a little as I watch her scamper through the door and into the hallway.

She returns a few minutes later with a pot of boiling water. She digs in one of the green garbage bags and pulls out a white plastic first aid kit.

"What kind of surgeon do you want to be?" I ask as she reaches for my arm at the elbow and pulls my palm into her lap.

"Brain or heart. I'm doing—or was doing—an internship in the cardiology department at Mass General."

"When you aren't riding horses and playing cello?"

"Lana plays the cello."

It occurs to me that maybe Lana is acting the way she is because she had to leave her cello at home, and now it's gone, like the rest of her house. I've heard that musicians can become insanely attached to their instruments.

Agnes stares down at dried blood and pus that have seeped out of the wound, and I feel like she's looking at my dirty boxers.

"Sorry, Agnes."

"It's all good," she says, smiling momentarily before zipping up the sweetness and studying my festering palm again like a jeweler with a rare gem.

I want to tell her to chill and stop trying to impress the world. Especially now that it's fallen apart. But I let her continue with her Florence Nightingale routine until I start to lose patience. The elephant in the room isn't really my palm. It's the houses. Hers, in the process of total collapse, and mine, which could be next.

"Lana's right, you know. We're going to have to leave soon. Probably in that dinghy."

"It's not that easy," she replies dryly.

"We're not going anywhere tonight, that's for sure."

She nods as she opens a package of sterile pads, dips the bleach-white mesh square into the pan of steaming water, and wipes it back and forth over my palm. I have to admit now that she does seem like a pro.

"How did you know it was time to leave?" I ask.

"The floors shifted and started to separate from the walls. Everything got damp. We could feel the porch sliding into the water."

"You could have been crushed."

"It won't be long before yours does the same thing," she replies, pulling a roll of gauze from the white box and wrapping my palm mummy-style.

She stares at me and says, "Wake me tonight, Billy. So I can dress the wound again."

"Okay," I respond, trying to keep it cool. "If you don't mind."

She presses hard on my palm with tape, but I don't flinch because I'm thinking about what she just said. And I'm staring at the pink top of her ear poking through strands of brown hair, reminding me of the wood nymph in *Circe's Grotto*, a video game I used to play. She moves off the bed onto the floor in front of me, sitting back on her heels.

As she packs up the white box, I wonder if she's ever been with a boy. I imagine her not sitting on my bed tonight but actually crawling into it while Lana sleeps in my parents' bed. I stare at her hunched shoulders and shapely biceps, which must have developed from galloping stallions across fields on weekends. I picture her hips rocking in the saddle, and I feel myself stir against my zipper. I shift on the mattress, put my good hand over my lap, and look away.

"Did I hurt you, Billy?"

"No. I'm fine," I say, focusing my breathing.

After an awkward minute of silence, we both stand up.

"Thanks, Agnes. You're a lifesaver."

She gives me a stunned look, as if I've called her a murderer instead of a healer. All her cute features seem to harden, her cheeks flush, and her eyes fill with tears again. Jesus, what have I done wrong? She puts her hands to her face and begins to sob uncontrollably.

I look at Salty on the floor and then over at the closed door and feel dizzy, as if someone has flipped George's room upside down, turning it into a puzzle with many missing pieces. How am I supposed to make sense of this behavior? I don't have a sister.

I swallow hard and then look down at my own hands and arms, which seem to belong to someone else now. Only when Agnes falls against my chest, do my arms rise somehow and embrace her. I never imagined that holding a girl like this could make me feel so grateful and a little melancholy. I put one hand on the back of her head and kiss her hair near her pink ear.

"What's wrong?" I whisper just as Lana turns the doorknob.

She barges in and stares.

"Okaaaaaaay," she says, and then seeing Agnes's state, bows her head as though the peace she'd found alone for twenty minutes has been swept away by floodwaters.

We turn on the two battery-operated lanterns, light a couple of candles, and place them around the room. When Lana orders us to pack immediately and put everything near the window in case we have to bolt, I refuse and tell her it can wait until morning.

"We'll know when it's time to go. Won't we?"

"You don't get it, Billy," she replies.

"First, it was the rugs," says Agnes. "Damp and smelly."

"Then the porch went," adds Lana. "Windows rattled, and the floors sunk."

"The floors feel fine," I say, jumping up and down to make my point.

"You'll see," says Lana, joining her sister on the mattress.

While they finish off a bag of Doritos, I go to George's closet and rummage through sneakers, sweatshirts, and an old blue and red lacrosse uniform. I kick at an empty vodka bottle and pull out a full six-pack of Budweiser along with a couple of board games because if we don't do something to tire ourselves out, we'll lie in bed driving each other bonkers.

"Monopoly, anyone?"

We set up the board on George's rug, and I place the warm six-pack next to it. Lana grabs a can, hooks the tab with her finger, and pops it back like a pro. She downs her beer quickly. Without hesitation, she buys every piece of real estate she can in the first half-hour, including Boardwalk and Park Place. Agnes takes a long time deciding on houses for each property, a few here, a few there. She nurses her beer, taking minuscule sips for show because, clearly, she despises the taste.

I begin to wonder where Mom and Mr. Featherstone have landed. Surely not at Logan Airport, which practically sits in the harbor, near the mouth of the Charles and Mystic Rivers. I imagine trying to text, telling them that the girls are okay and the house is holding up for now. While we're waiting for them to come get us, we're playing board games and drinking George's beer. But I know, from the rain and the clouds, that there's no signal tonight. I also begin to suspect that they may never get here, and it's up to us to get ourselves out.

When Agnes doesn't think I'm looking, my head bowed over the board as I pretend to strategize, she glances at my phone on George's table. Her eyes open wide, no matter the swelling and redness from tears that alter her expression and make her look like she has the flu. When she realizes I'm watching, she stares back at the growing piles of colorful bills in front of her. Lana, crazy with her purchases, is nearly bankrupt and that much more agitated. But Agnes is in it for the long haul. I can see that she's got the brain of a CEO as well as a surgeon.

"You keep staring at my phone," I finally say.

She laughs a little and shakes her head in denial but then asks, "Why did you keep it?"

"It's my business, not the government's."

"But it's toxic. Someone has to regulate it. Your decision affects other people, you know."

"You're right," I admit. "And I've told you that most of the time, it was archived in an alloy case behind two thick metal doors."

"In the basement."

"Correct."

"So that you can enjoy what the rest of us had to give up?"

I'm about to say, "To have a little fun ... do you know what that is?" but I keep my mouth shut. Nor do I tell her that I'm pretty sure Mom let me keep my phone because she was afraid I might go crazy without it, like my cousin, Jack, who disappeared a few days after the

Ban and hitchhiked to some place in Vermont called the Northeast Kingdom. My aunt Margo nearly went mad driving around in those mountains trying to find him.

Lana shakes the dice. She runs the tip of her tongue slowly over her thin top lip.

"What about you guys? What happened to yours?" I ask.

"Our parents took them up to the town hall, threw them into those lined containers, and got the rebate," Lana answers.

"My mom had a change of heart about that. She said if I archived it, I could keep it for a little while longer. She would have taken it from me sooner or later if all this hadn't happened."

"Have you tried to reach anyone else?" asks Agnes.

"No contacts anymore. There's no phone icon. Just the message box. Just my mom and Sam, who doesn't respond anymore."

"I don't see what the big deal is," says Lana. "You can still use a computer. They'll come up with something else soon, anyway, to brainwash us and take our money. Too much at stake not to." She pauses, looks down at the board, and scans the dozen or so square green houses and rectangular red hotels that we've all purchased on various plots. Looking back up, she tosses me the dice and asks, "Did you have to get hypnotized?"

"What do you mean?"

I jiggle the dice in my fist and scatter them. I've landed on GO TO JAIL for the third time.

"Some parents had to hypnotize images out of their kids' brains."

I look at her pale, tired face and chapped lips. Nothing in her expression has changed. Agnes is staring down at her money as though calculating how to double it within the next five minutes.

"Is that even possible?" I ask.

"Some parents thought so. Their kids had seen so much awful stuff that their brains had to be, sort of, rinsed."

"What, like porn?"

"Naturally, but also decapitations and shit with animals," says Lana, with a calm expression. "All kinds of abuse and whatnot."

I remember Mom, in one of her mood swings, saying that the phone was a portal to the inferno.

"Did it work?"

"Some people think so. It's like dialysis of the brain, I guess."

"Those images can stay with you forever," adds Agnes. "They get into the corners of your mind and come out when you least expect it."

I think about all the stuff I've seen—some of it pretty bad. "How do you know if you need it?"

"One of the tell-tale signs," says Lana, "is obsessively thinking about certain stuff at all hours of the night."

That sounds like me.

"You can't have normal relationships," says Agnes, sensibly tucking her hair behind her ears like she's looking for order. She gazes innocently at both of us. "You want to kill people."

"Or fuck them," says Lana. "But your dick doesn't work anymore."

I'm tired of Monopoly now, but not sure how to get out of it.

"Whose parents made them do it?"

"Like half our tennis club last Christmas, before the Ban. Parents got wind of it and forced it on their kids."

Our discussion has motivated Lana in some way because she buys two houses and a hotel for Marvin Gardens, smiling as she doles out the last of her cash.

"Sally Brady said that first, they put you in a white room. You go on a liquid diet. They purge your whole system with a vitamin and herb cocktail. Then they put special headphones on you that neutralize your brain with electromagnetic orgone energy."

"You're bullshitting me."

"No, it's true," says Lana, looking into my eyes. "They dilute your memory so that you can rebuild it in a wholesome way, with the help of professionals."

She reaches her fist out over the board and hands the dice to her sister. When their knuckles touch, they make eye contact and burst out laughing hysterically. I try to laugh with them, to be a good sport.

"No, but seriously," says Lana, catching her breath. "I know a couple of kids who did go crazy when their phones were taken. My boyfriend, Jonas, for one."

"And my cousin, Jack," I offer.

Lana, sitting cross-legged the whole time, rocks up onto her knees at the edge of the Monopoly board. She's giggling and then almost shrieking with phony laughter. She reaches her hand out and violently swipes away two hours of progress. Agnes joins her. The pastel money, green and red plastic houses and hotels, and metal charms fly everywhere and spill onto George's carpet and under his desk. In a frenzied, free-for-all, they destroy all evidence of who's gained the monopoly. Not that it matters tonight.

I sit back, watch, and try to laugh along with them, but frankly, it's not very funny. I'd pulled out the game to try to calm the situation and get our minds off the weather, but they've made everything worse. They're out of breath when they sit back down, still laughing with that artificial happiness slapped across their faces, which makes me worried for all of us.

We're avoiding the larger picture.

"Sorry," says Lana. "Family tradition."

"No worries," I reply, trying not to lose it.

Her smile vanishes, and she stands up and asks again if she can text her father.

"I already told you there's no service."

She picks up my phone and presses the home button anyway as if her warm palm can activate a connection. Her body is rigid, eyes glued to the blue glow with so much wishful thinking. When no box appears, she takes a few hesitant steps toward the window, pointing the phone screen at it.

"Not going to happen if the sky looks the way it does tonight," I tell her, recognizing the anxious hope to reach her dad, which clearly eats away at her. First, she worships the screen, then wants to smash it with a hammer or chuck it out the window into the floodwaters.

"I'm going to bed," says Agnes wearily.

I take the phone from Lana and place it back on George's desk. Grabbing one of Jonathan's L.L.Bean lanterns, I lead both girls into the bathroom, raise the big window to the left of the sink, and show them the two large soup pots and a big black plastic bucket of rainwater on the roof deck.

"Don't forget your towels and soap."

"Thank you, Billy," they say.

"Are you sure you don't want your own room?"

"No," replies Lana quietly, having worn herself out. "We should stick together."

"Especially at night," adds Agnes. "That's when the middle of our house began to split apart."

I push that image from my mind, leave them in the bathroom, and go back to George's room. I look out the window and shine my flashlight down at the dinghy, still there, bobbing against the house, knots tight and holding. Across the currents, I see the faintest dark shadow of Lana and Agnes's house and know we need to stop dicking around and make a plan. No more Monopoly, no more six-packs. We need to pack minimal stuff. We should probably leave as soon as the sun comes up.

Agnes and Lana come back from the bathroom smiling uncomfortably, as though they're in the wrong place and ready to exit. Their eyes look red again and slightly swollen, maybe from exhaustion, maybe from the repulsion they feel at being here with me. I, myself, was doing just fine without them.

"I'm tired," says Lana, reaching her hands behind her head and pulling out her ponytail.

Her long brown hair falls over her shoulders, making her look sleepy rather than restless. I confess that I'm worried about my house collapsing.

"We aren't fleeing in that boat tonight, Billy," says Agnes. "That would be suicide. Believe me. We should pack, though. Leave our stuff by the window just in case."

I look at Lana, waiting for her to nod, but she's crossed her arms. Her sealed lips and hard stare are clearly the result of stress, exhaustion, and rage, which she projects under pressure. I imagine her father is a little like this, too, because he always has a painfully serious expression at the end-of-the-year school barbecue when everyone else is line dancing and eating ice cream. It must be stressful to be so afraid of failure all the time. Mrs. Featherstone is probably like that, too, under all those smiles and well wishes. I'm about to ask them where she is when Lana's expression softens a bit more, and she says, "I like Agnes's plan: Pack now, leave in the morning."

CHAPTER TWENTY-FIVE

Juliet

The door to the room at the Comfort Motel is open despite the key given to us by the owner, Mr. Balam. He wouldn't take our cash but pleaded with us to stay anyway. Does a full house give the illusion of a normal Friday night in the suburbs west of Charlotte, North Carolina? Does it buffer the solitude of watery vacancy? Minimize the possibility of a night full of lawlessness?

Martin and I walk over the soggy rug and throw our bags on the bureau. He strips down to nothing so fast. It seems he does it to free up his hands so that he can help me remove my damp clothing, which he tugs at, gently pulling my shirt over my head and peeling down my underwear, his thumbs, intentionally or not, grazing my thighs and igniting a mix of fury and abandon. I don't care anymore about Peterson, the hotel, the rain, or my exhaustion. I just want to smash the expectations, failures, and setbacks despite days of effort. There are no more principles at this point. I'm perched on a precipice, and the only way off is to open my arms and do a free fall.

Martin puts his mouth to my neck and moans or sobs or both. With his warm, strong hands resting at the base of my back, he kisses me tenderly, like he did before, but with no intention of stopping this time. My hands are in his hair, on his shoulders, and then everywhere as he guides me down onto the bed.

"Is this what we want?" he whispers in a voice I hardly recognize. I have no reply left in me. I just open myself to him, ditching everything I've hoped for, letting the failure recede into foggy absolution. There are no more pressing questions. No more fears or explanations. No right or wrong.

PART TWO

Following the light of the sun, we left the
Old World.
—Christopher Columbus

CHAPTER TWENTY-SIX

Juliet

We lie in bed in the afternoon in the soggy, humid room at the Comfort Motel west of Charlotte. The belief yesterday that we were hours from reuniting with our families imploded on the tarmac, reverberated from Macon, through Augusta, into North Carolina, and drove us toward each other in this dank room as though we were the only resources left on the planet to manage the failures; this was how we would get back on our feet and start north again, even if it meant breaking the rules.

Martin puts a couple of clean white towels down on the other queen bed that we haven't used. It's drier, as we haven't been getting in and out of it from shin-deep water. He takes my hand gently, leads me over the submerged, sodden beige carpet, and pushes me face down onto the towels. The sound of his breath, through the silence, crushes all my trepidation. He dips a washcloth into a bucket of water and wipes the bristly cotton over the back of my neck. He scrubs my lower back, the back of my arms and legs, the inside of my thighs. I close my eyes and descend a notch above unconsciousness, where I can barely sense my own breath and the touch of his hand and his mouth and the weight of him behind me lost in his tender force.

When I wake up, someone is shuffling outside the hotel door. Muted light behind the filmy orange curtains suggests late afternoon going to dusk.

"It's that guy again who gave us the key," says Martin. "Mr. Balam."

"Whatever. He wants something."

He came to the door earlier, around noon, to leave a gallon jug of water on a patio chair below the window to compensate for the lack of plumbing.

I sit up on the edge of the mattress now, flinching as my toes sink into the mushy carpet. I stand up and walk through the pool of sepia sludge that laps at my lower legs. At the window, I part the curtains discreetly and peer out at Mr. Balam, his back to the door. When I strain my eyes down to the right, my mouth begins to water at the plate of rice and black beans on the seat of the metal chair painted white with rust bleeding through.

"He brought us food," I whisper, turning to Martin, naked on his back, no attempt to cover himself.

"Four-star room service."

We're both starving for a real meal. Reaching into my bag, I grab my yellow dress and throw it over my head, pull it down over my hips, and wait for Mr. Balam to leave.

When he's gone, I open the door against the water pressure and peer at the parking lot filled with cars, the floodwater up to their axles in latte muck. Ripples of it spill along the concrete curb, onto the raised walkway, across the threshold at the door, and over my ankles and bare feet. It streams into the room like a tributary. As I attempt to step through the doorway to grab the plate of food, Mr. Balam appears in my path, his short, thick-limbed body lumbering toward me with fatigue, as if he, too, has been up all night with the barking dogs and distant gunfire.

"Do you need anything?" he asks in a heavy Spanish accent. "More water, batteries, a flashlight? I might have gas tomorrow." He gestures toward the white metal chair. "Please, eat."

"That's so kind of you. Mil gracias," I reply, grasping for commonality in the unknown and because I am a Spanish professor who is happy to engage in anything reminiscent of the time before the flooding. "Y gracias por el agua más temprano."

"Por supuesto." He nods tersely, staring at the flooded concrete beneath us. "Venceremos. Si Dios quiere."

"Ojalá," is all I can muster.

His Spanish is slow and melodious, warm and easy to understand. I suspect he's from Mexico—possibly Chiapas—or the highlands of Guatemala—with a name like Balam.

When he finally looks at me, I see dark eyes rimmed with bruising shadows, a broad face, and full lips under a neatly trimmed black mustache. I can see the tracks of a comb he put through his shiny black hair earlier.

"Keep your door locked. There's looting in the mall across the road."

"We heard it last night."

"Can you and your husband stay another day?"

"Maybe," I say, crossing my arms tightly against my chest, squeezing my knees and bare feet together in my skimpy sleeveless sundress meant for a carefree day on the beach. "We might leave for Boston tonight."

His squinting eyes shift left, as if contemplating the fifty states and their new arrangement on a map.

"Maybe that's better," he says with an uneasy smile. "They've taken over the National Guard base nearby."

"Who?"

"Los armados."

"Have they been here?"

"Not yet."

We look up at the sound of an approaching helicopter. Not-so-distant automatic gunfire ricochets through the still air, and a baby starts to wail in one of the nearby rooms.

"Be careful," he says. "I can't help you."

Martin comes up behind me. I can see that he's slid into shorts and a T-shirt.

"We'll keep the door locked," he tells Mr. Balam, who turns from us and looks back at the flooded parking lot.

A yellow stain rings the edge of his white shirt collar. His sopping-wet brown leather loafers look as though they'll come apart if he continues to slog along through the flooded walkways of his motel.

"Any news about flooding further north?" I ask.

"Desastroso por la costa."

"What does that mean?" asks Martin, grabbing my shoulder, his grip so forceful, it's hard to believe he touched me with that same hand hours earlier. I want to lead him back to the bed and tell him to calm down, but Mr. Balam starts telling us that coastal cities are underwater.

"Where? How do you know this?" asks Martin.

"I heard yesterday on my radio."

The jumbled magnitude of science fiction that he's just conjured rebounds in my brain as Martin tries to press him for details he doesn't have. Maybe he misheard the transmissions. Is he exaggerating? I want to slam the door in this poor man's face and try Billy again, despite the dense, putty gray, late-afternoon sky hovering above the disappearing parking lot in front of our door. I look down at the water churning at our ankles, as if whatever comes in from the coast has a current and a tide.

"Thanks for your help," I say, stepping back from the door, my feet splashing the floodwater as I move to get away from him. Mr. Balam braces one hand on the door jamb, bends one knee, and folds slightly at the hip in his tired black slacks.

"There are lots of people coming now," he stutters, anchoring his eyes to mine, his accent sharper with this message he needs to unload. "They are coming north. Del sur. The walls? La migra? No importa," he scoffs. "I want to help. But every room here is full."

Martin is standing at my side now, nodding. I know from his hollow gaze that he's stopped listening and is trying to grasp the notion of a surge of ocean so strong that it has engulfed coastal American cities. He and Peterson are a little late to the game. That they didn't see this must make it that much harder to swallow. I suspect that not everyone's models were off.

"We'll keep the door locked until we leave," I say. "You stay safe, too."

"The food," he says, grabbing the plate from the chair and passing it to me.

As I reach for the rice and beans under sweating plastic wrap, the small fist of a child extends past the doorjamb. A little girl, not more than four, with big brown eyes and a tawny complexion, steps in front of the door. An oversized rhinestone barrette at the top of her head cinches her shiny black hair. She's been standing out there somewhere on the saturated walkway in her pink pajamas and rain boots, listening the whole time. She looks up at her father and, with her free hand, grabs the edge of his black dress pants, clinging tightly near the front pocket, while the other hand juts out at me.

"A gift," says Mr. Balam. "From Josie."

I hand Martin the plate of food and step forward. I put my hands on my knees, lean toward the little girl, and look into her bright eyes that are completely oblivious to the world she will inherit. They dart with uncertainty. But she stands firm, and finally, her gaze meets mine and stays fixed there.

"What is this?" I ask, pointing at her hand.

She unfurls her palm to reveal a piece of bubble gum.

"It's been hard on the children," says Mr. Balam, smiling wearily. I take the gum from Josie's palm and hold it in my fingers, wishing I had something to give in return.

"Thank you. Josie. I love your diamond barrette."

She smiles and turns her gaze to the room behind me, studying it as though it contains wonders rather than the same lackluster particle-board furniture she could find pickling in brown puddles in any of the rooms in her father's motel.

I look at the phone. I'm ready to say goodbye to the Balams and eat this food. Then I can try Billy again, even if it means venturing outside to shove the phone at the heavens. As I stand up straight, Josie lets go of her father's pant leg and takes a small step forward over the buried threshold, her pink rain boots splashing water.

She balls her hands into tight fists as though the thrill takes effort but is worth contact with a stranger. I take a step forward, too, to discourage her entry. I stand there, stiff, unrelenting, until her joy turns to confusion. I wish Mr. Balam would leave now and take her with him to a mother, a brother, an aunt, or any of the dozen or so relatives we saw sheltering in the back of the motel late last night. There's no time now for small talk or amusements. If things were different, I might show her something in my bag, like pictures of Billy and George on my phone. But I just don't have it in me anymore. She stands there in her preciousness, her smile barely holding out as her intuition tells her to turn back to her father.

"Dinner and then bedtime," says Mr. Balam.

"For all of us," I reply, doing my best to smile as I wave goodnight, shut the door, and slide the deadbolt in place.

Martin passes me the plate, and I peel back the plastic wrap. I dig into the rice and beans, shoveling them into my mouth with a plastic spoon as I find my way to the edge of the bed and sit cross-legged. I eat half of the food in five or six mouthfuls, and then it's his turn. While he's eating his half, I get up, grab the phone off the bureau, and think about Billy's unanswered questions lost in shattered infrastructure. The screen glows arctic-ice blue, and the tiny wheel in the upper-left corner spins endlessly, looking for residual networks.

"I think it's broken," I say to Martin, placing it back on the bureau's scarred veneer.

"Then don't keep trying," he replies, packing the beans and rice into his mouth and chewing vigorously.

"It's been twenty-four hours."

"And anything could have happened." He places the empty plate on the bedside table with indifference. "God. I'd love a Dos Equis. Even a Narragansett would do."

"What about the phone?"

"What about it?" he asks, with the same numb gaze he revealed when Mr. Balam talked about the deteriorating security in the area.

"I could take it out to the parking lot and walk around."

"Do what you want."

I look at him, sitting on the mattress, staring at his submerged ankles like a kid on a dock playing footsie with pond water. He catches me trying to read his expression and stares back.

"What, Juliet?"

"It'll only work if we're both in."

He cocks his head and smiles.

"The phone," I say.

"Oh, the phone. Well, then. I'm out."

"No, Martin."

"My wife's missing. So are your husband and son. That piece of shit device has done nothing. It can't even map us home."

"You know where your daughters are now."

"Ah, yes, the great connector."

The possibility that he's shutting down, refusing to go on, rattles me. I lunge back to the bed and sit next to him. Should I touch him? His face, even sad, is pleasing in its expressiveness. But I don't know how to move him forward. I'm afraid that the longer we sit in the brine of this hotel, the faster our regrets and fears will consume us.

His brow instantly hardens, jaw clenched. If we weren't together in this room, if we hadn't been intimate on this bed, I might embrace him with everything I've got. But that gesture now carries so much more intention. I don't want to topple what little tolerance we have left for disappointment. I reach for his knee anyway.

"Don't," he says. And then, "Sorry."

He puts his arm around me and pulls me close. We're side by side, sitting on the bed, our hips touching. I put my head on his shoulder for a second. I think about going further. Pulling him down on the bed, me on top this time, plunging into nothingness again. I brush my hair out of my face, dismayed by my thoughts, by everything. Mostly, though, dreading the distance that lies ahead, through flood conditions, the failures of the last few days trailing us like a turbulent wake.

I climb back under the sheet in my yellow dress. Martin sinks himself next to me with a deep sigh, his subdued voice in my ear, telling me that we are doing the best we can, his touch making me forget. I close my eyes and try to focus on the present, try to block the past and future, those fickle constructs against which so many decisions are made. He reaches for my fist, his fingers gently unfurling mine.

"What is this?" he asks, looking down at Josie's piece of gum, a talisman I've kept in the dimple of my palm.

We split the gum and chew for a long time, staring at the water stains on the walls, in the shadows. My mind stumbles, and I think about Billy and George walking over the dunes on the island at sunset, their knees rattling sea oats on long green blades of grass, the waves swilling and rushing in, obediently retreating, exposing a universe of shells.

Then I'm back to the last night on Dog Island, when Martin, my mother, and I headed to the beach for a walk at dusk to buoy our spirits. I wanted to show them the battlefield of marine life I'd seen right after the surge, thinking it might shed light on what happened. But as we crested the dune, I froze. Maybe it was a super tide, combined with more surge we'd seen that afternoon, that washed away the proof of nature's malfunction. I knew I hadn't dreamed it. I glanced at Martin's unruffled expression as he looked at the high-water line and the pockmarked dunes but not much else. The three of us stared at the vast roiling slate-blue sea and white caps beneath a steady drizzle, each crashing wave a reminder of our seclusion, severed from our families and unaware of their condition.

As we turned from the surf and dimming sky to head back, Captain Karl came over the dunes, walking one of his red-brindled hounds. Slightly bowlegged, Karl tottered back and forth as the dog pulled him over saturated sand, which made him look more enthusiastic about our presence than he probably was. He raised his arm and waved as the dog dragged him along until he unclipped the animal, and it sailed over the dunes, nose to the ground, smelling bits of leftovers from what the sea had regurgitated earlier.

Apart from knowing about the flooding in Tallahassee and inundation in Jacksonville, he had no further news and didn't seem concerned. He saw no explosion of light along the coast and felt no tremor. He also liked his scotch on the rocks after three in the afternoon and often chased it down with a six-pack. He did admit that water on the bay side, where the ferry launched, washed over the docks early in the morning, making it impossible to cross. An unusual event, but not an impossibility during hurricane season with a full moon.

"But this isn't hurricane season," said my mother.

"You're one of those worriers," he replied with a slight ridicule I found unnecessary. "The phones and the TVs will all be back up soon, and we'll get y'all over to the mainland."

"And then what?" asked Martin, looking at the three of us. "There are no flights out of Tallahassee. The streets are underwater, houses submerged."

Karl nodded, his shoulders bucking slightly with a soft chuckle, revealing his discomfort, his veiled recognition of the changes around us. But he disregarded his own intuition.

"Weather down here does a lot of damage," he said, sweeping his thick, callused fingers across the wedge of blond bangs at his brow like a little boy might do. "And there won't be no flights forever. The chop will ease, and you'll be good to go." He looked at me and smiled, "Don't you go worrying, too, Juliet."

"I am worried," I said, with mounting dread that sat with me like a bad meal. "We all should be."

Martin put his hand on my shoulder and held it there firmly, as Tom might do.

"We'll figure it out," he said, trying to compose himself by first comforting me because one person crumbling in these situations could easily bring down everyone else.

The four of us stood on the elevated sodden dunes that felt like pudding, my mother and Karl talking about contacting the marina in Carrabelle, and Martin confessing to me that he had a bad feeling about his family. His wife, Stephanie, wasn't very good at managing crises.

It began to drizzle. Agitated, Karl went on his way with his dog, and the three of us trudged silently back along the flooded sandy road, lost in our own thoughts.

By the time I saw the indigo porch railings, Martin was marching steadily up ahead, turning into the driveway. My mother, several yards behind, gazed down at the ground, her toes drilling into the sand to steady herself. I stared at Martin climbing the stairs, the same ones my boys climbed with Tom, with their cousins and my brother, and thought, *Where was everyone?* If we could just get off the island, we could find them.

I sit up in the dim glow that spills through the orange curtains.

"Let's make a run for it now."

"With vigilantes and no streetlights?"

"Less of a target."

"Too tired," he says, switching off the lantern and finding my hand again in the dark.

A few hours later, I wake to Martin shaking my arm.

"It's time, Juliet."

"It's pitch black. I thought you said—"

He pulls me up and turns on the electric lantern. I can see from the faint glow that he's wearing the same dirty navy shorts and T-shirt he wore yesterday. And the day before. A faint beard seems to have sprouted across his lower jaw overnight. He looks shipwrecked as he slaps his bare feet into the water, painstakingly packing the flashlight, a shriveled orange, a box of crackers, some toiletries, and a few spare clothes scattered around the room. He looks absolutely nothing like the neighbor I knew from PTO picnics and VERT classes in the high school gym.

"Get your stuff," he says, filling two plastic gallon water jugs with what's left of the container that Mr. Balam left us.

"It's too dark," I moan, rubbing my eyes.

"It's dawn."

Reluctantly, I get out of bed, grab the phone on the bureau, and poke the home button. Blue glow, no text box. No surprise. I change my underwear and throw on a pair of dusty rose shorts, a black T-shirt, and a bottle-green cotton sweatshirt. Sitting on the bed, I dry my feet with a towel before pulling on dirty socks and gray rain boots. Martin is already holding the door, peering up at the tinge of orange haloing the sky.

I pull the door closed against the pressure of the water and follow Martin onto the walkway, past dark windows and doors of other motel rooms, through air thick with briny rot. Bag slung over his shoulder, fingers of his left hand hooking the plastic jugs, his right hand beams the flashlight across flooded concrete and gravel, over cans and milk cartons that spill out from gutted white garbage bags, into the swampy lot under the drizzle. A scruffy shepherd mix lurks next to the mess, his vacant hazel eyes tracking me through the lantern light. Martin shoos him away, and he jogs off between two cars.

"Who's going to save the animals," I ask as we get into the rental.

"Not us. Not now," he replies, adjusting himself in the driver's seat.

There must be some semblance of order in the city, despite the gunshots earlier, because no one has siphoned off the last of our gas. I imagine that Mr. Balam's generosity and hard work have earned him some street credibility. Maybe somebody is watching out for him.

Martin slowly rolls the car forward in the darkness, headlights off, and nearly hits an approaching figure. I imagine armed thugs assaulting us. But it's just Mr. Balam. As he steps up to the driver's door, Martin rolls down his window.

"What is it?" Martin asks in a voice anticipating horrible news. Collapsed bridges, washed-out roads. Or worse.

Mr. Balam freezes at the window, stuttering as if he's forgotten his English.

"Qué pasó?" I ask.

"Un favor."

"Dime."

A figure appears behind him, holding a bundle.

"Please," he pleads. "This is my sister, Noemi. Please take her. And her daughter, Ana. Por favor."

"Where?" asks Martin. "Now?"

I can barely see Mr. Balam's shadowy face, the dark pools of his eyes. I hear what's in his voice, though.

"Ana needs medical care."

"We're going north on a long car ride," says Martin. "How could we possibly take her?"

"What about hospitals in Atlanta or Nashville?" I suggest. I'm about to say, "Or Columbia," but I remember Darrell and the pilots in Macon saying the routes there were now gone.

"She needs a pediatric specialist in Pittsburgh or Rochester. I have the names. Please."

Pennsylvania and New York seem like foreign countries, beyond blockades and borders. Was he crazy? He pulls out a wad of cash and thrusts it into Martin's face.

"If you can get her close to one of these hospitals, my cousin will meet her there."

"This is nuts," I exclaim to Martin. "Phones barely work anymore."

"We email by computer and generator." He hands Martin a piece of folded paper. "My cousin is waiting."

I grab the paper and drop it into the console with the charging phone and then look through the windshield at a black-gray sky fringed with glowing orange like the coals of a dying fire. Our breakaway is in jeopardy, delayed by Mr. Balam and our own wildly swinging moral compass.

"What if the hospitals aren't running or can't take her?" I ask.

"Or if we don't make it?" adds Martin.

"The hospitals there are inland. Please," Mr. Balam implores. "There's nothing here for her."

His sister, at his back, speaks up: "My cousin in Pittsburgh will help me. He knows I'm coming. I've got to get my daughter out of here. Believe me, we can travel in rough conditions."

Mr. Balam drops the money. Martin looks down at his lap, at the bills that have little value considering what's at stake. Mr. Balam moves faster now, along the side of the car. He opens the door and ushers in his sister, the bundle in her arms. I glimpse the shadowy contours of a sleeping child framed by a crocheted blanket and think, *Are we all mad?*

I look at Martin, still gaping at his lap, his usual resolve suspended. Glancing over my shoulder, I watch Mr. Balam, one knee on the back seat, as he ducks into the car and places a medium-sized black duffle bag next to his sister. Before withdrawing, he tenderly tucks the blanket around the sleeping child and kisses his sister's forehead.

"Animo," he says. "This is best."

"I can't guarantee anything," says Martin. "The roads are terrible. We don't know where we're going."

"I understand. But my niece needs help. Que ya no se la podemos dar."

I look at the child in Ana's arms. She's longer than an infant. I see through dawn's softening shadows that the blanket swaddles a very frail toddler.

"What about a car seat?" I ask.

"She'll kick," replies Noemi in a calm voice, a slight nonnative inflection.

Still pivoted in the seat, I introduce myself as I stare into her probing dark eyes, a tint of maroon below them, like Mr. Balam's. She has black hair, his same broad face, but more defined cheekbones, where the shadows hollow them.

Mr. Balam whispers something in Spanish that I don't catch and then closes the car door. Martin rolls up his window, and we slide away through the floodwaters and drizzle onto an empty road.

Soon, we reach Route 129 and drive in silence in the very early dawn with just enough glow behind cloud cover to get by without headlights if we concentrate hard enough on the blurry gray trajectory ahead. We see no one, no animals, nothing dead or alive, only murky water against our bumper, streaming under the car.

"The phone," says Martin.

"You're back in?" I ask, in a near whisper, reaching toward the console, through the bills and the slip of paper, looking at the disappointing glow.

He stares ahead silently through the windshield as the gray early morning peels away, revealing a depth to our rural route. I'm glad for the silence, for not having to worry about saying the right thing, explaining myself, or making small talk with another stranger. Noemi looks out the window at flooded farmland. Ana, thank God, asleep in her arms.

"Can you try again?" Martin whispers a little while later.

"There's nothing out here."

"Make it work," he says absurdly. "I need to ask my daughters where Stephanie went. Ask Billy what he knows."

But the phone sits lifeless in the console.

The road begins to dip. Water rises over our tires. I can hear it wicking off the rubber. The soot-gray sky turns to marble, which is all the light the day will offer. We turn onto Highway 77 and merge with other cars slogging through the flood. A tandem fleet of camouflaged military vehicles rolls by on our right, looking like it has plans that the rest of civilian society can only imagine. Where are they going? What do they know that we don't? The last truck in the convoy passes, opening the view to a swelling lake in a field of early crops, leaves buoyed on the surface like lily pads—soy, peanuts, corn that feed the world, gone to hell. Is there a backup plan?

"What's that?" asks Noemi, shifting in the back, trying to get comfortable.

"Drowning soy or peanuts," I reply.

"No, I mean up ahead. Coming at us."

Two large black pickups race in the opposite lane. Only, as they come upon us, we can see now that they aren't in the other lane at all.

"Holy fuck," says Martin, swerving and honking and somehow getting out of the way as the pickups reconfigure lanes across this highway.

Ana has woken up. As she flails and whimpers, Noemi, rocking against the back seat, does her best to settle her. Peterson was bad enough, I think, with guilt. But a sick baby deflates the little bit of hope that jingles in my ears every so often. I want to help her, but I can't. Just like I couldn't help Peterson.

We've slowed considerably for fear of more rogue traffic and soon edge along even slower as we drive close to four men in civilian clothing, jeans tucked into tall black rain boots, standing next to a police cruiser, its red-and-blue lights strobing. The men watch ineffectively as traffic going in the opposite direction diverges, crosses the median, and spills into our northbound lane again.

"This is psychotic," says Martin.

"Get us close to the cruiser so I can talk to them."

"No. Wait," pleads Noemi. "Not with me here."

"They don't care. Not now," I say.

"I can't cross again. Not with Ana." She looks left, staring hard through the glass at the sinking fields full of assurance that no one will interrogate her out here. "Okay. Ni modo. Bueno."

Martin veers out of our dissolving lane and pulls up next to the cruiser. He rolls down the window.

"Excuse me?" I shout past him before he can get his words out. "We're going north. Do you know what's going on in New England?"

"Nope," says the older man with thinning gray hair and a wizened look.

"Unviable, ma'am," says the younger one with light coffee-tone skin, a short Afro, and Coke-bottle glasses.

"What do you mean? Where? We're trying to get to our kids, near the coast."

"I can guide you to an information center," says the younger one.

I feel Martin's hand on mine in my lap.

"Forget it, Juliet."

He pulls off the shoulder and back onto the highway. Water in the opposite lane has receded, and the oncoming traffic returns to the southbound lane.

"What does that mean?" I ask as we drive on. "Billy and the girls aren't *unviable*. What the fuck is wrong with people!"

Ana whimpers.

"Shit. I'm sorry, Noemi," I whisper, turning to her. "How can I help?"

"She's just soothing herself," she answers, pulling the white crocheted blanket back from Ana's anemic form, buoyed by the sea of cotton, her blank gaze, mouth slack, bulb of her tongue against her full lips. Noemi breaks apart a soft fruit bar and feeds it to her in tiny pieces. "Do you want one?" she asks, looking up at me.

"No," I reply and turn back in my seat to watch the road.

I reach toward the console for one of the oranges the inmates gave us the day before. I peel it and split it into three parts. Chewing it only reminds me of my hunger for something substantial.

The traffic slows again. A line of fifteen or so men plodding through muddy puddles on the median catches our attention: the camo jackets, the AR-15s slung over their shoulders, the long pole with a black banner announcing "Christ's Army" in white script.

"The nuts are getting nuttier," I say.

"Amen," replies Martin, slowing further and making a wide berth so as not to splash them and call attention to our car.

He loosens his right hand from the wheel and touches my hand again at my knee.

"Try Billy."

I lift the phone from the console, put my finger on the screen, and recoil at the disturbing crack, crack,

crack, a magnified flipping of cards that knocks at my temples. I slink down and turn to peer around my seat, over Noemi's crouched body shielding Ana. The men are still pointing their guns upward, releasing their rage at the steel sky as if to bust open the clouds and initiate rapture.

"Holy fuck. The moment they've been waiting for," says Martin, sailing through the water, slick at the tires, whipping through the treads.

When I raise the phone toward my face, a text box appears. Martin sees the glow and says, "They're sitting ducks. Tell them to get out of there."

"And go where?"

"Where there's law and order."

He's losing it, I think, as I text, *Missed plane in Macon. Driving toward PA. You ok?*

"Tell them to go inland. Find something to float in. Tell Billy to ask the girls where Steph is."

I type a condensed version of Martin's message, hoping my industrious Morse-code sounds will help him focus on the road. But his hands slide loosely over the twitching wheel.

Billy doesn't respond.

"The houses are going to collapse. They've got to get out. I have to find Stephanie."

"Okay, Martin. I don't need the scenarios. I've got plenty of my own."

"You don't see it, do you?" he says, pointing to a patch of flooded highway to our right, where water rushes in and sloshes around as if live animals are thrashing beneath the surface. "The vortex effect. Warming oceans and cold glaciers fucking with the jet stream."

"This isn't the coast, though," Noemi pipes up.

"It is now. And pressure's pushing the ocean in on a conveyor from possibly thousands of miles away.

"I don't understand."

"Too much heat melting the ice shelves and calving the glaciers, tipping the earth's axis, or whatever," he mumbles. "It's hard to know anymore."

"It's desert where I come from," she says. "No corn, no coffee."

"Careful what you wish for. The Dry Corridor could be ocean now. Not very good for crops either."

More scenarios, more despair. I can't stand it anymore. "Find a high spot and pull over," I tell him. "It's my turn to drive."

CHAPTER TWENTY-SEVEN

Billy

At some point early in the morning, the hissing sound of the current outside of George's window wakes me. When I fully open my eyes, I realize it's not the water after all. Agnes and Lana are standing in the darkness near the door, whispering at each other like angry cats.

"You do it. I don't want to."

"You promised you would."

"I can't now. I'm too upset. I'm going into another room to be alone."

"Please, Lana, don't. We need to do it."

The bedroom door closes. I'm alone now with Agnes, who comes toward me. Something's seriously wrong. I feel it in the way she painstakingly pulls back the sheets, slips into my bed, and presses her trembling body against my back. She puts her right arm around my waist, her warm skin against mine, and burrows her forehead into my shoulder blades. I freeze like an idiot as she embraces me.

"Billy?" she whispers in a pleading tone, as though I can shift our reality and make it all go away.

"What is it?"

"I'm so scared."

I take a deep breath, trying to steady my heart rate.

"I can't stand this anymore. I want out. Now."

"We all do," I reply, hoping that Lana is taking a very long timeout in my parents' bedroom.

"Is it true that the water is going to keep rising?"

"I think so. We have to find dry land."

"In the dinghy?"

"Unless you have a better idea."

"Oh, my God. It's so flimsy in the current. There's no hope for us."

I flip myself over and feel her nose and mouth so close to mine. She fits her head under my chin against my chest, and I hold her tightly for a long time. She smells like marigolds or whatever girls spray all over their bodies. I turn on my back, and she adjusts her head against my shoulder. Her breathing is deep and irregular; her moist mouth on my collarbone stirs me up inside. But instead of pulling away, I turn my face to her again and put my lips against her forehead. This, I think, is enough to erase most of the destruction and rot I've seen. The dead dogs, the baby, the bodies. I don't care if she bawls her eyes out.

I wake up to Salty's nose in my face, her tongue on my cheek. She still smells like bleach and marsh. Agnes is asleep on the mattress on the floor, spreadeagle on her stomach. I didn't sense her leaving my side earlier, if she was even here in George's bed at all.

The early morning glow casts a faint gray sheen through the window, coating the provisions we left there last night: the electric camping lamp, the green garbage bag full of clothes, the last of the food, and a gallon jug of drinking water.

I scratch the top of Salty's head.

"You want some kibble, don't you, old girl?" I whisper. "And then a good shit on Jonathan's roof deck."

CHAPTER TWENTY-EIGHT

Juliet

Billy, I text, my finger hovering over the touch-screen as I think about how to put information into a sound bite that might motivate him to seek higher ground. *Leave now. More water coming.*

And then the ping that makes my heart sprint.

Where? How?

"This is all wrong," I tell Martin. "They don't need despair. Maybe staying put is best."

"They need to get out, Juliet."

Noemi, who keeps asking about the weather, tries again, "I still don't understand."

"A glacier in Greenland or Antarctica maybe," explains Martin. "Heat, expansion, melt, affecting thermohaline circulation, radically shifting everything you see."

Away from coast, I peck out hard with my pointer finger. *Get in boat. Go inland.*

Noemi, arms weighted down by her child, is shifting in the back seat as if her whole body is contending with what Martin has just said. I look back at her dull gaze, the mechanical motion of adjusting her elbow against the black duffle bag, habits of survival, void of the bustle of emotion.

"Do you want me to hold her?"

"No," she replies, shaking her head while staring wearily at the phone in my hand.

"Why'd you keep that? I mean, it's great that you can talk to your son when other people can't."

"It's a mixed bag."

"It's dangerous."

"It's complicated."

"Juliet's a skeptic," says Martin.

"That's not true. I just don't think we got all the information."

"What information?" asks Noemi.

"That they cause brain cancer," Martin says flatly.

"Who's profiting from the Ban. What devices are coming next—were coming next."

"And you, Martin?" asks Noemi.

"I don't know anymore."

"Do you have one?"

"No," he answers. "I've got a dead flip phone somewhere in my bag back there."

Ana makes a gagging sound through a listless body and an unresponsive gaze. Unfazed, Noemi rolls her gently to her side and rubs her upper back.

"You let your son keep it, though. What's his name?"

"Billy."

"Yeah. You let Billy keep it."

"It was vaulted most of the time, in a case, in a basement room, in a metal box. He didn't carry it around, sleep with it under his pillow, or anything like that."

"But still."

Her questions begin to annoy me. There are more pressing issues right now. Billy isn't answering.

"Rebelde," she mutters.

"I'm not a rebel. I meant to turn it in sooner or later."

"She's just stupid," says Martin with a slight grin, which makes me think maybe he's coming around.

"He's right," I reply. "Kids make you that way. When they get older."

"Oh, okay," she says.

"I'm sorry," I say, turning back and looking down at Ana.

"It's fine. We'll be okay," she replies, strands of her straight black hair buffing her daughter's face as she kisses her forehead and cheeks. "The doctor in Pennsylvania will help us."

We hear the ping again, which always stops the conversation. I look down at Billy's words.

How? Where do I go?

Higher ground.

Dad and George?

No news, I text, trying to think of something uplifting to tell him.

"Well?" says Martin.

"He's asking where they should go."

"Inland. Western Mass. I don't know," he stares hard at the road. "Tell them to go north to the mountains. Vermont. Burlington or Montpelier, and find help there."

I remember that Tom has friends in Stowe, but Billy won't remember that.

"Maybe they should stay in the house and wait for help."

"There is no help," says Noemi.

I look back at her again and then down at Ana's stunned expression. When Noemi reaches her hand over Ana's face to rearrange the blanket, Ana doesn't blink.

"She's blind. And deaf," Noemi says, meeting my gaze. "She has sight. It's just not visual like ours."

"I hope you find the help you're looking for."

"I hope you find your children. If you don't mind me saying, Martin is right. They should get away from the coast. Beto is an inflight refueling specialist in the air force. He flew over cities along the coast just after the water came in. But his plane went down two days ago."

"Shit," says Martin. "I'm so sorry."

"Esperamos," she replies, lifting a corner of the blanket and wiping a bit of spittle from Ana's mouth. "He told me before he left that New York, Philadelphia, Boston, and Providence were underwater. Others in his squadron had seen it, too."

"Was he rescuing people?"

"Just flyovers."

The phone pings again. I lift it from my lap.

Mom?

I can't get my finger to the keyboard fast enough and fumble with the device before pecking out, *Head north. Toward the mountains. NH or VT.*

Where?

A shelter. Concord, Hanover, Burlington?

I'm with the girls.

Good. Go together.

I turn to Martin.

"They're together now. They're leaving."

"What about Steph?"

Blue dots roll along with a speech bubble on the screen, and Billy texts, *Love you.* And then he's gone.

"I'll ask again in a bit," I say as I lean against the headrest, thinking about my house. My bed and pillows, the cross breeze, the lily of the valley and the lilac that blow through my windows at this time of year, making it easy to fall asleep with a book in my hand. I think about my kitchen, my children's voices at breakfast, Tom's laughter, my cherry tree, the stack of students' essays waiting for correction in my office, and all the things on that one plot of now-submersed land that used to make getting out of bed every morning worth the trouble.

My vision gets blurry for a second. I try to distract myself by the flipflop of the wipers sucking and slapping rivulets of rain, a default metronome for our long, circuitous ballad of a journey that lacks an itinerary. Does Billy know there is no plan? His texts are a plea for concrete motherly wisdom, while mine are fragments of confusing, disjointed warnings and fears, the special of the day on today's menu of anxious childrearing.

We bound through the water. I can hear the rain strafing the sides of the car again as Martin does his best to maneuver along the sinking highway. We all exhale for a moment when the road rises, giving us temporary relief from the flood, before another descent, and we plunge back in, our breath unpredictable like the weather outside. He grips the steering wheel, his knuckles taut. When the phone pings again, I grab it and stare down at Billy's words.

ru ok? Mr. F still there?

Yes.

"Ask about Steph," Martin reminds me, his right hand releasing the wheel just long enough for him to scratch the stubble at his chin.

Mrs. F?

No idea.

"If I could have a minute with the phone, I might figure out where my wife went."

"There's a rest stop up ahead on higher ground. Pull over, and you can text."

"I need to change Ana's diaper," says Noemi.

We slow down and pull off the road, up onto a muddy rest area that's elevated on the shoulder. I have just enough time to read Billy's last text—*What should I ask about their mom?*—before Martin finds a place to park and idle the engine.

There are so many things I want to say to Billy about his own safety and intuition. Questions about Tom and George that don't seem to congeal long enough to get me anywhere, as I'm confounded by the lag in real-time answers.

Martin opens his door just as I make a last-minute sprint with my texts.

Go to Burlington. Be careful. Stay away from crowds.

I feel horrible for the scare tactics, for suggesting his incompetency. The screen flickers. I shake the phone futilely, my thumb pad back at the glass dimple, finger on the glass, because I can't help myself.

Don't trust strangers. You're too trusting.

"Can I have it now?" Martin asks.

CHAPTER TWENTY-NINE

Billy

When I take Salty up to the roof deck of Jonathan's apartment and let her out through the door, I notice the rug is soaking wet. I reach out and touch the sweating wall. I can smell the dankness coming, the beginning of a domino effect that will end with the collapse of my beautiful home.

Salty does her business on the deck. She trots back inside and then hops down the stairs, and follows me back into George's room. I'm rubbing her dry with a towel, thinking about the weight of the damp wood, plaster, and studs in these walls, when I see the screen glowing silvery blue in the lamplight. Bubbles sputter on the left side of the screen, and a text box pops up.

Missed plane in Macon. Driving toward PA. You ok?

This irritates me. Then makes me panic. I really need to see Mom's face now. As if this dose of reality isn't enough, the next text reads:

Leave now. More water coming.

I sit down on George's swivel chair with the phone in my good palm. Does *now* mean this very instant? Where does she think we can go? I knew we'd have to get into that dinghy at some point, but no one's hammered out the details. I look out the window at the darkness fringed by a pale blue dawn. The three of us might as well be in a space capsule.

Where? How? I text as fast as I can.

Away from coast. Get in boat. Go inland.

I resent all this texting. It's a message in a bottle that keeps bobbing in the waves. Does she think we can just open the front door and swim away? Hoist sail and shove off? Her words swirl in my brain with hopelessness and more resentment. She and Mr. Featherstone should have found a way to call someone in to rescue us. The fact that they haven't means that things are probably more screwed up than I know. She isn't partying with the Featherstones in the Sunshine State. Their worlds have collided because something awful and far worse than monster high tides in the Boston Harbor brought them together.

I look at the screen.

How? I write again. *Where do I go?*

Higher ground.

I picture me, the girls, and the dog paddling away from my house in the dinghy, out toward the suburbs. The rolling currents from the sea are washing in this way. But if the tides turn and pull us back out, we won't have a chance.

Dad and George? I tap out with my pointer finger for what feels like the billionth time. I'm worried about them. Then I feel sorry for myself. But another part of me doesn't give a fuck anymore.

No news.

A pause. More bubbles.

Mom?

Head north. Toward the mountains. NH or VT.

Now, there's some logic that's escaped me: head for the hills. Dad is a hiker. Skied a ton in Vermont before he got married. Maybe he and George are up there, sitting in a cabin around a wood stove. Or fishing in a brook.

Where? I text back.

A shelter. Concord, Hanover, Burlington?

I'm with the girls.

Good. Go together.

Love you, I text, even though I feel so abandoned.

A little while later I try again, *ru ok? Mr. F still there?*

Yes. Mrs. F?

No idea. Should I ask about their mom? Lana, Agnes, and I haven't really discussed her.

The text bubbles rotate for several seconds before her messages appear in rapid fire:

Go to Burlington. Be careful. Stay away from crowds.

The horribleness of everything starts to sink in. I feel like an idiot for sitting around playing board games and drinking beer. No one is coming to rescue us. Not Dad and George, not Mom or Mr. Barrett. And not FEMA.

As if what Mom just told me isn't enough, she sends one last text before the screen goes black, *Don't trust strangers. You're too trusting.*

CHAPTER THIRTY

Juliet

Outside the car, his back against the driver's door, Martin tilts forward slightly and bows his head over the phone, shielding it from the drizzle as he focuses on the screen nestled close to his chest. He didn't hear me helping Noemi and Ana back into the car after we changed Ana's diaper under the hatchback. I close Noemi's door and move close to him, to where he stands in a foot of water. I lean against the car. The cool, damp metal sears my back through my thin cotton T-shirt. I watch cars and trucks rambling by, swerving to avoid pools, spraying water everywhere. Kale green sludge sloshes across the highway, burying the white lines between lanes that previously stood for law and order, for keeping everyone moving safely forward on the highway, the principal cog on the giant wheel of American progress that makes our world turn. If it weren't for this saturation and a few too many abandoned vehicles curing in the muck, it might seem like a normal, drizzly day on a freeway in the southern Atlantic states. Only it isn't.

A military caravan rolls by in a dozen hybrid vehicles: huge bulging potato-tan cabs attached to semi-flatbeds. I make eye contact for an instant with a woman in russet fatigues and cap, sitting in the passenger seat, surveying the changed landscape with a listless look of disbelief. Where are they going with their steely incursion? Which calamity are they tending to now? I saw a woman in the breakdown lane somewhere outside of Charlotte trying to flag down a convoy like this. They drove right past her as though she were a bleating sheep, and they were needed for larger missions, like mass civilian rescue on a scale no one had planned for.

"Come on, Agnes," Martin blurts out now as he jabs at the screen with his finger.

I inch closer to him, against the driver's door, my damp shoulder against his. I want to lean my head there and rest like I did in the hotel, but the glow cradled in his hand, at his chest, waltzes with bubbles and boxes full of text that consume him. I imagine him cradling me instead, looking into my soul for answers that will make us both feel better. Drops of rain clot on the skin and hair of his forearm, mixing with his sweat, beading on his silver watch band and thick gold wedding ring.

"It's going to get wet," I say.

"One more minute," he replies, tapping at the glass.

But I want it back now. He's followed the rules with the phone and kept his family safe while I've gambled like a neglectful mother. And now he's reaping the benefits of my lax decision-making. Does he understand that?

"Damn it, Agnes. Come on!" He pushes himself off the car with the heel of my brother's firefighter boot. "She's not answering."

I squeeze behind him, open the driver's door, glance at Noemi dozing in the back, and slide onto the seat.

"Get in," I say.

I twist the steering wheel and pulse the gas pedal, rocking us back and forth until we jolt forward onto the two-lane rural stretch of Route 79. Intense rainfall, tropical humidity, and atmospheric rivers have left a crust of muddy batter all over these elevated hills of northern Virginia. We can see water pooling in the valleys below, the surge that just keeps coming in, percolating through the maze of watersheds, irrigating the base of these mountain hamlets we pass.

"Tank's nearly empty."

"Take the next exit. Don't want to stall here."

I veer off the highway and glide toward a rural intersection.

A woman, probably in her mid-forties, flags us down at the stop sign at the end of the exit ramp. Long red hair falls into her narrow, sun-furrowed face. She's wearing a red and blue flannel with cut-off sleeves and tight, faded denim jeans torn at the knees and tucked into white rain boots. We can't possibly make room for her in this car if that's what she's asking. When Martin rolls down his window cautiously, she holds her hands up like a criminal caught in the act.

"I got no money," she shouts at us before I've even fully stopped the car. "Gas, food, overnight accommodations?"

For a moment, I think she's shopping for these things until she winks and adds, "We got it all."

"We need gas," says Martin.

I can hear Noemi shifting. The redhead's brash voice has woken her and, by extension, Ana, held in her firm embrace. The woman stretches out her right arm stiffly like a scarecrow. Her gameshow happiness clashes with tired eyes and the apprehension she continually suppresses with a false smile.

"Straight up the road here, around that massive puddle. Follow the tire marks around the edge of the field, but don't get stuck. You'll see a gas station and a line of cars a mile long. Go around it, along the field again, and take your first right down Abbots Lane. Look for my husband, Hal, in a gray T-shirt and Hawaii-print shorts."

We thank her and pull away.

"This means we'll pay through the roof," says Martin.

"It's either that or a two-hour wait at the gas station," I reply.

"Use my brother's money," says Noemi, rocking Ana in her arms, calming herself by whispering into her daughter's deaf ears.

We bypass the long line of cars at the gas station, turn onto Abbots Lane, and start to bicker about the risk of continuing through the thick pools of liquidy sediment in front of us. Noemi weighs in, saying we have no choice. We agree, and I drive for several more minutes, slow and cautious, before pulling into a sinking gravel driveway behind six other cars.

Hal, in his orange and blue Hawaii shorts, and two other men, in filthy white T-shirts and jeans, pump gas from a tanker truck into five-gallon red tubs. With a plastic siphon, they pour gas right into the tank of a green Dodge pickup at the head of the line.

"Fill it up," I tell one of the guys who comes up to my window.

"Ten bucks a gallon."

"Use my brother's money," repeats Noemi.

"You'll need that cash when you get to the hospital, or your cousin's, or wherever you end up," I say.

"Believe me, I have enough. You don't understand what you've done for us."

Martin pulls out his wallet and takes several bills. He digs more deeply around credit cards, hesitates, and then reaches for the console and takes two twenty-dollar bills from the wad that Mr. Balam so bountifully dropped in his lap.

"Who were the others staying in the back of the motel," I ask, remembering the small community crowded into the proprietor's suite, behind the front desk.

"My younger brother, Mateo, and a cousin and his family, and an uncle."

"Sounds crowded."

"I don't live there. I'm closer to Raleigh, near the air force base where Beto works. When the water came, I went to my brother's motel, thinking it would be drier. But the water made it to Charlotte."

I turn and stare out the window at the mention of the motel. I feel a weakness in my limbs, followed by regret now that Martin and I have salvaged ourselves and found our way back on the road toward home. I hope he doesn't notice. I don't want emotional entanglement to get in the way of our decisions from here on out. I turn back and keep my eyes focused on the black Prius in front of us.

"I left for the motel the day before Beto's plane went down."

"Have you heard anything?" I ask.

"Nada," she replies.

"Maybe—"

"He'll get back safely. Yes, ojalá. Ya veremos."

Martin lifts the phone from the console, looks at the screen, and then puts it back down. A minute later, he's checking again, staring at the black glass, when one of the guys with a crest of curly blond hair and a beard to match appears at our window. He tells Martin to pay the teenage boy sitting with two friends on a rickety, soggy staircase attached to a white bungalow long overdue for a paint job. Martin gets out of the car, cash in hand. I can hear his boots smacking the water, grinding against gravel as he plods away from us. The phone pings. I grab it, look at the screen, and see his last words to his daughters.

What is it, love?

Above that box, one of the girls texted:

I have something to tell you dad.

I look at Martin's back, his shoulders slightly stooped from fatigue, as he counts out the bills. I think of his wife, Stephanie. Her kind face is beautifully wholesome. Her goodwill, always delivered with raw candor, has unmoored me once or twice.

Billy? I text hastily. *What do the girls want to tell their father?* I can see from the spinning bubbles that someone is reading my text, but the bubbles roll on with no reply. And then, just as Martin turns from the boy on the staircase and heads back toward us, someone texts:

Leaving now. Getting in a boat.

"Holy shit," I mutter. *Be careful.*

CHAPTER THIRTY-ONE

Billy

Realizing that we forgot to pack Salty's food last night with the rest of the stuff, I go into the hallway toward my room to grab it. I pass Lana in the bathroom, sitting on the toilet lid, tapping her pointer finger against my phone, and frowning at the screen. Her brown hair wilts around her face and down her shoulders in a scruffy, tomboy kind of way. Her moodiness really annoys me now. It's like she's waging battle with everyone, including herself. I've always had trouble with girls whose emotional state requires so much decoding. It's exhausting.

I let her go at it with the phone, with her father, I'm guessing, even though she didn't ask permission. How could I intrude on her sorrow and disrupt her determination that seems hard-wired?

"Where are they?" I finally ask.

"Not sure. Battery is low."

I go into my room and grab Salty's food and the last portable charger.

Back in the hallway, I ask, "What's your dad saying?"

"Give me a minute," she replies, both thumbs drumming at the keypad.

What could she possibly be telling him?

"Are they okay?"

"They aren't responding. I'm trying to figure out a way to get to Gregory Allen. He has one, too."

"You can't just add contacts. It doesn't work like that anymore."

Her extracurricular Russian math school might be good for equations, but I think it has gotten in the way of life's basic intuition.

"There's a way to get to an alternative screen. I've read about it."

She's bullshitting me again, but I'm not falling for it this time.

"You're wasting power, Lana. This battery in my hand is the last one. No more after that. Do you hear me?"

"Your mom wants us to go to the mountains."

I step toward her and put my hand out.

"You're reading my private texts."

"Jesus, Billy. This is an emergency. The more shared information, the better." She twists her head at a weird angle. "Fine. Never mind," she says, slapping the phone into my good palm.

With the bag of dog food in my arm, I go back into George's room, Lana following close behind. She flops herself down on the mattress and cuddles up against her sister, who's waking up. I try to make eye contact with Agnes, but she doesn't stir much. I pour kibble on the newspaper and stuff the near-empty bag into the garbage bag on the floor. Then, I head back into the hallway toward my room to boil water for tea. I'm just about to step into my room when I hear Agnes whisper:

"Did you tell him?"

I pause and lean against the wall.

"I texted him. No response."

"What did you say?"

"Just that I had something important to tell him."

"But did you say it?"

Lana doesn't have an answer to this question.

"One of us has to tell him," says Agnes. "If you can't, I will."

After a long pause, I go into my room. I strike a match, light the propane stove under a pot of water, and head back to George's room, an air pocket of silence. I knot the garbage bag so that it's ready to load when it's time to go. I can't help but shift my gaze toward the mattress, where the girls spoon in a tight embrace. I grab a T-shirt, a pair of shorts, and three loose socks off the floor and throw them into the closet. Then my fingers pluck at vagrant kibble nuggets, which I place back onto Salty's newspaper. I feel clumsy and, frankly, not very welcome in my own home. They clearly don't want to let me in on their secret.

"Everyone want tea?" I ask, going toward the door, hoping that Agnes will look at me and smile.

She acknowledges what happened between us last night with complete silence.

I pour boiling water into jelly jars I found the previous day in the cabinet below the bathroom sink, slip in Jonathan's tasteless tea bags of ginger whatnot, and go back into George's room.

When I pass the girls their tea, neither acknowledges my hospitality. It dawns on me that Lana probably has her period, which is why she lounges around like a cat with her claws out, ready to pounce at the smallest peep out of anyone. But I notice that Agnes is lethargic, too. It's a melancholic lethargy, I realize, not a menstrual one. Lana's muteness, in particular, worries me.

"My mom always brings me tea when I'm not feeling well," I say in the cheeriest tone I can muster. "Isn't it nice to be served by someone? I mean, moms are good at that."

I want them to understand that mine is a super-mom, too.

The phone glows on the desk. I lunge at it, look down at the screen, and see Mr. Featherstone's earlier message:
What is it, love?
In the box above, Lana wrote:
I have something to tell you dad.
I stare at their heavy eyelids, bodies compressed against each other, spooning silently on the mattress.

"Where's your mother?" I ask.

Agnes bursts into tears, and Lana, stroking Agnes's hair, can't contain herself either and joins her sister, tears seeping from the corners of her eyes and rolling down her cheeks.

Good God, I say to myself. If I could make a run for it out my door and down the street, I would. I begin to sweat. Not only under my arms but at the back of my neck and my pant waist, where the material starts to feel very tight. I look at the floor and then out the window at a chunk of the girls' imploded house, and I get a very bad feeling. I could change the subject, but I need an answer to my question because I know Mom and Mr. Featherstone will keep asking. How can we possibly leave in a flimsy rubber dinghy in a state like this?

"What happened to her?" I ask with more urgency.

Lana, spooning in back, squeezes her eyes shut and burrows her face into the back of Agnes's head as if doing so will clear her mind, hypnotize all the bad memories out of it, so to speak. Agnes licks tears from her top lip. In the silence that follows, I feel guilty for beefing with Lana near the bathroom. I should have been more forgiving. I think of the message I read on a tea bag last spring. Something like: "Even too much love is not enough."

Agnes opens her eyes slowly as if it's physically painful. Her left arm is folded underneath her, her left palm against her cheek. She raises her right hand, her fingers wiping away tears.

"Billy," she says. "Water poured through the front door, the walls, the floors." Her voice trembles and then breaks, like it did the first time she spoke from the ladder that still scrapes across the clapboards, in case we've forgotten it's there.

"We barely made it to the car."

"It filled the first floor like a fucking bathtub," mutters Lana, gripping her sister around the waist, burying her face into Agnes's messy brown hair.

"We waded to the Prius in the driveway," Agnes says, her voice soft and distant. "I pulled Wagner through the water by his collar and got him into the back seat. I don't know why Mom turned back. Maybe for her flip phone. When she came back out, the current surged and pulled her under."

"It lifted the car and slammed us into the garage," says Lana.

"I'm so, so, so sorry," I mumble.

"She came back up and swam toward us," Agnes continues, wiping her eyes. "Grabbed the driver's door with both hands, slamming her fist against the glass. But the car flipped. And she was gone."

Lana, sitting up on the mattress, pulls at her blue T-shirt bunched at her waist and wipes away more tears. I don't know what to say. Do they want me to leave or keep listening? I stand up and make some cowardly bullshit excuse about needing something from the hallway.

"We don't mean to freak you out," says Lana just as I get to the door.

"It's not about me."

"Your dad and brother are missing."

"But they got out," I manage to sputter.

The girls stare at me with a numb expression.

"Didn't they?" I ask, as though their experience has made them clairvoyant.

"I hope so," says Lana, pushing her knuckles into her eye sockets.

"Billy?" asks Agnes. "How could you not have heard it? It was so horrible."

"I really don't know."

"There was no help," she continues. "Just crushing water, bobbing us in our flipped car."

"In our coffin," mutters Lana.

"How did you get out?"

"Lana kicked the door open—that was now the roof. We climbed on top."

"We got shoved against the house. And grabbed the railings. It was dumb luck."

As Agnes squeezes her eyes shut, tears leach out across her flushed cheeks and onto the pillow.

"We know what the current is like out there," says Lana.

I go back to my room to catch my breath. I feel like I've just run ten miles. My heart is pounding; my mind feels hot. I look down at the tiny propane stove below the window. Agnes, who packed the food, left salt and pepper, oil, ketchup, and two eggs sitting in their carton. I strike a match and light the stove, pour in some oil, crack the eggs, and scramble them. Then I scrape the eggs onto the two white porcelain plates we've been using and carry them back into George's room because these girls need to eat so they don't crash.

They both try to smile—not very successfully—sit up on the mattress against the pillows and eat. I wrack my brain for something else I can do to make them feel better. If I had known last night what I know now, I might have tried to comfort Agnes as she pressed her warm body against mine, holding my waist and pushing the madness away. If Lana wasn't here, I'd put my arms around her again.

"What was that?" asks Agnes, putting her empty plate on the floor and sitting up straight, eyes bulging. She kneels on the mattress. Then she's on her feet, moving toward the window. "Did you feel it?" she asks, peering outside.

"I felt it," says Lana, scraping her spoon against her plate for the last scrap of eggs.

"Billy?"

"I'm not sure."

The next tremor is unmistakable. It's as if a 550-horse-power Mac truck just crashed into my house. Lana and I are on our feet immediately and join Agnes at the window.

Tree limbs, wood and metal debris, mattresses, and uprooted shrubs drift through the canal between our houses. I watch the gray-brown bloated body of a coyote float by, caught in orange construction mesh. Or maybe it's someone's German shepherd?

The boat beneath the window, tethered to the top of the ladder, knocks against the house again.

"Did you pack Salty's food?" asks Agnes.

"It's right there," I reply, pointing at the bag, lantern, and water near our feet.

Lana nods toward George's desk, where my phone pings again, the screen glowing ice blue. I pick it up.

Billy? What do the girls want to tell their father?

Lana has stopped moving. She stares at me with an empty gaze, her skin paler than before.

"What should I say to your dad?"

She looks away.

"Tell him we're leaving now," answers Agnes.

Leaving now, I text as fast as I can. *Getting in a boat.*

"We need to go," says Lana, grabbing her yellow rain jacket and slipping it on. She moves closer to the window and leans her body out as if she's ready to hurl herself as far away as possible from her father's question. "I just felt it again," she says.

Agnes raises her hands to her face, covering her eyes. Warmth surges through me. I want to grab her and hold her so badly, like I did last night, even for just a few seconds. I don't care if Lana stares. But we have to move, or we'll get buried alive.

"Agnes?"

"I'm fine. I'm fine." She pulls her hands away. "Wait," she says. "It never works out when you lie."

"Not now," says Lana, stuffing a pastel pink blanket into the garbage bag full of clothes.

"It's cruel not to tell him the truth."

"Better if we're with him when he hears it."

"That might not happen."

"Don't be negative."

"Don't be stupid."

"Stop," I say, holding up my phone. "We don't have time for this. What should I tell your father?"

"Whatever you like," says Lana from the edge of the window, where she turns to grab the ropes.

She pulls on them to check their strength, climbs onto the sill, and slips out the window feet first. When she lands on the bottom rung of the ladder, Agnes passes her the garbage bag.

Heading away from the coast in a dinghy, I type as the girls continue to lower the bag, jug of water, and lantern out the window.

Agnes reaches down and picks up Salty, whose legs immediately stiffen. She looks at me pleadingly with her glossy brown eyes as if to say: Why would you take me back down that ladder after what we went through?

There's no time to wait for Mom's reply. I grab George's green rain jacket from the floor and pull it on, zip my phone tightly into the pocket, and follow the girls and dog out the window.

CHAPTER THIRTY-TWO

Juliet

Back on Route 79, Noemi falls asleep against the door with Ana in her arms, propped up with the blanket and black bag. My lower back is aching from eight hours in the same position.

"I'm hungry," I say, gripping the wheel, focusing on the road, and fighting fatigue and low blood sugar.

"I'm hungry, too," replies Martin, staring out his window at drenched West Virginia farmland, tall oaks, and gangly longleaf pines. "What are you thinking?"

"Pizza. Fried chicken. Cucumber, feta, and tomato salad. Anything smothered in hollandaise."

"An eggs benedict girl."

"Breakfast for dinner. I'd kill for that."

Drizzle begins to mist the glass. It takes effort to hold the wheel. My elbows and shoulders ache. The body can get tired from sitting. But it isn't immobility or the usual suspects of hunger and thirst that deplete us.

"Turn on the wipers," says Martin.

His tone sounds bland, so unlike him. Full of regret and disappointment at what happened at the motel outside of Charlotte, perhaps? I glance down at his hand, resting on his thigh, and think about reaching for it. But then what? Twenty-four hours in that motel felt like quarantine during the pandemic, both of us running on fumes, disaster squatters in the remnants of a local business taking its last breath. We got out, though. We got back into the car, northbound, trying to solve the riddle of our families, which looms darker than any storm cloud. I guess you could say we're recuperating from each other.

"I'm not sure I meant for that to happen in the motel," I say faintly, even though Noemi is asleep.

"Not much we can do now."

"I'm sorry," I say.

"For what?"

"I'm just telling you that I'm okay with everything."

"Me, too."

I swerve right, around a small pond in the center of the road.

"Ready to be home," he adds.

What does that mean, I wonder. Reaching his saturated house that has probably imploded from what we've concluded from Billy's texts? Reuniting with his family in another location? *Go back home* is a primitive, nostalgic euphemism for trying to recover what we both know doesn't exist anymore. Something that together we altered. Which parts of *home* does he think are salvageable? And, by the way, where are we actually going? When will we be forced to ditch the car because it can't carry us through an aquatic landscape that has slurped up landmarks we long took for granted? The ones that can't map us home anymore. How will we get to our children? And where are they? I want to tell Martin how the panic I feel for what's coming buzzes in my head and ties my stomach in knots. But he slouches in his seat, turns from me, and stares out the window.

"I need to eat something other than crackers," I say.

"There are no more crackers."

I listen to the swish of the wipers and look at the eruption of marbleized clouds above us and the subdued grays in a dimming sky that announces the end of the day. Broken white lines separating the lanes shimmer under the water. My focus slides just for an instant to the deep green kudzu all around us that devours whole stands of trees, boulders, and meadows, an orchestra of foliage consumed at its base by a maple syrup sludge. I glance down at Martin's hands again, forming tight, impenetrable fists that seem to want to work things out for themselves. But mostly, I think about being with him in the motel room. How our time together there rescued us from a punishing resignation because to do what we did was to mutiny against forces that were fueling our misery and defeat. You only break those rules if all else fails. Unless you're stupid or heartless or out of control, which neither one of us is.

I finally reach out anyway and awkwardly fumble with his stiff fingers until they open, and he gropes for mine and squeezes my hand, just as he did in the motel, on the bed, in the heat, with the dogs barking, my heart racing, and the automatic gunfire nearby.

"Sometimes I get this feeling," he says.

I strain for air, afraid of what will follow. My pulse thumps in my wrists. I'm not up for a confession or a guilt trip. Even compassion seems unbearable. I just want him to hold my hand and be quiet. I glance at Noemi's placid face in the rearview mirror. Strands of her straight black hair fall over her closed eyelids, along the hollows of her bronze cheeks, and into the fissure of her parted lips. I wonder what her story is. How the drought, long before the flooding, unfolded to push her north on an earlier journey. How she actually got here. The awful details. But those aren't questions you ask.

"I've had this feeling before, a couple of times," continues Martin, roping me back in. "Several times, really. It's not good. But it's always right on the money."

He lets go of my hand, and I grab the steering wheel. We've hit a low valley. The hovering green canopy opens to once-green pastures that are now a sloppy paint-by-numbers pastiche of gray, green, silver, and brown, where water seems to bubble up from creeks and rivers and roll into our path, slowing us once again.

"I just don't feel right."

"Who does, now?"

"No, no. It's not about me or you. Or the shit going on around us." He scans the panorama through the windshield. "It's the colors. The light's too bright."

I have no idea what he's talking about because there is no sunshine.

"The glow, everywhere. The deep, layered dimensions."

A rumbling, nervous chuckle stirs in his throat and tumbles out of his mouth.

"You don't see it, do you, Juliet?"

"Not really."

"There's so much minute detail in the trees over there, messaging me, assaulting my senses, and filling me with dread."

I let him go on. What can I say? We need food and sleep.

"The light is hitting my brain with such force. God, it's a battle. And how do I fight it?"

"Are you okay, Martin?"

"Probably not."

We rise on an incline and then hit a shallower slope, where the road soaks in eight or so inches of khaki liquid. I press the gas, hoping that velocity might shake him out of it.

"It's a big fat fucking warning sign is what it is." He claws his hand through the air in an arc in front of his face. "It says: 'You know damn well where your wife is, Martin.'"

Heat smolders in my neck and spreads to my cheeks. I think of Tom, how much I wish he were here next to me, in Martin's seat.

He taps his hand against his thigh, looks right, and studies the floodwaters.

"Don't get me wrong," he says. "I have fears. About my kids, for example. But this isn't anxiety."

I'm glad to be in the driver's seat, at the wheel. That security is the best I can offer any of us right now.

"Do you get what I'm saying, Juliet?"

"You're getting a bad feeling?"

"It's not a *feeling*. It's what I *know*. And the knowledge says: 'Open your eyes, Martin Featherstone, and face the truth.'"

I nod, hoping he'll calm down as we speed through water and mud. I pray that the few cars in my periphery keep to their lanes, marked by blurry disappearing white lines under the surface.

"We've been on the road for a long time," I say. "Why don't you put your head back and try to close your eyes."

He laughs dolefully and asks if I think he's nuts.

"Of course not. Try and rest."

Rain begins to fall hard against the windshield, rapping the glass. I'm not sure if the feeling of the car sliding left and then right is real or not. I wish there was a rest stop along this highway where we could pull over, have a hot plate of spaghetti and meatballs, and text Billy again. Intentionally keeping west to avoid what's left of DC has landed us on this rural highway with nothing but flooded farmland for miles.

"I'll stop asking if you know what I mean. If you've ever had this feeling before. I know it's weird. But I can tell you right now." He sucks in a deep breath and exhales, "Stephanie is dead."

I shake my head, but he doesn't want any of it.

"You're thinking that you've had the same thoughts about Tom and George. Maybe they didn't make it. Maybe they did, but you're not sure."

"Stop, Martin."

"Those are normal thoughts, Juliet. Your family is probably alive."

He begins to choke up, his hands in front of his face, gesticulating with a ferocity I've never seen. In the gym, on the street corner, at the morning PTO coffee hour, I'd always wanted a little emotion, a little vulnerability from him, to bring us closer as friends and neighbors, instead of calculated conversations with some captivating humor thrown in to deflect my deeper questions, my need to tell him who I was. But now I just want him to be quiet. Tufts of his brown curls fall across his brow into his eyes, which have always been so expressive with spirit and drive.

"She's gone."

"Okay. I believe you."

The wheel begins to slip from my grip, and my arms feel rubbery. How do I shut him up before we sail off the road and drown in a culvert?

He rolls down the window. Warm rain falls into the car, misting our skin. His eyes are closed, but he focuses them upward, toward the sky, pitching his head side to side, laughing sorrowfully as tears meld with rain and stream down his cheeks.

"It feels so goddamned liberating to finally shout that Stephanie is dead!"

Withdrawing from the window, he drops his head into his hands and sobs. I put my hand on his knee, my skin against his, permissible this time. I can see, in the rearview, that Noemi is awake. How much has she heard? She has a banana in her hand and begins to peel and feed small bits to Ana, who gums it with surprising alertness. I step on the gas, risking a skid into the flooded guardrails. We need to get off this road, out of the car, and away from each other for a while. Even just fifteen minutes. As much as I try to keep my thoughts on the road ahead, my mind digresses to the bed in the hotel, the two of us lying in the heat, our judgment evaporating with our hope.

I don't want to take care of strangers anymore or spend hours decoding our kids' fragmented texts. And now Martin's internal battle waged against a predictable life fraying at the edges because of rapid and outsized changes, most of it beyond our control. I try to reason that I'm feeling it slightly less because my life, frankly, is a patchwork of intuition, instinct, and inspiration that sometimes lacks the discipline he's refined. This may also be why I caved to Billy, and he kept his phone while Martin's children surrendered theirs, no questions asked, no push-back.

We drive in silence, past cars in the breakdown lane, military pachyderms plodding by every so often. Martin catches his breath, closes the window, and checks the phone in the console. His steady movements seem to intentionally contradict the fact that he just announced the presumptive death of his wife out the window.

Noemi clears her throat.

"I got a feeling like that once. Right after Ana was born."

Martin nods his head slowly.

"The air got thick and swallowed me. A different dimension, everything upside down, blinding light from the corners of the earth. I really can't explain it with words, so, disculpa. But in the end, I knew." She shifts Ana in her lap and kisses her on the forehead. "Is this too personal?"

"Please continue," says Martin.

"I was pregnant. I was sick. I bled. I'd already been deported once, but I crossed the border again anyway, found Beto, and made it to my brother's place. At the clinic in Charlotte, they said my baby was small but healthy. I knew better."

"Why don't they listen to mothers?" mutters Martin.

"I should not have left my mother and my aunts, buried now, in the dry soil that once fed us."

I curse the weather that separates people. Then, glance again at Noemi in the rearview mirror, shifting Ana, placing her on the seat, head on her lap. I saw Ana's anemic legs when we changed her diaper and imagine them now, the bowed appendages in tight pink leggings and white lace socks, flopping against the gray velour seat of the rental.

"They sent her straight to the NICU and me to a room with large windows looking out on the grounds. I spent two days there, staring at a tree that pressed against the glass, its leaves, like daggers, shimmering under a blinding sun."

"It was the light, wasn't it?" asks Martin.

"So bright. It was like I was sitting in the branches, searching for a burning core, wondering what I had done wrong. I thought it was all the walking."

"Sounds like delirium," I say.

"I had a high fever, sin duda. And my baby was sick."

"You knew, though," says Martin. "No one can dispute that. You don't fight for that knowledge."

"I just stared at the greens and yellows, the glowing ball of fire, sparks at the edges like the twinkling lights of tiny stars in the daytime. Dios mío, I was so comfortable and warm in the leaves and branches that tossed me up and down like the tiovivo at the feria en Tuxtla Gutierrez. How could I give that up? Even for a sick baby?"

Her words seem to fuse, exaggerating her accent. For a split second, it sounds almost like she's chanting.

"But I did. Because the nurse called my name from miles away. I saw the kindness in her eyes, felt the cold alcohol wipe across my cheeks and forehead. 'Who will take care of your baby, Noemi?'"

"That's upsetting," I say.

"I let go of the tree and fell for miles. When I woke up in intensive care three days later, I knew that Ana wasn't just small. Like you said, Martin, you don't fight for that knowledge. If you think your wife is dead, then maybe—"

"We don't know that," I interrupt.

"Venga, por favor! Let him say it."

The phone pings in the console. I reach for it, but Martin gets there first. "They're leaving."

"How?"

"In some kind of boat."

He swipes his finger up and stares at the screen.

"It's Lana. I know it. And she wants to tell me something," he mutters, tucking the phone back into the console, leaning his head back and closing his eyes.

CHAPTER THIRTY-THREE

Billy

Lana and I take the two seats in the dinghy. Agnes sits on the floor, crammed between the green garbage bag, her sister's knees, and my back. Somehow, she fits Salty into the knot of her lap.

"Is this thing going to hold together?" she asks.

"This is what we have," replies Lana, shifting on the seat, pointlessly trying to find her own space as she grips the paddle.

Drizzle coats our skin and the surface of the orange rubber dinghy. The water is so close now, I could touch it. It smells like an old fish tank and whatever the sewers cough up when they're overloaded. This flimsy rubber boat is already flexing under us, even though we're still tied to the ladder, knocking our knees against the bag, the jug of water, and each other, terrified to leave what had felt pretty solid until this morning.

From where I'm sitting, I see loose gutters and wooden casing around my sagging bedroom window. Some of the clapboards and most of the railings around the second-floor deck, where Mr. Barrett flapped his paddle, have been plucked by moisture and gravity, like gumdrops and peppermint candies from a stale gingerbread house. But truthfully, my house is a death trap. The sooner we get away, the better. I wish I had ropes to tie stuff down because I get a desperate feeling that we're going to lose the food, the water, and the dog. I lean forward and feel the phone at my hip, zipped into my rain jacket pocket.

"Okay, Lana, untie us."

She wobbles, steps onto the bottom rung of the ladder, and unknots the rope. When she pulls it into the boat, I let go of the smooth, damp, familiar wood that Dad cut and sanded for me and George years ago. It was his handyman's way of helping us climb, but I've just used it to sink close to the flood line. It thumps back against the clapboards, and we slide away.

We start to paddle with the current, over submerged streets, maybe twelve feet below, over buried lawns, sidewalks, and driveways. Brown-green gumbo liquid laps at the second floors of the houses that are still standing, more or less. We coast down Aspinwall Avenue, past the Episcopal church that's held up pretty well despite the rushing water and crushing pressure. Dark stains ring the old gray stone walls as though the rock and mortar have absorbed all they can. The dwarfed spire with its metal cross is like a lighthouse for the soul. When mom was going through her Christianity phase, she joined the church and dragged me and George to a bunch of potluck dinners, Christmas sing-alongs, fall fairs with homemade cider donuts, and lots of praying. But that's not happening anymore. I'm struggling with the paddle, to move past the church and leave it behind with the rest of my neighborhood.

I'm heavier than Lana, so I'm on the back seat. She's in front of me, facing forward until the boat begins to twist, and we move backward through the current, which really freaks her out. She flaps her paddle like a maniac, plunging it through the surface, not getting much done.

"Save your energy," I shout. "We can't control this."

"It's going to pull us under."

"Just go with it. The current's our best chance."

"Where are we going?"

"Inland."

Agnes is curled up on the floor with Salty, eyes closed, leaning against the garbage bag. She seems hypnotized by the rocking and bucking. Or she's just holding on for dear life. Hoping not to upchuck that egg I made her less than an hour ago.

At the intersection, we pitch and bob onto Harvard Street, right over the bus stop, dangerously close to its disappearing rectangular black and yellow signs that now look like enlarged razor blades. Gray brownish-green water laps at the dinghy, soaking our arms like it wants to pull us over the edge because, in the end, we have no fucking say in what's happening. We're heading toward a spinning current that pulls us along the edge of a concrete Walgreens, its windows under the surface. I can just make out the top half of the red plastic cursive letters that arch above the glass.

"Lana, use your paddle," I shout as I jab mine against the concrete, pushing us back toward the center of the sludgy water. I try not to focus on my stinging palm, but I know I've split open the wound again. I have to push through the pain, or we'll capsize.

Lana is muttering something and attempting to hit the wall with her paddle but missing. She continues to do her best until we head straight toward a half-submerged streetlamp.

"Push off," I shout, wishing I were in front now.

"We're going to flip, Billy."

"Don't fight it. You're rocking the boat."

"I can't do this."

As we rub against the metal pole, Lana finds the strength to push us away. Agnes yelps and grips the dog. I have no idea where this much water could have come from or how it's wrecked so much of my town. It churns, sucks, and slurps at steel, concrete, brick, two-by-fours coated with plaster—all things humanmade that were meant to withstand weather. But it's coming apart, sloshing around us in small islands of debris.

"What should I do, Billy?" shouts Agnes from the floor, her face twisted with worry.

"Sit still and hold Salty."

"I'm trying," she cries, squeezing the dog around the neck in the cove of her lap.

I touch the pocket of my rain jacket to make sure the phone is still safe and dry. Then I look left as we pass my friend's house.

"Holy shit. That's Jack's house."

His crumpled white triple-decker with black trim, where I'd smoked my fat share of spliffs in the basement, is smashed, the first floor nearly under the surface; the top floor splays out on all sides as though Godzilla stepped on it. We pass Annabelle's hollowed-out yellow house next door. Water swills inside and spills out the missing second-floor windows. Sections of a white picket fence and a telephone pole bump against the clapboards, looking like they want to topple what's left.

"Jesus. Did she and her family get out?" I mutter to myself as I pull at the paddle and grit my teeth to stop the pressure building in my throat and the back of my eyes. But there's no time for tears because a slab of gray shingled roof and two flipped cars in a sea of other junk come slamming at us every which way.

"Do something, Billy!" screams Lana. "We're going to go under."

"Use your paddle and help me!" I yell back.

She leans a little too far over the edge. She's pushing her paddle against wood and metal, jamming it at a muddy yellow couch, a bike, a telephone pole, when a body rolls out from beneath the debris.

"Oh, God, no," she cries, dropping the paddle and covering her face with her hands.

I jam my paddle in the water, wince pointlessly at the pain in my palm, and paddle in reverse. The bloated, pale-gray figure slides back under the surface.

"Oh, God. That smell," says Agnes, shaking her head violently and wobbling the dinghy.

I want to tell her to cut the shit with the drama before it kills us, but instead, shout, "Hold onto the dog," as I stab at the bobbing yellow couch to get us back to the center of the current.

"Lana?" I say, trying to calm her down. But there's no time to comfort her. We're hurtling toward a nest of wires hanging from bowed tips of telephone poles at the end of Marion Street.

"Pick up the goddamned paddle, Lana, and row!"

"I can't," she stammers, looking down at her hands in her lap. "I can't do this anymore."

"For fuck sakes, Lana. Do it for your father."

She picks up the paddle again and, with crazy energy, begins to beat at the water. Soon, we're both gasping for air, swearing, and trying like hell to keep away from the wires. Agnes is squeezing Salty, grounding herself, hunched cross-legged now in the bottom of the boat to help keep it from keeling over.

We miss the tangle of dead wires and spin past the glass and concrete of what used to be a bank or law office, bumping against the top of the door and scraping along the silver metal casing at the roofline. We get dragged backward again toward the center of the current, where the water runs fastest. We bob and shift and grip the dinghy's black nylon ropes at the sides. I can't tell if the boat is bucking from hitting junk underneath us or flexing because of our uneven weight.

The water pushes us onto Beacon Street, into a wider plain of floodwaters where two people in a dinghy like ours twist on an angry current a block ahead. We shout and wave our paddles, but their boat has slipped out of sight around a bend of buildings, their flat concrete rooftops like giant steppingstones marking where the street used to run. The current slows a little as if to brag about all the things it has devoured: the T, with its tracks winding through neighborhoods, the bookstore, the theater that shows weird films my parents like to watch, bagel shops, and cafés.

"Where are you taking us?" asks Agnes. "Why'd we leave?"

She, of all people, should know.

"We're going west. Away from the harbor, toward Newton, maybe Arlington."

It doesn't seem to matter that streets used to dip and rise; the surface is churning like an ocean, the current so strong, we can ride with it if the dinghy stays upright.

As we're carried toward Washington Square, I think I see concrete a few feet below, which makes me want to jump out just to bounce against solid ground. But

I'd get pulled under, like Agnes and Lana's mom. In the distance, up on a steep hill behind a sinking middle school, some houses look whole. I wonder if we should try to make our way there and wait. But now that I'm looking closely, I see that they also sag from the surge and never-ending rain.

I touch my jacket pocket again, feeling my phone tightly zipped in, and I imagine texting: *Dear Mom, nearly shitting my pants as I sail through our town on an inflated magic carpet, heading toward The Magic Kingdom, or whatever that place in Vermont is called. Where the fuck did you and Mr. Featherstone go? Did you forget you have children?* Then I want to burst into tears. But I can't because we've just sailed over something that scrapes the bottom of the boat. The three of us freeze and hold our breath, getting ready to possibly abandon ship, afraid the water will seep in through a puncture in the rubber seams and kill us.

Only it doesn't. It wants us alive to see the family of four standing on a flat, speckled gray rooftop near the school, waving a piece of black fabric in the air and shouting, "Water, water."

No shit, I say to myself, as we bob in it through lanes of liquid, until I realize the shipwrecked family is shaking an empty gallon jug at us. I look down at ours, which is full. I want to help these people so badly, but the current hauls us past them into a low-lying area on the Chestnut Hill border, between what used to be a convenience store, a pizzeria, take-out restaurants, and a jewelry boutique. My guilt for the thirsty family slides into the water with other regrets as we pass more brick buildings swallowed by the surge. We could dock next to them and climb onto the masonry and sticky tar roofs if we were in a dream or shitfaced on a Saturday night with a spliff and a handle of Pink Whitney. But we're desperate. We're battling with the paddles and this river from hell because we know nothing about anything anymore, not to mention where we're going.

Toward afternoon, we roll forward on a slowing current. Lana and I dip the paddle to jab at flipped cars. She points at a refurbished industrial building the color of brown mustard. Two enormous old windows in front look like the glassy eyes of a monster amphibian, half-submerged in marshy wetlands, watching us sail by.

"I know that building," she says. "I took an art history course somewhere around here last summer."

Her voice bloats with sadness. She says she feels like she's in *Charon Crossing the River Styx*, one of the paintings she studied by some old Dutch dude.

"Patinir. 1515. Flemish. Northern Renaissance," she mutters, ever the A student, just like Agnes. She's slightly hunched, the paddle resting on her knees, elbows there, too, for a moment. "Angels, devils, fire. The tiny soul is on a boat just like us. Poor idiot has his back to paradise because he's doom scrolling the scene in front of him." Her eyes dart around at the heap of standing and collapsed buildings, the flipped cars we graze chaotically, and the invading ocean that fuses with streams and rivers so it can erase everything.

I think about our surreal journey, this psychotic obstacle course that seems designed by someone with a sick sense of humor. It's like one of those virtual reality games with nauseating motion and fucked-up images, only we can't exactly take off the headset.

"What's the point in studying art like that, Lana? I mean, for a grade and everything?" I ask.

"The human condition. A glimpse of your soul before the final assessment. For God's sake, Billy, what do you do in school all day?"

"Eyeball chicks, eat hamburgers, and smoke weed," I say with a smirk.

Truth is, I got an A in Calc II, just like her.

We seem to be floating now in the Charles River, which apparently has changed direction and flows inland. We aren't worrying much anymore about sharp stuff puncturing our boat because the water has breached the banks so completely and risen so high that it's just a slick plain of brown, sludgy liquid as far as we can see. I try to imagine how the ocean obliterated Southie, Quincy, and the airport before crashing in and breaching the dams and locks near the Science Museum and the Old North Church, gobbling footpaths and bridges over Storrow Drive. I stare at the thick cables, railings, and tops of telephone poles poking through a distant green-black mercurial landscape. Then I look back at the city skyline behind us that's dwarfed, futuristic like a bad sci-fi film. I'm scared shitless at what's around the bend but also numbed by the strange silence that keeps me dipping my paddle so that we can move forward. It's like we're on one of those glacial lakes I read about in *National Geographic,* with shards of our city at its edges.

Hours later, we coast over a calm area of sunken highway with stunted green and silver Lexington and Concord signs. You don't have to be a climate genius to figure out that some of this liquid is bubbling up from inland watersheds that can't take any more saturation, just like Ms. Fagan said.

Agnes sits up. Her hair is damp and tangled, and strands of it stick to her face.

"It's my turn to paddle," she says, her eyes meeting mine. She gently pushes Salty off her lap and rolls onto her knees, wobbling on the rubbery bottom and elbowing me in the back. "Did you hear me, Lana? I want to sit now. It's my turn."

Lana looks down at the ripples left by her paddle.

"Not yet."

"I'm tired of doing nothing. I've been down here for hours."

"Fair enough. But let me eat something first."

I don't think any of us has an appetite. Lana's buying more time on the seat so that she can fool herself into thinking she has some control. I'm not going to take sides. I'm just too exhausted.

To get herself closer to a turn with the paddle, Agnes digs in the garbage bag and finds a box of crackers, which we share. We chug from the gallon jug that's been sitting at Lana's feet. Paralyzed by fear, Salty has no interest in eating, drinking, or moving, for that matter.

"Billy, do you want a turn down here on the floor?"

"Maybe in a little while."

"We need his weight in the back," says Lana.

"Well, I can't be down here for much longer."

I think about giving her my paddle, but I don't want to end up floating out of the current that carries us west. Neither girl seems very good with direction. AP exams, maybe, but not navigating water, tracking the sun and stars, and looking at the larger nonscholastic picture.

CHAPTER THIRTY-FOUR

Juliet

We continue along Route 79, the two-lane rural interstate with little traffic, tucked into the hills of West Virginia. It takes us through Morgantown, across the western edge of the Mason-Dixon Line. Martin is mostly silent. Noemi, cradling Ana, shifts uncomfortably; even a light parcel on a long car ride can begin to chafe, no matter how precious.

I'm stuck on Billy's last text: *Heading away from the coast in a dinghy.*

Part of my brain shouts, Hooray! Get out while you can! But that thin ray of light is soon eclipsed by thoughts of the turbulent currents, the general peril of unknowns, a flimsy rubber boat up against a sinking abandoned city. I want to talk to Martin and spit out all my fears at his silence. But I can feel the steering wheel bobbling in my grip, joining in the fray of me against myself. I grip the hard plastic and floor the gas through cascades and outflows, past anywheresville, with Saxon names like Wickersham, Rutledge, and Hastings that evoke bucolic Old World hamlets rather than residential districts surrounded by flooded generic shopping plazas constructed on farmland that rolls out to the tree line, the lower spots small lakes, the plateaus slick with mud and water.

Noemi grapples again with Ana and the white blanket. I'm about to turn around and ask if she wants me to pull over when I hear her sigh.

"Oh, God. The hospital," she mutters.

I saw the blue H sign pass us by, like so many others, and thought nothing of it.

"Are you sure that's it?"

"Por Dios. It's right there!"

"Ok. Let's go."

"I need to talk to my brother. And Beto. Dónde estás, mi amor?" she mutters. "And I could use a smartphone."

"It's hardly helped," says Martin.

"If I could just find him." She shifts Ana in her arms and then reaches into her bag. "I've still got this pedazo de mierda," she says, pulling out her flip phone and holding it up so that I can see it in the mirror.

I hear her punching numbers halfheartedly.

"Nada," she says, placing it down somewhere.

"Old habits," mumbles Martin.

I slow the car in water that has receded to about half a foot or so as we glide along an incline. Better conditions mean more cars on the road. But the earlier surge, combined with bursting lakes and streams, has left saturated fields, flipped cars, and disemboweled houses with their contents scattered everywhere. I imagine, for a moment, that it's the day after a bad hurricane, and soon, people will salvage and rebuild because that's what human beings are so good at. But it isn't just the physical world we've scrambled. The human psyche, with all its convolutions and insecurities, is now in uncharted waters that will require a whole new set of coordinates to adapt to whatever is sailing toward us in the coming years.

"Drop me at the front," she says. "I'll walk in. You can swing back to the highway."

"Nonsense. I'm going with you," I reply.

"You're wasting time. Aren't you close to home now?"

"No. Yes. Kind of. I don't know. Around six hours under normal circumstances."

"We could be in Siberia," says Martin.

"Only we're not. We're in Pennsylvania, and we're going to find everyone. Including Stephanie."

Martin shakes his head, nods, and then shakes it again in a battle that I can't help him with right now. We've slowed in traffic under a twilight sky. The cars ahead of us sift themselves through the shadows of an intersection below unresponsive traffic lights hanging in black boxes.

"We're far from the coast," he continues. "From the onset of that flooding, whatever it was. Boston will be different. Roadblocks, sandbags, no way in."

"We'll cross that bridge when we get to it."

"Bridges wash out."

"Right," I mutter meaninglessly as we join a slow-moving line of cars heading toward a complex of boxy brick buildings covered in glass and silver panels. The faint orange glow of dusk, nearly extinguished, fringes the peaks of distant evergreens, bringing us another night on the road.

Traffic stops, and we sit for fifteen minutes. Just enough time for the ache at the nape of my neck to radiate into my skull, restlessness kindling in my arms and legs, the futility of everything smoldering around me.

I can hear the sucking sound of Ana gumming her own fist. What are we all doing here? How can doctors help her in this mess? I try to push back the questions spinning at me: Where are Tom and George? How high is the water on Dog Island? I picture Billy in a dinghy, floating into oblivion.

"I need some air," I say, turning to Martin. "You drive. I'll meet you up ahead at the hospital entrance."

I unbuckle, open the door, and slip into near darkness, passing him silently on his way to the driver's side, our forearms grazing, the sudden warmth of his skin. I know his touch, and it makes me hesitate. But he just keeps going, gets into the driver's seat, shuts the door, and leaves me in the cool air, a moist, pungent stew of rotting leaves and logs, mud, moss, and fungus, seemingly just an ordinary forest in the Northeast after nightfall. I walk onto the shoulder of the road, splashing alongside the line of cars, kicking my rain boots through the slurry.

Someone honks.

"Fuck you, too," I say under my breath as I march alongside the stop-and-go traffic.

I keep my eyes on the rental, sometimes ahead of me, sometimes behind, until I lose track in the darkness and begin to reflect on all the difficulty. Getting to Billy and finding George and Tom is like clawing at a latch that just won't give. Perseverance has a purpose, but at some point, I fear, the effort will become aimless. I kick my rain boots as hard as I can at the channels of muddy floodwater that feel eternal now and bent on upending this journey for good.

CHAPTER THIRTY-FIVE

Billy

Later that afternoon, the current drags us over a highway where it has swallowed guardrails and mile markers. It ripples out to a horizon of treetops and flooded glass office buildings in the distance. If we look hard alongside the boat, in certain places, gray asphalt arcs under the surface like a giant whale accompanying our boat until it dips again into the abyss.

"What about the phone, Billy?" asks Agnes now that the water is calmer. She's back on the floor of the boat after a brief turn up front. She'd rather lean against a garbage bag, snug between me and Lana, knees up, Salty's head in her lap.

"There's nothing. I checked."

"We left my dad hanging. I'm worried."

"Now's not the time for the phone."

"But where is it?" Lana chimes in as if plotting how to take it from me again without asking.

"Right here," I reply, slapping my hip. "Zipped in the pocket of my rain jacket."

"Are you going to check it again at some point?"

"We aren't using the phone out here, Lana."

I have no intention of pulling it out and trying to text. My arms are killing me. My infected palm throbs, shooting pain into my elbow. I've tried to use just my good hand as much as I can, but it's nearly impossible with the paddle.

Both Lana and I rest our forearms on our knees when we aren't centering the boat in the current. We glide along the wide, buried highway, past drowning green direction signs—Concord and Bedford. We still bob around and knock against debris sometimes, but it's calmer out here, away from the city, the harbor and tides, and the Charles River.

The sky turns yellow-gray in the late afternoon. Lana, hunched, rests her paddle on her thighs and stares off to her left at a silver bar rocking on the water in front of a stand of trees.

"What is that?" she says as an aluminum canoe drifts toward us.

"Oh, God. Is there someone inside?" asks Agnes.

Lana and I pick up our paddles and place them in the water.

"Where did it come from?" asks Lana, striking the surface. "From over there, through the trees?"

"No," I answer, positioning myself carefully so that I can grab the canoe with my good hand.

I pull it in, parallel to the dinghy, in the milky daylight that's rapidly disappearing.

"Oh, no. Look," whispers Agnes, peering at the floor of the canoe. "A sneaker." She stares at the sky-blue Converse, about her size, as though it were a whole person with a story to tell. "This water is so fucking evil."

"It's demonic," adds Lana. "Never let your guard down, even when things seem calm."

There's no proof that someone fell out of this canoe. But after what they've seen, I don't dare say so.

"We should secure these boats together," I say loudly. "While we still have light."

I do my best, one-handed, to lash the dinghy's black plastic rope through its rungs and thread it around the two metal bars that run from one side of the canoe to the other, loosely binding the boats side by side.

"There's a backpack under the seat," says Agnes, leaning left, grabbing the navy pack and lifting it into our dinghy, causing us to rock.

"I wouldn't do that again," says Lana.

Agnes doesn't answer. She's busy rummaging in the bag, pulling out a full bottle of seltzer, pretzels, cheese sticks, and a bag of almonds and raisins.

"Agnes, can you help me first?" I ask. "We need to secure these boats."

Ignoring me, she yanks a purple bandana from the bottom of the backpack and studies it. She brings it close to her face, holds it there, and breathes in.

"Agnes. I really could use your help."

"Sorry, Billy."

"My hand is killing me," I say, standing up as best I can, slightly crouched, good hand on the side of the dinghy, knees wobbling. The thread of dim, pearly light in the sky is almost gone now.

"I'm going to transfer the bag and jug of water. It'll give us more room in the dinghy tonight."

I step one foot into the canoe and then the other. I kneel on the hard metal floor and settle into an inch or two of puddled water that smells like mud, cut grass, and low tide. The metal and rubber boats chafe against each other, followed by a hollow plunk as the water sucks and slaps the aluminum belly of the canoe.

Although I can still see what my hand is doing in the last bit of daylight, Lana helps out by turning on the lantern and raising it.

"Pass me the stuff, Agnes. Before it gets pitch black."

She kneels unsteadily as she shifts Salty off her lap and onto the floor of the dinghy.

"Who do you suppose this canoe belongs to?" she asks, passing me the garbage bag.

"Someone like us. Trying to find solid ground."

"Maybe they got there and abandoned ship," she says, passing me the two-gallon plastic jugs. "Don't you think so?"

Her eyebrows arch with hope. But her strained voice says she doesn't believe the story any more than we do.

I arrange things in the canoe as evenly as I can.

"This will make it easier tonight for two of us to navigate in the canoe while one of us sleeps on the floor of the dinghy."

"Brilliant, Billy," says Lana.

I'm beyond exhausted. My palm is pounding. I can't wait until it's my turn to rest, but I offer it to Lana. I don't feel confident yet to pass out and let them take the helm. But at some point, soon, I won't have a choice.

"Go ahead, Lana. Agnes and I will navigate in the canoe."

"Okay," she says, passing the lantern to Agnes.

I start to shiver until a wave of heat buries my chills, and I peel off the rain jacket. I unzip the pocket, grab the phone very carefully, and stare down at a glowing screen.

"Did they text?" asks Agnes. "I'm worried about my dad."

"There's no service out here."

I stuff the phone deep into the back pocket of my shorts and then stand up slowly in the aluminum canoe so that I can help Agnes onto the seat, where she'll sit facing forward. The canoe is light and rocks under my weight, making everything feel that much more unstable in the near darkness, with the lantern glowing around us. Holding on to the knotted ropes that bind the boats together, I step one foot back into the dinghy so that I'm straddling both boats, knees slightly bent, trying to use the strength in my thighs to avoid using my sore hand.

"Billy, the phone," says Lana. "It's going to fall out of your pocket."

"It's fine," I reply.

"I'll hold it while you help Agnes into the canoe. We can't risk it."

Because she seems to be the keeper of the lantern and water, and she's pretty anchored there to the front seat of the dinghy, I pull the phone out slowly. I look down at the screen again to make sure there are no messages.

"We aren't texting now, Lana," I remind her as I bend my knees for balance and steady myself by grabbing the knotted ropes between my legs with my good hand, my sore one, handing her the phone.

Just as I slide the device into her palm and let go, the water swells slightly and detaches the two boats where I've bound them, just enough to separate our fingertips and swallow the phone, as it has so much else.

"For fuck's sake!" I shout, staring at the slick, black, briny surface. "Mom. Oh, God, Mom. Mom!"

"Holy shit," Lana yelps, lifting her empty palms to her face.

"I told you to hold it. Now we're fucked."

I want to grab her by the shoulders and shake her violently. God, I'm pissed at her, sick to my stomach, shivering with confusion, with the heat and then chills overtaking me. I feel a tight sensation creeping into my neck and the back of my eyes, which I close for a split second to get a grip so I don't do anything stupid. I'm so dizzy and I have to sit back on my heels in the canoe so I don't keel over and follow the phone.

Agnes reaches her hand out to try to calm Lana, who, in a fit of sobbing rage, begins to rock the boat involuntarily, looking as though she might hurl herself overboard without my help.

"This is a disaster," Agnes says, putting her hand on my thigh.

"No shit!" *And no need to cry*, I say under my breath. "We would have run out of power soon anyway."

Agnes tugs Lana down toward the floor of the dinghy and puts Salty in her lap before slowly stepping into the canoe and taking the front seat. She helps me untie the boats and then rearrange them so that we are in the canoe with the paddles, lantern at her feet, pulling Lana and Salty behind us in the dinghy. We drift in darkness for a couple of hours, past submerged buildings, constellations of broken trees, and who knows what else in the ghoulishly mangled shadows that make up this new nightscape in the suburbs of Boston.

Only Lana sleeps. I hope she feels horrible about what she's done when she wakes up. I'll find it in me to forgive her, I guess. But first, I want a heartfelt apology and some gratitude for everything I've done. I'm sick about what happened to her mom. I need to tell her that, but my sympathies are tangled in the latest clusterfuck of collaboration between humans and nature.

The drizzle has finally stopped, and a cool breeze picks up. I close my eyes for a moment and imagine we're canoeing on a lake in Rangely, Maine, in early August. Me, Dad, and George, pretending we're fishing, but really just giving Mom some space. Then I'm back here, in this disaster zone, with two girls whose lifelong academic achievements just don't make the grade right now. Why aren't schools preparing us for this shit? How to forage and purify dirty water?

Evidently, I'm brainwashed by the phone, like Mom always says, because I can't stop thinking about all the care I've taken with it, the hours I've spent in the nook waiting for her texts, responding as best I can, checking the screen more than I ever have.

I think about how Mom's done her best to understand me and George, although it's hard for her sometimes. She's honest to the point of being a little naïve. She probably would have loved to see my phone disappear like this before the Ban, before the weather got so crazy, before the ocean expanded and separated all of us. I once dropped my phone in the toilet, on purpose, thinking my parents would upgrade me. But they sat back and let me deal with it: the bowls of rice and the $70 repair bill. They did their best with me. I know I'm difficult sometimes, even without George telling me all the time.

A gentle breeze blows across my skin, like a lonesome whisper coming from behind the green hills. A half-moon stuffed into layers of frothy, dirty-gray clouds dribbles a little light over us. I wonder if I'm seeing a reflection of it falling onto water through the trees in the distance or actual lights. I imagine Mom again, regretful this time that the one thing that's caused so many problems between us is actually gone for good. I picture her watching the phone fall, slapping her palm to her forehead and saying, "How could you, Billy? After all this?" Mostly, though, as we drift along in silence, I'm thinking about George and how my idiotic hope that he'd text me somehow, from somewhere, evaporated when my fingers brushed against Lana's at the exact moment that the water decided to act up again.

Lana finally wakes up on the floor of the dinghy after who knows how long.

"It's okay," I tell her.

Although it's not.

"I'm such a fucking dumb ass."

"It's the current."

"It's always the current!"

Agnes stirs her paddle, going through the motions of paddling more for the sake of distraction than navigation.

"Where are we going, anyway."

"Northish," I reply.

"Where's Vermont?"

"I don't know."

"We're screwed without the phone."

"Was it really helping all that much?" I ask, trying to make her feel better. "We texted our parents, and they couldn't help. We got out on our own."

"It has been a distraction," she admits.

"You sound like my grandma."

"You're an addict, Billy, face it," she declares sedately, her back on the floor of the dinghy behind us. "I've seen all that dumb shit that you and Sam and Gavin post. Weed and skateboards, rapping and fake parkour."

I want to tell her to shut the fuck up for once. After what she's done, she's pushing it. But I bite my tongue because she's lost her mom.

"How long are we going to drift in this wasteland with some nuts and dried fruit?" she asks sullenly. "And a dog that has to take a shit and can't?"

CHAPTER THIRTY-SIX

Juliet

I walk past the hospital sign and turn into the entrance. Martin pulls up beside me in the rental car and rolls down his window.

"You okay?" he asks in his pre-apocalypse voice, which gives me some relief.

"Been better," I answer as I get in on the passenger side.

He crawls the car toward the brightly lit hospital doors. Noemi is rustling in the back, the constant calisthenics of caring for Ana. Again, I ask if I can help, and she says we already have. Then, she offers us the last of Ana's snacks.

"Thanks, but we need a real meal," says Martin.

He jerks the wheel right and presses the gas, lurching us forward to get around a car that has abruptly stopped in the drop-off lane.

"The child," I say.

"I'm sorry. But I'm done with this shit. The endless waiting." He passes two cars, drives right past the front doors, past hospital staff assisting people, and pulls up to the flooded curb. Noemi has already slung her bag over her shoulder. She swaddles Ana close to her chest and opens the door. I get out to help her, but a woman in jeans, a T-shirt, and a brown canvas Carhartt vest beats me to it, grabbing Noemi's bag.

I splash around to the door anyway.

"Can I take Ana for you?"

"You need to go home, Juliet."

"I'm sorry we're dropping you in the middle of nowhere."

"This car ride wasn't easy, but it was better than some of the routes I've taken. Thank you."

"Of course," I say, embracing her and Ana.

"Qué les vaya bien. I hope it works out."

"Igual," I reply.

She turns away and walks toward the hospital doors under the theater lights. When I reach the passenger side, about to duck in, I look back at her. She's answering questions from a young woman in scrubs. Just before turning and following the woman through the glass doors, she looks at me with a placid expression, her brow slightly worried.

"Andale pues! Keep going!" she calls.

I can only nod, as Martin is calling my name, telling me to hurry the fuck up. I slide onto the seat and close the door.

A couple of hours after leaving the hospital, Martin pulls the car into the dark, empty parking lot of a shuttered McDonald's on the side of a rural highway in New York State. I'd do anything for a grilled chicken sandwich with cheese and extra pickles and a large order of greasy fries.

There's no service, of course, so I climb into the back seat with my backpack as a pillow. Martin stays in front, on the driver's side, reclining his seat as far down as it will go. As I drift off, I hear him lifting the phone, turning it in his palm, brushing his fingers over the screen, and kneading the home button with his thumb.

When I wake up, I see the sky out the back window, tightly packed with pink and yellow layers of dawn. The small highway to our left is empty. I feel cold and confined. The inside of my mouth is taut with dryness, and I'm starving.

"Martin?"

"Yes," he replies, raising the seat.

"We need food."

"And coffee."

I sit up on my sore hips that have been compressed against the back seat all night. When I put my feet on the floor, I kick into a navy lunch box that Noemi left under the driver's seat. I unzip it and find a rubbery grilled cheese sandwich wrapped in tinfoil and slices of mushy brown peaches in a plastic bag. Martin and I devour it all, like a dog would, gulping without savoring much, as that isn't the point.

Soon, we're back on 81 North, then 88, lurching through a foot of water, passing other flood nomads, adjusting our speed when the plateaus descend and deliver us back into more deluge and debris.

At Exit 7, we come off a ramp into deeper flood-waters that lap at the top of the hubcaps. We push through it at a slow pace alongside other drivers. We try to merge onto Route 87, back toward the steel and concrete barriers that have been erected at every junction, bridge, and exit. Our only option is to skirt Albany, bypass Troy and Schenectady, and double back on 87 to hit the turnpike if it's still there. We make it past Stockbridge and Blandford, but more barriers block the route to Springfield.

As I stare at the impenetrable blockade, my body begins its own protest, hands trembling, my lungs trying to keep up, my mind spiraling so fast I don't know where I am for a moment.

"Juliet," shouts Martin, grabbing my shoulder and shaking me. "Don't, don't," he pleads. "I can't fucking take this anymore."

He presses the gas, heads to an overpass beyond a barricaded exit, and pulls into the breakdown lane. Despite traffic that speeds by, he gets out, comes around to my door, and opens it.

"Hurry," he says, grabbing my elbow and pulling me out.

"Stop it, Martin."

"We have to look."

He guides me out of the passenger side and along the slick asphalt to the guardrail, where he takes my hand in his and puts an arm around my shoulder, finally showing some affection.

"Okay, I see it," I say, staring at the brown-green liquid iridescence in the distance, carpeting the valley. Slabs of rooftops cluster where there had been small towns, schools and municipal buildings, businesses, ballparks, a maze of road and avenue networks, now sunk deep in a Jurassic muck. I think of Tom and George, and I close my eyes. Clearly, as Noemi indicated, there will be limited search and rescue from here out to the coast.

Martin pulls me in and holds me tightly until I open my eyes and can walk again.

"We gotta get going," he says, his arm around my shoulder as he walks me back to the passenger side.

But he stops short of helping me back in because the sinking valley has caught his attention again.

"Should we try somehow? Get a boat or something? Hire someone?" he mutters, slowly reaching for my door. "I guess not."

We reach Route 7 and drive into southern Vermont, through the eastern corner of New York State. The phone sleeps after that, forgotten in the console.

CHAPTER THIRTY-SEVEN

Billy

My head hurts, and my whole body is stiff and damp from sitting on the canoe seat for so long. I just need a few minutes on the floor of the dinghy, eyes closed, holding Salty, cradling my pounding palm. The water is calmer, the ride smoother, but I'm not sure what state these girls are in. They don't talk anymore. I reach into the navy backpack and grab a handful of nuts and raisins, shove it into my mouth and chew what feels like wood chips. I've never understood trail mix. I try to find some hope in the few stars that flicker through gauzy clouds.

We've drifted toward a large concrete platform, probably the top of a low-lying building. Like a giant solid dock, it goes on and on into darkness. Instead of pushing away from it with our paddles, we decide to dock the boats here so that we can climb out and go to the bathroom. As we glide alongside the metal and concrete ridge, Agnes holding the lantern, I see a rusty brown metal pipe sticking out of the side of the roof. Agnes tosses me the black rope, and I tie it around the cool metal. The canoe kicks back, the dinghy bounces against it, and we're docked.

Agnes climbs out of the canoe first, Lana following from the tandem dinghy, their sneakers finding a ledge as they scramble over the rough beige concrete edge that disappears into the night. I carefully pass them the dog and the lantern, trying to steady the tipsy canoe. They walk away, leaving me in the darkness.

To give them privacy, I turn my back and look out at the inky plain. There are no rushing, hissing currents anymore, no crushing, crackling sound of debris. I pray to a god that I've never been sure of for the safety of George, Mom, Dad, and Grandma. If we've gotten this far, I pray, please don't spring any surprises on us. I remind myself that good things do happen; sometimes, people and families get lucky. But then my mind goes haywire, and I'm swatting away the other thought that sometimes they don't. The girls shuffle back across the roof. I turn and see the lantern casting a spotlight around their sneakers.

I grab the dog from the edge and lift her off, careful to guard my throbbing palm. Agnes slides into the dinghy, and I pass Salty to her. I stand firm, anchoring myself to the back floor of the canoe while Lana slips onto the front seat. Rather than pressing my palms to the roof, I use my elbows and forearms to hoist myself onto the damp, grainy concrete, first onto my knees and then my feet. Distorted shadows dance through the light of the lantern dangling in my fist; my sore legs and damp sneakers make me feel like I'm going to stumble and never get up.

As soon as I get fifty feet or so away from the girls, I switch off the light, unzip, and piss for a good minute. As I turn around to head back, I think I feel my phone for a moment, snug against my lower back, like a phantom limb of sorts. I even reach for it. But my pocket is flat, and it's all Lana's fault.

About an hour after our bathroom break, I feel like I can't sit up anymore. The stars are gone, and everything's black, although Agnes swears she's seen sparkles of light through the tree line.

"People in their homes, maybe?" she suggests.

"Doubtful," replies Lana, breaking her punishing silence.

"I gotta lie down," I growl.

Agnes, who's tried to convince me to rest a handful of times, shuffles in the darkness and makes room for me in the dinghy. Could we both fit together on the floor, spooning the way we did in George's bed? She'd never do it unless Lana went overboard.

"Billy, give me your paddle. I'll sit in the back," says Agnes. "Don't worry. We'll be okay."

Once on the floor of the dinghy, I ball up Lana's pink blanket under my head and curl on my side with Salty tucked in at my waist and thighs. I have no strength left to pet her.

The next time I open my eyes, it's to the sound of voices in the dark. Someone far away is hammering wood; the hollow echo is unmistakable. I'm too tired to lift my head. I can't see anything since the girls either turned off the lantern or it ran out of power. I'm hot and cold. I shiver and can't get comfortable, twitching on the floor of the dinghy, in and out of sleep, until the faintest glow from the very early morning wakes me.

"Billy," whispers Agnes. "Do you hear that?"

I try to sit up but can't. So I roll onto my back with my knees up and listen to faint, distant voices.

"They don't sound very close," I say.

"Why are you shivering so much?" she asks.

"My bones hurt."

Someone shouts for help. Another screams, "Jimmy, where are you?"

"Hello," Agnes calls. "Can someone help us?"

"Hello," shouts Lana. "Hello? Can you help?"

No answer, so we drift on.

When I wake again, I'm on the cold, hard floor of the aluminum canoe, not sure how I got here from the floor of the dinghy that, in comparison to this, felt like goose-down. Lana is curled in a ball on the floor of the dinghy. Agnes, on the seat in front of me, has navigated through the morning. I think she's gotten the hang of it, switching hands and keeping to the center of the gentle current. I pull myself up onto the back seat and grab the other paddle.

"I don't feel so good," I say.

She passes me the last of the water in the plastic gallon jug, and I gulp it down.

"Look, Billy," she says, sounding joyous in this wreck we're in. "There's someone in a boat."

I turn my stiff neck and see four people in a Zodiac coasting toward us, its motor humming. The tree line has opened to a wider, flooded plain with submerged buildings and houses scattered in the distance. Some of them, up on a hill, look dry. But down here, on the soupy plain, the tops of telephone poles and green highway signs poke out of deep waters, and clumps of unrecognizable plastic, metal, and wood slosh against the swamped tree line.

I'm not sure what the girls have been doing, but the accelerating hum of the Zodiac motor vaporizes our inertia, and we all sit up straight as though it's the first day of school and we're waiting for someone to take attendance. Two women, probably moms or sisters, and a blond kid my age stare miserably at us from beneath yellow ponchos, heads bowed as if they're crouching under something more solid than the hazy, damp dawn. An older man in a silver windbreaker, his hand on the tiller, shouts out that we're close to the highway. I look down through the murky liquid surface and see that we're still gliding over it.

"Solid, dry highway," he corrects himself.

I nod at the kid in the boat, and he bobs his head in reply. The two women smile, but their eyes are full of fatigue and concern. Who knows what they've gone through to make it into that rescue boat?

"Where are we?" I ask the old man.

But he doesn't seem to hear me. It takes all my energy to speak.

"Do you know where we are?" asks Agnes in a loud voice.

"Ninety-five, near the air force base."

"Can we get help there?"

"Yes, there's a rescue station close by."

The old man has a friendly smile framed with some serious wrinkles and watery eyes that make him seem like the gentle type, truly overjoyed to help people. His enthusiasm fills me with hope I haven't felt for a while. Even Lana, awake and sitting up now from the commotion, forces a pathetic grin for a few brief seconds before looking at Agnes, who is slouched a little on the front canoe seat, her back to me, probably looking worried: arched eyebrows and lips parted in discomfort.

"You see here," says the old man, plunging his paddle through the surface and hitting solid ground. "Highway," tap, tap. "Right here. There's solid land straight up a bit, around that bend, where those people are."

I see ten or twelve of them standing at the water's edge on a solid bank that rises to more scattered homes on hills in the distance.

"You'll get help there. You'll see. Where are you all coming from?"

"Boston."

"That's a ways away. What's it like there?"

Lana shakes her head, and he nods thoughtfully, not surprised at all.

"Keep going straight, over there. It'll be okay."

I look at the back of Agnes's head and then glance at Lana in the dinghy behind me. She stares down at the dog in her lap. I hope the man won't ask any more questions about where we've come from and what we've seen.

Something's flapping now to the left, beyond the buried highway. When I look, I can just make out someone on the roof of a brick building with broken windows waving an old white T-shirt or pillowcase.

"Gotta get him," says the man, turning the tiller. He accelerates and glides away from us as though he doesn't want to hear our story. He's pure future tense, which helps him maintain that hopeful smile. "You're almost there," he shouts as if we're running one of those ultra-marathons that make people heave their carbs along the route.

Agnes and I lift our paddles. I find a bit more strength, and together, we paddle like hell on each side of the canoe toward the curve in the broad, milky brown canal. We hear faint chatter and then voices building as we coast around a bend of flooded trees, past a green and white sign sticking out of the mud that reads Bedford. A strip of blacktop, stitched with a broken white line, rises out of the soup we've been in and winds through terrain and along the solid bend that runs parallel to us. I've never been so happy to see asphalt, which is basically fermented plankton, bacteria, and dinosaurs mixed with sand, and, according to Ms. Fagan, is what got us into this trouble in the first place.

A car door slams, pulling me from my environmental science class daydream. Then, the voices of children, someone shouting. Grassy hills surround the road and extend back to a landscape that hasn't seen what we have.

"Who are they?" asks Agnes, staring at the people standing on the bank, along the road, and in the fields.

"People just like us," says Lana, peering at the crowd, at parents with babies and cats in their arms, dogs at their feet, and a few belongings spilling from haphazard luggage, garbage bags and knotted sheets.

I know the girls are searching for their mom in the crowd. I see it in how Lana tilts her head, her eyes darting back and forth. And in Agnes's arched back, hands resting on her thighs as she anxiously scans the crowd.

"There are buses," she says. "People are boarding."

"They're going inland," replies Lana.

Some people have formed lines in front of a half-dozen white tents pitched on the hill that must offer emergency care and whatnot. Standing near a cluster of tables, others sip from white paper cups and eat from napkins. I hope there's something left for us.

Agnes begins to laugh as she jabs her paddle at the road below and waves at three people who wade out to our boats, asking if we're okay if they can help us out of the boat, and if we can walk on our own. I barely understand how we've gotten here, how many miles we traveled, why a young woman with a short Afro, dyed orange at its tips, is holding up my swollen bandaged hand that doesn't have much feeling to it anymore.

"Dehydrated. Infection. Possibly shock. Might need a stretcher," someone says.

Two grandpa-type guys in beige and navy baseball caps, black raincoats, and jeans tucked into green rubber boots grab Agnes by the elbows to help her step out of the canoe. I'm overwhelmed by all the help and encouraging words from the same two men who now hold me up by my arms.

"We've got you," they say as I put my foot onto the flooded asphalt, more water seeping through my sneakers and drenching my toes. I'm dizzy and can barely stand up straight.

"What's your name?" asks the one with a gentle but serious expression, his probing eyes glued to my face.

"Billy."

"You've done a good job, Billy. And so have these girls."

Through my dizziness, I smile and nod. I manage to turn and loosen myself from the men's gentle grip for a moment so that I can face Lana, still sitting in the dinghy. I wobble forward, my legs cramping, and take Salty from her arms so that she can step out. My bad hand feels like an inflated balloon that someone inserted into my numb wrist.

"Don't drop her, Billy," says Lana with a frail smile.

I shake my head, unable to form words through the blur of voices in my ear, a hand on my shoulder again, words I can't decipher. Once Lana stands, I hand Salty back and look out one more time at the muddy green sea that has washed in from the Boston Harbor and beyond, changing our world.

CHAPTER THIRTY-EIGHT

Juliet

The long lines extend out of a former military base's hulking corrugated steel hangar at the end of a dead-end dirt road surrounded by a pine and maple forest. I'm waiting in mud and sawdust, hoping for a warm meal, while Martin looks for someone from the Reunification Team. As I watch him disappear into the crowd, I wonder if he'll return. Together, we've made this trip possible, bearable, and complicated. There's no sodden highway to battle anymore. No more phone to wrangle.

The lines lead me through the gaping front entrance into the bulky steel shell that once held planes and armored vehicles. Two men in front of me, who look like dads from my neighborhood, gone scruffy with beards, rumpled jeans, and T-shirts, are talking about the extent of damage in their town in a New York City suburb. As one plunges his fist into the front pockets of his jeans, and the other shakes his head in disbelief at his own story, a woman behind me, in a gray sweatshirt and matching baggie sweatpants, steps out of line and stands by my side to listen. She moves closer to the men while adjusting a pink bandana that swaddles her long, frizzy, auburn hair, brindled with gray.

"Is it true?" she asks the men, the muscles in her face hardening into anguish. "That they opened up the outer barrier and the gateway into the city?"

"I didn't hear about that," answers one of the men.

"They did," she snaps, her misty eyes swelling open. "They flooded the city to relieve the surge at the coast. They killed people deliberately."

Boston, I say to myself, is a coastal city, too, with recently constructed Army Corps of Engineer sea gates, just like New York's.

"I-I-I don't know about a barrier or a gateway," the man stutters; his tight grimace and tired eyes seem about to collapse in on themselves if she continues.

"My girlfriend disappeared in front of me, into the East River, when the bastards let the water in. She was in our kitchen, and then she wasn't."

A few people in line turn to listen. No one replies. None of us puts a hand on her shoulder. We just glare grimly at her, the only solidarity we can muster. She stares down at her mud-caked hiking boots and slips back into line behind me. I think about looking back at her, reaching for her hand, but I'm distracted by the smell of the food. We all are. Garlic, onions, tomato sauce, hamburger: the institutional mainstay that keeps bodies going during a disaster. To my right, people begin to pass in the opposite direction, carrying paper bowls of chili topped with a slice of bread. God, it smells good. Unable to hold back until they leave the hangar, they slurp as they push by.

I stand on my toes and look through the crowd, trying to locate Martin to bring him a warm bowl of food when our turn comes. But word soon passes that they've run out of chili. It will be another forty-five excruciating minutes before the next batch. I'm not going to stand here and do nothing with Billy on my mind, a charged phone in my backpack, and the slim possibility of service despite the silence on his end.

"Excuse me," I say, turning to the woman in the pink bandana and gray sweats. "I'm having a slight emergency. Would you mind holding my place?"

She stares at me suspiciously.

"Where are you going?"

"To find a bathroom."

Her gaze falls on my backpack and stays there for several seconds until she replies, "Sure. No problem."

I turn, squeeze through the crowd, and head toward the arching entryway at the front of the hangar, where Martin and I plan to meet at four pm. I look for him through the commotion of bobbing heads, gesturing hands, and reclining figures, a few resilient smiles amid solemn expressions. Has he finally ditched me to go it alone for practicality's sake? And because there are no more texts anymore to raise our hopes? To connect him with his family? Again, I search for him in the crowd through the murmuring fragmented language of many voices, the lulls, and more conversation.

Someone pushes me into a pack of people staring at a large map of the United States taped to the wall that shows levels of inundation and is color-coded to denote the severity level. The Eastern Seaboard is outlined in crimson marker from Maine to South Carolina. Red fading to orange, then yellow where water has retreated, somewhere east of the Berkshires in Massachusetts, down through the inland communities of the Southeast. The orange line south of the Carolinas and Georgia turns crimson again around Jacksonville and down the peninsula until it swells and swallows Miami. At Tampa, the line fades to orange and then a hopeful yellow along the coast of the Panhandle, where I last saw my mother.

I think of the sugar-white sand on the island that slopes back from the water's edge. The drifting dunes covered with sea oats, frost weed, beach elder, and wild rosemary, rising high in some places and spreading back like a natural sea wall. I picture my mother's indigo house on stilts behind the swamp full of snakes, alligators, and blue and green herons. In August, it dries up and cracks like the inside of an old paint can, but in the spring, the basin is deep and swells with rain, a buffer between her house and the ocean.

I don't register the muted pinging coming from my backpack until I see the crowd closest to me stop talking. Seven or eight people turn from the map, from the dirty corrugated walls of sheet metal covered in tarnished yellow spray foam and cobwebs. They begin to search for the source. Two women to my right reach for their bags in a Pavlovian gesture, though they seem to have nothing to show. Taking advantage of the confusion, I slip a hand into my bag and mute the sound so it doesn't ping again. The haywire knot of both dread and possibility tightens in my throat as I look in all directions for a way out of the hangar, a path to Billy again, through the phone.

It's been over forty hours since we've had news, so why now? My cheeks prickle at the flash of horrors I know how to conjure so well. If he needs help, I'm powerless to provide it, making me not want to look at all. I've done that before, at two in the morning: *He's nearly an adult. He can deal with it.* But this isn't a late-night party on the outskirts of our town. I take a deep breath and exhale through clenched teeth, trying to slow the thoughts that flip through my mind like a shuffled deck of cards. I try to be hopeful. He's come through with the girls, just like I knew he would. He's texting again, paddling upstream against the obstacles of this new world.

And what about Martin? Where did he go? We've deciphered the texts mostly together, plodding side by side through the cluttered fragments, taking turns shoring each other up, trying to be resilient and making mistakes. I search for him in the crowd one last time, at every six-foot-tall man with curly brown hair mottled with white at the temples. But the pack of restless people to my left begins to push me toward the archway that opens to cool mountain air and shreds of fibrous clouds in a cobalt sky.

Shoved forward, I move with the crowd through air that smells sour from too many unbathed people, past a crying toddler, until I'm pushed out toward the lines of humanity waiting to enter the hangar. I walk through a stew of gravel, whipped up from rain and foot traffic. I begin to jog now along the expanse of mud, searching for privacy, passing a steady flow of families slogging toward the hangar. My arm still deep in my bag, fingers gripping the phone, I veer off the road toward the forest, through moss and new ferns with bearded fiddleheads. But the line of trees is too dense for a connection, and people on the road stare at my divergence. I have to text back. But where? I turn toward the dozen latrines that some heroes dug in a field bordering the forest and covered with two-by-fours and blue plastic tarps.

Out of breath and low blood sugar, I slip into line behind a mother and her two small children, shivering in the cool afternoon. I smile at them, but they look away.

"Do they want my sweatshirt?" I ask the mother, reaching for the knotted arms of green cotton at my waist.

"You'll need it up here. But thank you," she nods. "We'll find a way to get warm when we're done doing our business."

A young man emerges from the layers of blue tarp, flipping back the corner like a teepee. He holds it cordially for the mother and her two children, and they duck under his arm and disappear. When he lets go, our eyes meet, and he smiles as though we aren't all in this unfathomable mess, shitting, pissing, and puking in a hole in a field next to a decommissioned military hangar somewhere in southern Vermont.

When my turn comes, I duck under the opening and enter the muddy space, breathing only through my mouth. As I turn to close the tarp, a figure slips in behind me and pulls it down.

"Don't be scared," she hisses. "It's me."

I recognize the worried face, plump cheeks, pink bandana, and wooly hair.

"What are you doing?" I ask, moving away from her, my head grazing the sloped edge of rumpled blue plastic. I gulp air and breathe a putrid gust through my nose before I can staunch it again. "Do you mind waiting your turn?"

"I heard the ping back there," she says. "It came from your backpack."

"Did you follow me out of line?"

She nods, emotion roiling in her brow and trembling lower lip.

"I knew you were up to something. You're in here to text people."

"I'm here to use that," I say, pointing at the four blocks of wood stacked over a hole to form a crude toilet seat. "Can you leave?" I look into her flittering eyes. "You're barking up the wrong tree. I heard it, too. But it wasn't me."

She glances at my backpack and slowly nods.

"Yes, it was. I saw you slip your hand in your bag. You're holding your smartphone right now."

"Those phones don't work anymore," I counter, my fingers clamping the smooth plastic as though it's alive and can pop out of my palm if I'm not careful.

"They do if you know how," she whispers.

"Don't bullshit me."

I can feel my arm, the phone in my palm, rising out of the bag, shedding the secrecy for Billy's sake. I need to read his text.

"I can get you to a site. It only takes a minute." She steps toward me. "You'd be surprised how many people have lied to their loved ones about keeping it."

Tom and George, I wonder. If Billy and I have kept our phones, why not them? Is it worth a try? Handing my phone to this fruitcake and her fairy tales?

"Where's yours?"

"In the East River."

I stare at her flat palm, levitating toward me. Then I parade my gaze up her arm to her slumping shoulders under her dirty sweatshirt. We're all suffering from the same filth and exhaustion. The same sickening speculation of which of our loved ones survived. What's next?

"They're worried about you. Wondering why you haven't contacted them."

An image of George and Tom staring at a screen with my name flashing at the top of the screen plows through my brain.

"Give it here." She plies me again with her smile. "You can go first into your world. Then, I'll get a turn in mine."

"There's only one world. Lift the tarp and see for yourself." I loosen my grip on the phone inside my bag and sweep my hand over the bottle of water, a useless wallet, a lip balm, and the unlatched case. My fingers grope for the phone again, desperate to text Billy. I open the bag and stare deep into it at the glowing disappointment. It wasn't my phone that pinged after all because all I see now are the same texts I saw a day and a half ago:

Heading away from the coast in a dinghy.

The woman steps left and blocks the door, looking more formidable in this small space than she did in the enormity of the hangar, lost in her sorrows. I pull out the phone and hold it up, showing her the obsolete texts.

"It wasn't me," I say, hoping she'll turn and leave.

"We can still try," she replies, staring at her thrusted-out hand and smiling expectantly. Her gaze jumps from her empty palm to mine, where the phone sits. "Look at it. You've taken such good care under the circumstances."

"It's just a phone."

But she's right. I have treated it like a living creature, protecting it from the rain, putting it to bed, encouraging it.

She lunges forward and grabs my wrist before I know what's happening. Her grip against my skin, bones, and veins is solid and enraged. She yanks the phone toward her, twisting my wrist back and forth, her mouth warped with furious effort.

"Jesus, what are you doing?" I shout, trying to shake her off me. Her other hand swings around, trying to grab the device. I hold her back with my free hand but can't quite break loose.

"I just want to try her," she spits. "Please. Just a minute. I know I can get through."

"You can't though. It won't help you. Or me."

One of us pinches the power button, and Billy's last words light up again. The end of a long archive of disjointed messages that have trailed my journey with Martin—from the listing deck of Karl's sopping boat, through the drenched roads of rural Franklin County, into Georgia, the failed plane ride, the hotel, the southern states, across the Mason-Dixon, Pennsylvania, southern New England. We've sloshed through water and more water, always reaching for the phone, cradling it, checking it, pecking out messages, waiting, worrying, weighing our words. Is it enough? Have we said the right thing?

It's always been like this with the phone. Another minute, and we'll solve the problem, connect with our children, and become happy again. There *is* such a thing as too much information, vapid and pointless, that muddles what's going on outside the window—heat waves, glaciers breaking off, blooming infectious diseases, firestorms in California, the Amazon, Canada, and Australia, a thawing Arctic blanketing our world with expanding rivers.

My throbbing wrist curls in her grasp. As the phone begins to slip into her fingers, I manage to knee her in the stomach and pry her from me. She falls on the filthy, muddy floor against the tarp, her hands braced behind her in the sludge. This only makes her infuriated, her mouth open; the words stick because I've knocked the wind out of her. She pushes herself up with effort, scrambles to her feet, and comes back at me with every last bit of energy focused on the phone. My phone. My conduit to Billy. My discord. My failures with him there in my palm. His failures, too. He meant well and tried to use it as best he could before the Ban, through seventh and eighth grade and two years of high school, sitting in the dark on his bed, the phone spotlighting his stupor as he punched buttons, figuring out life, looking at God knows what, swiping up and left, page after digital page.

The woman loses her footing in the mud—her grip weakening, fingers grabbing at mine. She stumbles just enough for me to pull the phone away, look down at the black screen, and know I will never communicate again with Billy through it. So when she comes back at me, anger in her features blending with confusion, it dawns on me that she might believe the phone can resurrect someone she saw disappear into the East River days ago. My arm rises, phone in my palm.

"Here you go. Go to town."

She finds her balance and reaches out. With incredible sadness, she touches the phone and lets me slide it into her palm, where she cradles it with reverence. She spins from me, walks toward the tarp door, bats it open with her free hand, and disappears.

"Ma'am, are you okay?" asks a voice from outside.

"I'm fine. Thanks."

The smell in the latrine chafes my nose and throat. I duck under the tarp, stumble into the cool air, and shuffle past the long line of people next to the dense woods. Instead of returning to the hangar, I pause and look through the tall stands of sugar maple and blue spruce, different from the short, scrubby sand pines on Dog Island. I pray that my mother is safe with Duncan, a seasoned pilot who knows the airstrip as intimately as one knows his driveway.

A breeze blows and jangles the smaller limbs of trees as I head into the woods, shedding all the fallout from my journey. The leaves have a peculiar thickness, a layered dimension I've never seen before. Tiny droplets of water, like minuscule diamonds, hang on threads of sterling spider webs draped over twigs and branches, shimmying in the light. I stare at the canopy of color with a wide periphery that busts the edges of all my constraints. It's like looking through a brown, green, and silvery-yellow prism that swallows my vision and intensifies what I've felt all along. I remember Martin's words in the car about Stephanie and Noemi's story about Ana's birth. A buttery glow penetrates the thick woods and strikes the leaves, some of which are still unfurling with a chartreuse luminescence that lasts only a few days before the warm weather draws out the deeper greens and stretches the leaves to their full summer size. Watching them swivel on their branches, I know I will find Billy, George, and Tom somewhere inland. Maybe up here in the mountains.

ACKNOWLEDGMENTS

I began this novel in September 2018, a month before Hurricane Michael slammed into the Florida Panhandle. Rated Category 5 and the strongest ever to hit that area, Michael caused catastrophic damage. Houses were there one day and gone the next. Driving through Mexico Beach, I saw a forest of tall palms snapped in half and families rebuilding along the Gulf Shore with hope and optimism.

While the aftermath of the hurricane fueled my imagination, this narrative is about more permanent changes we can't address by rebuilding. Climate scientists say global temperatures have exceeded the 1.5 degrees Celsius threshold we've known about since before the 2015 Paris Agreement. This past year was the warmest on record, as were global ocean surface temperatures. News outlets and science journals have announced the possibility that the ocean's current system, including the Gulf Stream, could be in the early stages of collapse. I hope that this worst-case scenario I've conjured remains in fiction.

I am especially grateful to Steven Long at 12 Willows Press for his insight, patience, and focus. I also thank Mariella Travis at Alleiram Studios for the book's interior design and Judith West and Annaliese Jakimides for their thoughtful input.

This novel was written with the support and encouragement of my writing group and the Island Writers Retreat. I am deeply grateful for the thirty-five years of enduring friendship and camaraderie shared with Sally Brady, Anna Kovel, James Lansill, Stephanie Fleischmann, Chris Lynch, Alice Holstein, Kate Kruschwitz, Cindy Linkas, Glenn Morrow, P.K. Simonds, John Altobello, and Tim Traver.

Katherine Stewart was the first reader of my completed manuscript. I am grateful for her friendship and enthusiasm and the many conversations about climate, politics, and family that have impacted my writing.

Thank you to the Tufts community for giving me so many diverse experiences. I am grateful to my students, who keep me researching and learning. Thank you to the faculty and staff in Romance Studies, the Tufts Institute of the Environment for sending me as an observer to Cop25, where I learned a year's worth of environmental and climate information in a week, and the Tufts Green Fund Board.

Most importantly, thank you to my big family of Risses, Cazorts, Lockwoods, and Nyhans: audience and storytellers. Thank you, especially to my daughters, Claire and Camille, for always cheering me on and for your probing questions; keep up the inquiry! To my husband, Jim, for his habit of happiness. To my brother,

John: *we got this*. To my mother, whose quest for adventure and connection to the natural world brought me to the Emerald Coast for the first time when I was a baby. And finally, I thank my father, Bob, my mother-in-law, Margo, and my brother, Greg, for their support and memories.

ABOUT THE AUTHOR

Kate Risse teaches Spanish language and culture at Tufts University. She lives with her family in Brookline, Massachusetts, and spends time on Dog Island and in the mountains of Vermont.